MOUNTAIN MAN

Also by Keith C. Blackmore

Mountain Man

Mountain Man
Safari
Hellifax
Well Fed
Make Me King
Mindless
Skull Road
Mountain Man Prequel
Mountain Man 2nd Prequel: Them Early Days
The Hospital: A Mountain Man Story
Mountain Man Omnibus: Books 1–3

131 Days

131 Days
House of Pain
Spikes and Edges
About the Blood
To Thunderous Applause
131 Days Omnibus: Books 1–3

Breeds

Breeds
Breeds 2
Breeds 3
Breeds: The Complete Trilogy

Isosceles Moon

Isosceles Moon
Isosceles Moon 2

The Bear That Fell from the Stars
Bones and Needles
Cauldron Gristle
Flight of the Cookie Dough Mansion
The Majestic 311
The Missing Boatman
Private Property
The Troll Hunter
White Sands, Red Steel

MOUNTAIN MAN

BOOK 1

KEITH C. BLACKMORE

Podium

Special thank you to Donna Beck, Ken Maidment, and Rob Richter for help with those little things.

Cover design by Podium Publishing

ISBN: 978-1-0394-4414-0

Published in 2023 by Podium Publishing, ULC
www.podiumaudio.com

MOUNTAIN MAN

1

Augustus Berry rolled over to the edge of the stained hardwood deck and vomited. He squeezed his eyes closed, the pressure behind them forceful enough to almost pop them from their orbital cavities. He emptied his guts, took a deep breath, and heaved again, feeling as if someone had taken a fistful of his innards and were wringing them out through his mouth. Once that blast passed, he let one arm drop while he panted for air. He cracked open an eye and gazed at the autumn foliage forty feet below. He took in the concrete blocks and the iron support poles that kept up his deck. He thought he saw the splatter where he had just yarked. He realized he was on the deck itself and had damn near rolled off into oblivion. The night before, he had passed out on the comfortable lawn chair and had later moved to the harder, treated surface of the wood.

Seeing the ground far below made him dry heave twice more and then puke when he thought he had nothing left in his stomach. And he roared, not caring in the least who heard him as he voided, just wanting it over and done. When he finished, he stayed where he lay, gut down, ass up, and felt that sensation of wellness settle in, the kind that formed within one's core after the body ejected whatever shit had made it sick in the first place.

In his case, it had been Uncle Jack, the South's finest sour mash whiskey. At least, that was what the bottle said, and Gus was one to believe everything he read in print. Especially print found on a whiskey bottle. Booze didn't lie.

But it sure as hell gave him the shits sometimes.

A cool breeze rose up and slapped him on his bearded cheeks, hard enough to cause him to wrinkle up his face. He took a deep, shuddering breath and cracked open his eyes again while rolling over onto his back. Gray clouds. Fine and billowy like fat intestinal tracts. October clouds. He sat up with his legs stretched out in a V. He

1

scratched at his beard, a great length of facial hair resembling an old rug. The thing was getting grayer, and he absently thought about mowing it with the clippers. He drew his hand across his face, wincing at the contact of stomach juice there and in his whiskers, then checked his hands before rubbing them on his blue sweatshirt and jeans.

"Shit," Gus grumbled. A broken bottle of Uncle Jack lay to his left, splayed over the wooden deck like a jagged bear trap. He sighed. That stuff was gold, and he couldn't remember if he had drunk it or not. He had probably thought, *One more drink before bed,* then downed whatever was left in the bottle and passed out.

Here. Jesus Christ. Right on the edge of a forty-foot drop. The thought of passing out, then rolling over and splattering on the rocks and scrub below almost made him heave again. He'd have had to clear the wooden railing, which didn't offer much room below the lowest plank and the deck, but Gus knew stranger things had happened. Looking toward the front of his house, he found some small relief in seeing that the curtains were drawn. At least some part of him had remembered to do that.

Casting his attention toward the city and the bay that lay beyond, Gus sniffed, hoarked, and ejected a gob over the edge of the deck. Rooftops looked back at him, some black, some gunmetal gray. Silence buzzed in his ears, and in the distance, a seagull allowed an updraft to take it up a few levels. The bird hung in the air for moments before Gus realized it was flying away from him, toward the bay. Smart, for a sea chicken. Gus sniffed hard again, clearing his sinuses, and scratched his balls before rubbing his bald crown. He sat and stared, looking for anything of interest or concern. Nothing. Just another morning in the valley.

Then, he remembered he had things to do in the city. Just the thought made him shudder. It was much safer to just stay home, be safe, and get comfortably ripped out of his mind. Being drunk helped a lot at night, so he probably had a drinking problem. He thought back to his long-dead father, how he had been pleasantly plastered for most of his life, and realized that maybe the old man had been right all along in keeping a bottle nearby. It helped with reality. Whatever. He wouldn't worry about it until the neighbors called the cops.

That thought made him smirk.

He drew in another breath, scratched his junk once more, and looked back at his house. Perched on the side of the mountain, the two-story timber-frame design had high peaks and plenty of picture windows facing the city. Every window had black curtains. Privacy. It was all about privacy. Gus didn't need anyone from below seeing lights on in his house. He didn't need the attention. Attention was bad. As bad as going down into the city.

His stomach rumbled, and he felt the urge to get to a toilet. Grumbling, he got to his feet, wincing at the pain in his hip joints and lower back. He walked off the deck, grimacing at the broken glass and vowing to sweep it up later. He moved past the propane barbeque and the sea-green pool half-filled with rain water and yellow leaves. Shambling, he skirted the edge of his house and made for the outhouse at the far end of the lawn. Gus had dug the hole on the lower slope, away from the main house, then fitted thick planks over it and lugged a blue porta-potty to cover the hole. It was a lot of work for one man, and Gus had lost a chunk of body fat from the exertion. His hand lingered on the scar made by crazy Alice six months ago, back when his potbelly had saved his life. The beer paunch had eroded with time and effort, but the scar remained. Ancient Roman gladiators subsisted on a daily diet of barley and rice, fattening themselves for their fights as the body fat served as armor and protected vitals from their foes' weapons. Gus thought about trying to get his armor back on, but food was scarce, and until he solved the problem of how to grow his own, he would probably keep on losing weight.

And become more of an alcoholic.

He entered the outhouse and emerged a good twenty minutes later, feeling cleaner and somewhat more alert. He had gotten some good thinking done in there and, standing on the planks with the door banging behind him, thought that the quicker he got into town and did his business, the quicker he could be back in his fortress of solitude. Getting comfortably shitfaced. That sounded like a plan.

He went around to the back of the house and entered through the sliding door which he'd reinforced with a wall of wooden planks nailed to the frame. He closed the door behind him, locked it, and studied the inside of the house. Natural light from the upper windows peeked around the curtains. They were too high to barricade, but when the curtains were drawn back, they illuminated the rustic wood of the interior. Not bothering to remove his sneakers, he walked through the open space of the first level and went to the kitchen to remove a jug of drinking water from the fridge. He drained a liter and belched hard enough for it to hurt. After another sinus-clearing sniff, he moseyed out to the door leading to the garage. He thought about breakfast. His stomach probably wouldn't let him. He'd be hungry later, though. Maybe.

He opened the door to the garage and stepped into an interior big enough to hold four cars. The black van waited, like a battered, dead bull elephant. He walked around the front, mindful of the thick grill guard that looked as if it had once gone through a wall. He gripped the vehicle's door handle and sighed in exasperation. Had he really been about to head out without his gear? The thought mocked him, and he shook his head. It was too early in the morning for such shit. He had to focus.

Gus went to a storage locker in the back of the garage and opened the two doors. He reached to the top shelf and pulled down a forty-ouncer of Captain Morgan black rum. He sloshed the half-empty contents around in the bottle, staring into the depths of his locker in a morning malaise. He sipped on the rum once, twice, made a face of war, and took a heavier third.

"Christ on a stick." He looked at the label. The foppish captain smiled back at him, unconcerned with the world. "Happy fucker, ain'tcha?"

He took a fourth shot of rum, then returned the bottle to its shelf and got to work. He'd finished armoring himself on the inside; it was time for the exterior. Leather pants went over his jeans. A hockey vest of protective padding for his chest and shoulders went on next. Snarling at the burn in his guts, he hauled on his worn leather jacket, noting that the padding made up for the missing fat mass, filling out the jacket. A thick neck brace clamped around his throat. Shin guards and hard plastic knee and elbow pads followed, and he huffed as he slapped them into place. Lastly, he pulled on fingerless black leather gloves. With a groan, he opened the rear van door and threw his weapons into the back. Belching again, he fixed his motorcycle helmet over his head and stood in the shadows of the garage for a moment, waiting for the booze to kick in.

"Bad idea, this," he said. A guy he'd once worked with used to say that repeatedly before climbing ladders. He'd said it often enough to get on Gus's nerves. The thought of what might have happened to the guy stayed with Gus as he crawled inside the van. The doors closed with metallic groans, and he knew he'd have to get some WD-40 on the joints. Snarling in that day-after-a- monster-drunk way, he stowed his equipment on interior racks, then stopped for a moment and flipped the black visor of the helmet up and down.

He sighed. He didn't need to go anywhere. He could just lie on the deck and read and drink, or watch TV and drink, or contemplate life and *really* fucking drink. God drank above. Gus knew it. The Almighty probably got shitfaced all the time. So why couldn't he? He didn't need to go down there, imagining his frayed nerves pulling taut like bare piano wire, or exposed veins being strummed with knife tips.

"Bad idea." He took a deep breath. But he intended to go *today*.

He shook his head, exited the van, and went over to the crank to manually open the garage door. When the door was up just enough for the vehicle to slide under it, he got back in the van. Hands shaking on the wheel, he steered toward the closed gate set into a ten-foot-high stone wall. The barricade encompassed the property from cliff edge around to cliff wall. The place was something of a fortress, and Gus wondered when he would be placed under siege. Not if, *when*. It happened in the movies.

4

Always. He had to bank on it happening sometime. Everything he had done was in preparation for that day. The day when *they* finally got in.

He slowed the van to a stop, where it trembled and died. He got out, bent over, and lifted the timber braced against the gate, swearing at the weight and the pinch of pain in his back.

"Sweet *Christ* and titties," came from him as he did the same for the other four. He was no carpenter, but he had managed to reinforce the gate with layers of measured and cut softwood, wire twist-offs, and nails. Lots of nails. The gate opened with a girlish squeak and swung inward. He drove the van through, then got out and closed the gates behind it. He returned to the driver's seat and stared out at the cleared brush and trees, fifty feet out. It was a killing field, laced with shallow trenches and wooden planks spiked with nails. He had gotten that idea from an old *Death Wish* movie. He wanted to do more to reinforce his meager defenses, but he couldn't think of anything. Sooner or later, he'd have to go to the library again and see if he could find anything on home defense.

Before *they* found him.

Hunched over the steering wheel, he looked at the road and sighed again. The rum had taken off some of the edge, but only a little. Well, fuck. He'd have to drink *more* in the future. His system was building up a tolerance. The thought of no longer being a cheap drunk bothered him. Booze had become his mental armor, but there was only so much booze left in the world.

Placing the van into *Reverse*, which was really *Drive* for the old war wagon, he eased the van down the winding snake of a dirt road. Tall elms leaned in overheard, fragmenting the dim light. He arrived at a wooden lattice concealing the road from the highway. That was his first defense. With a grunt and quick rub of his hip, he got out and shoved the wall back, noticing how the creepers and vines were turning yellow. It wasn't much concealment anymore, and he wondered how he could hide the side road come winter.

Or maybe he just wouldn't.

He drove the van through and replaced the lattice, yanking it across the dirt road. Standing back, he could easily discern the road behind it, but that was a problem for another day. He just wanted to get into town and get out before nightfall. Pausing at the driver's side door, he looked down one strip of the main road, leading into the city of Annapolis, population just shy of a hundred thousand.

You don't have to go there. This is stupid. You're still *hung over*, for Christ's sake.

Gus belched again and felt the burn rise over his gizzard.

He jumped aboard his van. He cranked the stick into *Reverse* again and barrelled down the highway like a meteor skidding across the atmosphere. He drove for several minutes, not appreciating the brightening day or the fence of trees on either side. Every once in a while, his eyes would flick to the left or right for quick scans of the thinning brush, and then a few houses that appeared along the way. An emptiness opened inside him and made him feel abysmally alone. Back when there were people around, he'd been something of a loner, only able to take socializing for so long before wanting to just shut himself away in his apartment. Lately, he sometimes wished for those crowds.

The gas tank was half full, and Gus figured he would get to where he was going and back again without running out, as long as he didn't have any trouble. It was still another chance he was taking, though. He hadn't been like that before. Only recently did the sense of *fuck it* seep into him, like that odorless, colorless gas that roughnecks encountered when drilling for oil. The same gas that would kill a person without them knowing it. He was doing stupid things. Pushing it. And God help him, he was tired of caring.

Cars dotted the sides of the road, deserted and picked over. A scorched black skeleton of a truck loomed ahead. A semi lay dead just past that, driven through a roadside billboard, its empty trailer busted open and scoured clean of whatever it had contained. A motorcycle was on its side with the seat gutted, yellow foam fluttering. Skid marks and dark stains covered the pavement while occasional flicks of white gleamed. More cars littered the highway, and though Gus had already cleared a path through the worst over the past year, seeing the dead things still made him feel even more empty. And grim.

Doors hung off their frames. Windshields were smashed in. A roadside collage of broken glass, bent steel, and bruised fiberglass, all under an October sky of blah.

But no people.

For that alone, Gus felt a pang of relief. The booze coursed through his head, softening the bludgeon of the wrecks he passed. He lifted his hand and saw that it trembled. It shook often these days. He made a fist. His father once had the same problem, and Gus had sworn never to be like *that*. There was no cure for him until the booze finally ran out, and he wondered what would happen when that time came. There was never a doctor around when he needed one. But then, he had avoided hospitals since the last one. Since Alice.

The houses thickened on both sides, and suburbia bloomed with rotten magnificence. Bones picked clean dressed some front lawns, laid out before garden gnomes with their heads bitten off at their ceramic grin. Some cars and trucks stayed in the driveways, and he figured there had been a second vehicle to take the residents to safety. Maybe. He scowled as he slowed, driving a comfortable forty kilometers per hour through the residential area gutted by flame and mobs of flesh. He came to an intersection and, while scratching his balls again, turned right, not bothering to signal in the somber dawn. More houses. Big ones, with pools in back no doubt. They were slapped together so close he had to wonder what the city planners had been thinking, or expecting.

Ahead, a pedestrian staggered onto the road. Gus shook his head. The bastard could *not* have timed it better. He would reach the center of the lane at the same time as the van. The figure lurched on, its features as smoky as the clouds above. White hair hung off its head like a half-eaten wreath. The thing slowed to a stop, right in the middle of the street, skull cocking at the sound of the approaching vehicle.

Gus exhaled and flexed his fingers on the steering wheel. He glanced at his speed. Forty all the way. He gripped the wheel harder. *Full ahead, Mr. Robinson, full ahead.*

The figure in the road turned to face the van, arms rising as if in worship.

Gus's attention flicked from the pedestrian to his grill guard, then back.

"Unlucky fuck," he growled.

He caught a glimpse of empty eye sockets and a widening mouth with cheeks that had been chewed through by shards of teeth. The arms went up higher, and a moan wasn't far behind, a sound that would issue from shrivelled lungs that did not breathe.

The grill guard smashed into the figure dead on, splashing the front of the van in a cloudburst of grime and sludge that might have been blood at one time, something Gus didn't want to think about. Arms buckled, flopped, and flattened against the front of the van, all in a split second. The head whipped forward and cracked open on the grill. White brain matter spurted like bad jam from an expired jar. Gus couldn't see the face—pulverized upon impact—but gravity eventually did its job. One of the legs of the thing got caught underneath the right tire and pulled the body down. The van bumped once, twice, and continued smoothly.

The needle stayed at forty.

Gus let out his breath and started breathing again. He blinked. He had just run down a pedestrian. Probably would get a ticket for that one. He felt the subtle smirk on his face. He knew what he'd just run down.

He'd killed enough of them.

2

The van plunged deeper into a desolate suburbia where the only color to the world seemed to be the skid marks left by tires on the asphalt. Gus slowed to thirty, hunched over the wheel and attentive, watching the empty sidewalks and yellowing front lawns, the grass grown high enough to resemble wheat. He'd seen it yesterday when he was housing-picking in this part of the city where he hadn't been before. A red and blue mailbox looking as if it had had the living shit kicked out of it leaned against a street lamp on the corner of another intersection. Place could be like a goddamn maze, and Gus had lived there for almost forty years.

Movement in his peripheral vision made him jerk his head to his left, but he didn't see anything. He took a breath and concentrated on the road and the landmarks. It was there, somewhere.

There.

A mini-mart. Part of the *Needs* chain. The glass of the shop's front dull in the daylight.

Clenching his jaw, Gus fumbled as he fastened his seatbelt and increased his speed to sixty. The shop lay across a T-intersection, welcoming him like a steel-tipped torpedo leaping from a concrete surf.

In his experience, it was always better to drive *through* than walk in, whenever possible.

The van crunched through the glass storefront, accordionizing at least one shelf, the counter, and the zombified clerk standing at attention behind it. The grill guard rammed into the clerk's shoulder, shoving it and its head into the wall beyond. On impact, the engine fumed, shuddered, and raged like the beast it was. Gus cranked it into *Drive* and reversed out of the store. Glass and metal debris tinkled to the ground. He did a three-point turn, and shoved the van's respectable ass up to the hole it had just made. The engine died with a gasp, and the length of the van trembled and shook on its chassis, as if its guts struggled to get something out of its hide. He opened the rear doors and hopped to the ground with a clatter of motorcycle boots on pavement.

With his short-barrel twelve-gauge primed and ready, Gus stepped inside the *Needs* shop. He had slung an aluminum bat across his back, samurai style. He looked right, then left. Seeing the coast was clear, he advanced.

The gimp behind the demolished counter moved and hissed. Gus examined the not-yet-dead undead and pointed the barrel of the shotgun at the creature's head. The weapon hung in the air, wavered, and dropped.

His boot heel crushed the skull on the first kick, but Gus stomped twice more on the thing just to be sure. When it stopped moving, he grimaced and wiped his boot on the dust-coated shirt of the once-employee. As protected as he was in leather and hard plastic, he was still vulnerable to the stink of the things.

Leaving the gimp where it lay, he quickly went back into combat mode. He slapped his visor up and raised the shotgun. He edged out from behind the wrecked counter, watching his step, and moved like he remembered seeing U.S. Marines doing in action movies. He sidestepped from one aisle to the next, noting the shelves were ransacked. Upon reaching the last, he quickly walked up its length and checked the rear. Marking it all as clear, he went to the storage door at the back of the shop. It swung both ways, and he took a deep breath before opening it. Anything could be behind that door, and the risk increased if it was dark on the other side. Keeping the butt of his weapon planted firmly against his shoulder, he kicked open the door.

A memory popped into his head, of once surprising his girlfriend in a similar shop while she was doing the tedious task of taking inventory. Tammy's startled face had made him laugh, and when he'd tried tickling her, she'd gotten furious. He'd apologized and cooked for her later that night, which softened her up and won her back. He'd never done such a thing to her again, remembering her angry face.

Gus forced the image from his mind and returned to the present.

Inky shadows. More aisles and shelves full of canned goods and dry foodstuffs. A veritable gold mine in goods. He shifted his back to a wall, made certain the line he was going to proceed in was clear, and advanced. He snaked in and around the aisles, eyeing the corners and whirling left and right when reaching them.

All clear.

Gus relaxed, but only a little. He spotted a washroom. He moved to the door, noting the pile of toilet paper stacked on the concrete floor and smiling in spite of himself. *Gold.* His ass felt happy already. Who would've thought that the second most important thing in the world after the fall would be ass wipe. He paused before smashing through the door, and exhaled when he found the room empty. He went back out front and briefly sized up the neighbourhood through the remaining glass windows.

Nothing. No activity. *Yet.* There would be soon.

Gus stood by a row of freezers full of a sludge of melted ice cream, water, and rotting containers. He placed his shotgun on the glass top of a freezer and grabbed two of the wire baskets from a nearby stack. He rushed back to the small hill of toilet paper and began scooping up the rolls, stacking them in the basket as rapidly as possible. He returned to the back of his van and dumped the basket into one of three gray plastic storage bins he had appropriated from the docks so very long ago. Hunched over, he glanced out the windshield. The coast was still clear.

He made two more runs to the storeroom for toilet paper. Each time he boarded the van, he peered out the front and glanced around before going back inside for further pickings. Once all of the toilet paper was safely aboard, Gus began going through the back shelves, taking boxes of unopened canned food, as well as bags of snacks. He found some cases of soda and struggled back to the van with them.

On the fourth aching armload of soda, he spotted a figure emerging from between two houses. It slowly banked in his direction. Gus froze on the threshold between the store and the van, watching the thing do a drunk man's shuffle down the street. He still wasn't sure if they saw or smelled or heard, but they sure as fuck ate—ate like his uncle Leo at an all-you-can Chinese food buffet. The features were indistinct in the distance, but the way it moved told him it was a gimp.

A zombie.

And where there was one . . .

A sense of urgency cut through the haze of booze in his system, and he sped up his packing. He stacked the soda inside the van and ran back into the store, knowing other boxes of goods waited: cleaning products, batteries, even porn magazines still in their plastic wrappers. He scooped up a box of beef stew and speed-walked back to the beast, dumping it into the back. The gimp shambled toward the store, still a good hundred meters away, but closing. Worse still, through the front windshield, he spotted three more dark forms, which froze him to the spot. They approached the van with ungainly steps, spread apart like three gunslingers looking to drive the black-garbed stranger from their town, else they reckoned shit would happen. Ayup.

Time was something Gus still had, so he sprinted back into the store, feeling sour sweat seeping from his pores and catching a whiff of his own bad breath rebounding from inside his helmet, despite the visor being up. There were still dry goods in the back, and he wanted them all. He might not need them or like them, but he knew when one was hungry and desperate, they would make do with anything. He grabbed bunches of beige work gloves, beef jerky, packets of instant coffee, and a huge cardboard box of breakfast cereal, then spotted some huge flats of bottled water under a tarp. If he had missed that, he would have never forgiven himself, but in the end, he left it, deeming it too heavy for his aching arms. He dumped everything into the back of the van with an increasing sense of dwindling time. The three gimps in front of the van had tripled. Doors to houses banged open, and zombies came out of their homes as if hearing the cheery ring of an ice cream truck. The image put Gus in mind of old vampire movies, where the dead rose from their coffins. The first gimp, coming in from the side, had picked up friends as well, perhaps more than two dozen, and the pack had covered half the distance to him.

But there was still *more* stuff back in the storage area, enough for months perhaps. Gus stalled in the doorway, wasting seconds vacillating on what to do. Ever since the end of civilization not quite two years ago, he prided himself on one rule when foraging for supplies. That one rule had kept him alive when all others died. He had learned it from a youth gorged on action and horror movies—flicks where the main cast were a bunch of unknowns screaming their heads off in the face of a sadistic killer or monster or alien.

Don't be stupid.

Followed closely by: *Don't take any risks.* The risk part was optional, as Gus felt any trip into the city was a risk. But any risk he took was a calculated one, like the one today. The tried-and-true routine was to get in, check things out, pick up whatever, and retreat before the gimps showed.

And the gimps were presently showing.

With a glance at the closed backroom door, Gus decided he would have to come back another time. He snatched up his shotgun and jumped aboard the rear of the van. The doors shrieked as he slammed them. He thumped his way through the supplies and hooked his shotgun overhead on a gun rack nailed into the roof above the driver's seat.

Before him, the zombies thickened, filling the road. He looked out his side window and realized dozens more were only ten feet away and closing.

Realizing the slight booze buzz had left him and that his breath was coming in rapid huffs, he found the keys and started the beast. The engine roared to life.

Inhaling deeply, Gus steered his van to the right of the mob ahead, aiming toward the thinnest point. He had tried bashing his way through a mass of zombies before, at much higher speeds, but the mess afterward had left him reluctant to try such a thing again. Accelerating, the beast got to thirty before he bumped into the edge of the undead, the grill guard spinning the walking corpses away like broken robots. Hands and arms thumped against the left side of the van, hitting it hard enough to make him grimace. He ran down four shambling stiffs, bouncing in the seat as he drove over their flailing bodies. He felt his sphincter clinch and swore to sunny Jesus he wouldn't shit himself.

He grabbed for his seatbelt and struggled to fasten it. He took his eyes off the road for a split second to get the seatbelt secured, and the van thumped as it went over a curb and onto a yellow front lawn. He snapped forward, almost crashing into the steering wheel. He glimpsed lawn gnomes going under the van, their half-destroyed faces going dark as the vehicle rushed over their heads. He regained control of the beast and steered left, catching a peek of the mob turning around for him. He longed for side mirrors, but one encounter where the gimps had actually hung onto them, grinning and hissing until he shot them off, had left him no choice but to remove the things. He wondered if he would have to do that with the door handles someday.

The van bounced back onto the asphalt, narrowly avoiding a fire hydrant and a punched-in mailbox. Gus got the vehicle back on course and looked ahead, seeing nothing but open road. Getting his breathing under control, he drove a block before stopping and glancing back at his merchandise. He had almost a full load, but there was still room for more. The question was where to look for more. How he had missed that particular convenience store was beyond him, as he'd been up and down that particular stretch of town many times. He thought he knew the area.

Don't be stupid. Don't be greedy.

With that thought, he eased the van up to forty. He took a turn down another road and drove on the main drag of Annapolis, weaving in and around the derelict vehicles still on the road. On the left and right, he saw food warehouses, shopping malls, drugstores, and gas stations, all looking as if they had had the living shit kicked out of them. Gus wasn't the first person to pick through the larger shops, as there had been plenty of looting going on back when the world up and died. There had been enough looting and danger to make him steal away to the wilds beyond South Mountain, where he waited for almost a month until he ran out of camping supplies and was forced to return. Return to a civilization gone mad. Feral.

He drove by the fast food restaurants, McDonald's, Burger King, Dairy Queen, all broken into and left gutted. On his left, he passed a ramshackle Canadian Tire and Home Hardware, where Gus had gone several times to find building supplies and weapons. Two years ago, he had sometimes seen other people. He remembered seeing police and even a squad or two of green uniformed soldiers, but not anymore. In fact, getting right down to it, Gus figured he hadn't seen another living soul since . . . last spring. Not anyone. He heard people at times, up on his mountain estate, gunshots and cries of terror and agony that always went on for too long, haunting the hills and valley and either fading away or abruptly stopping.

Last spring. The thought made him frown. It was fall and heading into winter.

He turned onto the highway that led out of Annapolis, up a ramp that warned he was headed the WRONG WAY, like he gave a shit. Out of reflex, he looked over his shoulder as he merged with the major road, even though traffic wasn't an issue anymore. As he drove home, weaving in and out of abandoned cars, he glanced at the forests, and sometimes the houses, but he usually kept his eyes on the road, just in case a gimp wandered into his path.

He turned off the highway and got back with his load in the afternoon. It happened like that at times. If the pickings were slim—as they were growing more and more—he would be out longer, but getting what he wanted and returning before dark was fine by him. He wouldn't go back to that part of the city until a few days had passed and the nest relaxed.

Satisfied with the day's events, he parked his van and went about unloading his newly found supplies.

3

After parking the van in the garage, he got out of his gear, returning it to his locker. He took a welcome home shot of Captain Morgan, then another because it tasted good, and knew he'd have to replace the bottle soon.

"Saucy fucker." He glowered at the captain's grinning face. Gus turned around and took in the van full of booty. It would keep him for a while and fill the storeroom nicely. With a huff, he jumped into the back of the van and studied what he had scavenged. He liked keeping it in the packaging for as long as he could, as it reminded him of new, the concept of new, and perhaps fresh, even though each of the canned goods would have to be checked before he ate it. The packaging and preserving process the food went through seemed near perfect, and most times the canned food was fine. If he did open a bad can, it usually smelled or looked off and went into the garbage.

With a resigned sigh, Gus got to work. He lugged the drinks and boxes of food into his house and down to his basement. Two bedrooms converted into storerooms were filled with supplies, and in one of those, he stowed the new food. He spent a good two hours restocking the room, checking dates on the new canned food, and rotating the old out so he could access and eat that first. Old meant little to Gus, as all food production had halted when everything went to hell. Most of the canned food had passed the expiration dates, but it was still edible, as the polymers kept the food preserved. Gus would eat anything, but he recognized the problem facing him. The canned food would run out eventually, and when it did, he either had to grow his own or perish.

With the day moving into evening, Gus figured to relax and have himself a smile. He entered the second storeroom, which was filled with boxes of alcohol. Rum, whiskey, gin, Irish cream liqueur, vodka—though he hated that shit—liqueurs, wine, and plenty of others. He even had a case of apple brandy, though he had only opened one bottle of it. The one place that people seemed to ignore was the liquor store for whatever reason, and he had been able to clean out what was on the main floor's shelves alone in six separate runs. He had gone back several times, taking more from the store-room behind the liquor store. Someday, that would change. A scavenger like him would find it eventually.

However, he had stockpiled enough spirits in the downstairs room to go into business for himself. He took out two forty-ounce bottles of a Crown Royal special reserve and another bottle of Captain Morgan dark rum. The Captain Morgan he walked back to the garage and placed on the shelf as reinforcement to the dwindling supply there. The Crown Royal whiskey he brought out front.

The air had turned cold, which forced him to get a couple of sweaters and change into a double layer of sweatpants. When he returned, the sun was dropping in the west, and the clouds parted, colored a reddish violet. He walked out to the edge of the wooden deck, seeing the broken glass from the night before and telling himself he had to clean that shit up—tomorrow. Anytime he made it back from Annapolis still intact was something to celebrate. He plopped down in one of two plush chairs situated underneath a huge green garden umbrella. He wanted a drink—a smile, as his grandfather used to say. Maybe four drinks, before getting something for dinner. Just to relax.

Facing Annapolis, he unscrewed the top of the bottle and sipped. The rush and burn woke up his taste buds, throat, and stomach. *Fire one,* he thought, and then, *Fire two.* He settled back into the lawn chair, keeping the whiskey bottle in his lap, and spotted the blanket on the other, just out of reach. That might be needed a little later, but he was content to sit, drink, and watch the city go to sleep.

Wind cut across his bearded face, and for a moment, he wondered if he needed a toque. Another sip. Another grimace. The booze took the thought away. He adjusted himself in the chair, the material squeaking, and scratched his balls. The events of the day replayed in his mind. Fear. Diluted by the booze—the only and best way he knew of calming himself before going into action—and the driving of his van into the front of the store. Toilet paper. Good stuff. Had to have the shit to wipe yourself. In the movies, it was food, water, and ammo. Never said anything about crap wrap. That was something they didn't cover in the movies. Someone fucked up.

Gus chuckled, took another shot of the Crown Royal, and studied the darkening cityscape and the Bay of Fundy beyond it. His thoughts became a slow drip of anesthesia as he watched and sipped. Somewhere, he forgot his limit again and lost count of the shots he downed. The city became a basin of black and as biting as the dragging wind. He could see no lights at all, which was, he supposed, a good thing. He didn't know what he would do if he ever spotted light out there in the void. He certainly wouldn't do anything at night. That was as certain as all fuck. Sometimes, he caught a scream, or the end of one, waking him from a doze. Sometimes it might repeat, and mostly, he convinced himself it was just his mind becoming a little more unhinged.

Things might have been a little more bearable if he had company, but with company came another set of rules, and he felt, no, he *knew* that being on his own for so long had both saved and warped him. The angst of laying those rules out to a person who might not be receptive to following them turned him off from the idea of company entirely. In the movies, it was always the same—the greater number of people in a group, the higher the probability of there being an idiotic douchebag, which led to a higher chance of the douchebag placing the others at risk. That thought made him shake his head. He'd considered finding a dog at one point, but most of the dogs had long perished, especially the short-legged breeds, not having the speed to escape the zombies. In fact, he couldn't remember the last time he'd seen any kind of wildlife other than birds. Something probably existed out there, but he just hadn't seen it yet.

No, it was better to be alone in this world.

It was better.

Another long draw of whiskey took away any argument that another part of his mind might have voiced.

4

"Jesus *Christ*," Gus moaned upon waking and squinting out at a red sky. He woke up stiff, hung over, and facing the cityscape of Annapolis from the comfort of his lawn chair. Sometime during the night, he had hooked the blanket off the nearby bed and covered up with it. He squinted at the nearby bottle of Crown Royal and realized it was half gone.

"Goddamn alkie." He stared at the morning sun. Perhaps seven thirty or around there. He sat up, snarling out a yawn. Deep blue, the likes never seen before due to eighty thousand or more flights a day, greeted him warmly. That was one good thing about the apocalypse. The absence of flights cleared the sky of the usual silk worm gauziness that paled the color. Car emissions had once added to it as well, but the airplanes were just as guilty of fucking up the atmosphere. People just didn't hear about it as often, if ever. The sky that he opened his eyes to was the color of paintings. He wondered if that was a conspiracy of some kind. Fuck it. The only conspiracy he wanted to hear about at the moment concerned breakfast. Rising to his feet with a grunt, he turned to the kitchen with a long lingering scratch of his nether regions. He threw down his blanket and left the whiskey on the table. His core complained of a chill, and he wondered if he could pick up a cold without other people around. That was that. No more sleeping in the great outdoors, even if it was in a plush lawn chair.

In the kitchen, he boiled water on the electric range and unpackaged a bowl of instant noodles. Gus thought about checking the solar panels on the roof, but decided against it. He wouldn't know what to do with them anyway, beyond clearing them off. There was a wind turbine to supplement the limited power supplied by the solar panels, but it didn't seem to work. The batteries in the storage shed collected and stored enough power from the panels to keep the house going, as long as he didn't do anything too heavy. He had no idea how long the power was going to last, and trips to the shed where the batteries were housed gave him no clues. The meters and their numbers meant nothing to him. Any day, he fully expected the things to die on him, and whatever electricity the batteries had stored up to that point would be the last.

He opened the fridge and mixed himself a glass of powdered milk, which he swore curdled as it splashed down onto the contrary pad of his stomach. No dry heaves, which was good. He held out his hand, flat, as if he were about to walk like an Egyptian. It quivered slightly.

Gus grunted. He stared out a mostly boarded-up window that gave him a nice view of his wall out front. Moving to a cabinet, he got out a rare can of Coke, as well as a bottle of rum, and mixed a drink. *Half a smile, Pop,* he thought to his long-gone grandfather. Sighing, he shook out four aspirin from a bottle and palmed them all into his mouth. Raising the drink in a toast to the outer wall, he downed it. With the Coke, the rum tasted sweeter. His grandfather and father had it right after all. It *was* better than milk.

Gus gasped as the mix and medicine went down, then took a deep breath. When the noodles were cool enough, he ate, feeling the revulsion in his guts, but determined to get something in there besides booze. After breakfast, he rinsed the dishes in the sink and dumped the plastic packaging from the noodles into a garbage can. The sofa in the living room called out to him, and he walked to it, half in a daze. Lying down and getting comfortable, he realized that he hadn't opened the curtains in the last two days. A deep weariness settled over him then, and he knew he wasn't about to open them now.

Wasn't it bad to take drugs and booze together? was his last conscious thought before drifting off.

Six hours later, he woke up, still feeling hung over. He lounged about the house, carrying a bottle of rum with him wherever he roamed. He went down into the rec room, opposite the storerooms, and flopped down on the soft sofa there. He lit candles, both for the light and the relaxing effect. There was something pure about candles. Something even Christmasy, if that was a word. Tammy had gotten him into the practice, as she often had rooms illuminated with candles, some scented, most not, as they were the cheap variety. It never bothered her, as they all burned the same.

For the next four hours, Gus watched Disney animated movies, chuckling while drinking water from a four-liter plastic bottle with a chaser of Bacardi White and cola, not thinking about having Tammy snuggled up next to him. After the last movie, he flicked off the screen and covered up on the sofa. Thoughts seeped into his mind like vines forcing their way through the mortar of a brick wall. He lay there in the semi-dark of the basement, basking in the calmness of scented candles, and listened to the house creak above, noting that the sounds were only caused by a hungry October wind. He took another glittery-eyed sip of his rum and Coke. It was a big house, and he remembered when he first found it, how he would get up and investigate every sound he heard. He had stopped doing that perhaps a year ago. Winter was coming to Annapolis. It would be his second on the mountain.

Winter was coming, and its breath made the bones of the house ache.

The next day, Gus stayed off the rum and whiskey all morning. Work needed to be done, and he was feeling industrious. The good weather stayed, and he decided to get on the things that both needed to be done, and what he wanted to do.

A book he'd picked up from the library had taken up his reading time when he actually felt like reading. In the book entitled *Medieval Campaigns And How They Were Won*, Gus came across the idea of defenses. He'd gone out and studied the wall about his world, ten feet high and a foot thick. The wall wouldn't be enough if *they* ever got up there, and he had to count on the day when they would . . . and what would stop them when they did.

He was only one man, and he could only do so much, but he had *time* aplenty. He lived on the side of a mountain, with the ground on one side still soft. That would change with the colder weather. He had wanted a second wall, but didn't know where he could find the brick to do it, and he didn't know how to prepare mortar to stick it all together. But for the month of August, when he started having ideas of improving his defenses, he made the effort to get digging supplies from the warehouses in town. Picks and sharp black-bladed spades, crowbars and long iron bars for leveraging, chainsaws and handsaws for cutting. All of those things and more he loaded into his van and brought to his garage.

Moats were effective in throwing off armies. He didn't have enough water to fill one, but he would worry about that later. He wanted to *dig*. His wall extended from one side of the mountain, curved around his property, and ended with a forty-foot drop. Some small spruce trees had to be removed, but Gus meant to encircle the entire length of the wall with a deep trench. How deep he would be able to get it, he had no idea. He had already marked the earth with a shallow groove, no more than a couple of inches deep, that ran parallel with the wall.

September was already a write-off. He had gotten very little done, with the exception of cutting down the trees in his way near and on the mountainside. Today, he meant to start digging deeper. With a wheel barrel, he lugged the pick and spade through the crack he had opened in the gate and, counting off five feet from the base of his wall, started hacking out his trench. He took short gouges with the pick to tear up the turf and loosen the topsoil. After ten minutes of picking, he stopped and looked back at his progress. Three feet. Three feet not even cleared of the loose dirt. He sucked at ditch-digging.

"Fuck," he breathed, feeling the sweat rolling down his face. It would take a year to do what he wanted to do. There was no way he could get an excavator up without drawing the gimps. And the sound of the work would only bring more. It was with the pick and shovel or nothing at all.

Jesus.

His hands became raw as he worked, reminding him of a time he'd had to quit a construction job because he got too many blisters. He stopped at the top of the hour for a shot of water, wishing it were rum. He was fine with that, though, knowing full well he'd treat himself after the day's work. He inspected his hands and swore at them for becoming sore so quickly. He returned to the house to fetch some work gloves from the garage. He quickly found a pair next to the skin magazines he'd liberated from the shop. His brow arched in interest, but in the end, he left it.

He stepped outside the house and heard a gunshot.

The sound froze him in place. Another shot rang out, the echo of a *pop* coming from the front of the house. Gus ran to the deck and gripped the railing as he leaned into the wind, listening. The city looked deserted, cold, and while he watched, didn't make a sound. Gus strained to hear something, anything.

A scream.

It was a long drawn-out thing, full of pain and grating on the nerves. A man's scream. It continued on for seconds before finally faltering and petering out. Gus strained to hear more, but there wasn't any more to hear. After a long minute, he half-turned, scanning the city for a sign of some kind. The scream had originated from the center, but that was as much as he knew. The man had taken a long time to die, and he wondered why only the two shots. Perhaps he only had two shots left. Two shots to take on a small city's populace? If Gus were caught in some situation where he was faced with certain death, he knew what he would do, and how he would use those last two shots. The thought entered his mind to go down there and investigate, but he decided against it. Whatever had happened down there had happened, and that was that. Gus wasn't about to venture into the city for a stranger.

But he did return to the house for three calming shots of rum.

With the booze in his belly, he went back out to the trench, placing the scream behind him.

In the days that followed, Gus learned that it was going to take a long time to complete the moat. He had gotten almost to the end of the wall, and that was only a shallow and narrow cut that widened the initial groove. Expanding it and making it deep would take longer, perhaps even a year, with just him working on it. That thought alone almost made him abandon the project, but after watching a few more zombie movies, the more he felt he needed extra barriers to protect his home. The trench would be the new first defense.

And he rigged a surprise as well, one he was particularly proud of.

On the slope of the mountain, he cleared an area and rolled two plastic drums, capable of holding thirty liters of gasoline, into place. With a hammer, some wood, nails, and caulking, he rigged a pen for the drum, filled it with gasoline, and placed it on an angle on the mountainside, hidden by brush, but positioned above a shallow groove. He stoppered the gas drum with a rubber plug attached to a length of rope knotted to other lengths, making it long enough to run over the wall at the far end. If he yanked on the rope, the gas drum would spill and empty into the groove, running down its length and filling the little trench in front of the wall.

In theory, it looked good. Sounded great.

He even made a few Molotov cocktails for throwing, just for added *oomph*.

Looking at his work, he thought that starting a fire was only a drop in the bucket. With the trees he removed, he could use the brush and wood for fuel. The more he worked on it, the more Gus liked home defense.

When it was time, he dined on noodles, canned stew, meatballs and gravy, and even sardines, though he found them to be quite salty. He drank conservatively while he worked. He had almost gone through a case of Bacardi White, and he thought about the liquor store below with its remaining treasure trove. There wasn't a need to go yet. Not yet.

In the evenings, he relaxed and watched movies on the television. At night, he read books by the light of a single, environment-friendly bulb in his room, with all windows facing the city curtained. The wind snaked around the house in the late-October evenings, sounding as if it searched for just him. On the evenings when the wind was especially strong, he would simply lay on his bed upstairs in the master bedroom illuminated by candlelight and listen as it struggled. Every sound pricked his ears and made him pause just to see if there was a pattern, above or below. Those nights were spent sipping on straight whiskey or rum—Uncle Jack and Captain Morgan, his favorite companions—as well as the occasional visit by the women pictured in the skin magazines. And memories of Tammy.

There were no other screams from the city. Nor gunfire.

At the beginning of November, Gus had begun to dig down into the cold earth, grimacing at his back, which still disliked what he was doing. His hips ached from time to time, forcing him to take some generic painkillers to silence them. At the far end of the wall, he dug down a respectable foot and widened it about the same for about a hundred feet. Only five hundred or so more to go. Then, he would work on the deepening and the widening of the defense.

Smacking woolly lips, he felt he needed to go house picking again to stock up before the snow came in December. He would have to go down to the city soon. The van wore all-seasons, but he didn't fully trust them in a full-blown Nova Scotia winter. He didn't have snow tires, nor did he have any idea how to get them on the beast if he managed to find some. Last winter, he had stayed on his mountain for the duration. It was extreme and monotonous. But safe.

He thought about finding another vehicle. As much as he hated to admit it, he would lose the beast sooner or later. It would be wise to have a replacement on hand, as much as the old war wagon would hate sharing the garage with another machine. The image made him smile. *The beast*. He'd given the van human qualities. With the absence of living companions, the vehicle was a friend, as loyal as any dog, and he would do what he could to keep it running as long as possible. Gus carried those thoughts into the evening, while he stood on the deck and sipped on a hot rum toddy. He studied the shell of the city and made a list of the things he would need. He needed more gas, since he'd used so much for the home defenses. More food, tools, water, toilet paper—his current stock was fine, but he could never have enough in his opinion— and entertainment. Meaning . . . books. The world had existed on electronic tablets for the most part in the days leading up to the end, but at that time, Gus really hadn't been much into reading at all. That had changed. The house had come with a huge library of digital movies on the terabyte video unit hooked up to the television, as well as several bookshelves full of hardcovers and paperbacks. He had to admit there was something peaceful in simply lying on a couch or bed and just reading. There were books by Sun Tzu, Charles Dickens, Stephen King, Robert McCammon, Tom Clancy, J.A. Konrath, William Meikle, Steve Vernon, and countless others. Whoever had owned the place enjoyed a lot of military and horror fiction, which was fine with Gus.

Oddly enough, he could deal with the horror in fiction.

The hot rum and buttery goodness slicked his throat. He'd learned how to make the drink from another friend who had once lived up in Antigonish. Taking a second sip, Gus nodded. He would head into town the next day and see what he could find. It would take multiple trips, in shorter daylight hours—not that he screwed around with the nonsense known as daylight savings anymore. He knew that the time would come when nothing was going to get off the mountain. Unless he had a snowmobile. That thought had merit.

The trench would have to wait. Tomorrow would be the beginning of the last great rush before the holiday season. The idea made him feel a little brighter. Perhaps he would grab some Christmas decorations. He never knew what he might find when house picking.

Just as long as whatever he found didn't try to eat him.

5

It couldn't have been any more than five or six degrees the next morning. He suited up, saluted the Captain in his locker, downed four quick shots, and prepped the beast. Frost had turned the lawn to crystal, and he breathed out steam for a few minutes before getting in the van and driving into Annapolis. With the heat on and the heated driver's seat, he felt wonderful in the early morning sun, even while wearing all of his combat gear. With a scratch or two at his crotch for luck, Gus felt that the day would be a busy one. He wanted to haul ass in and out of the city before sunset, roughly eight hours away. The drive into the city took twenty minutes, all to the music of John Denver coming from the CD player. It wasn't the morning music he wanted, but he didn't have anything else in the glove compartment.

The beast sped by the intersection where he had run down the gimp the previous month. The dead husk was missing, but that didn't really concern him. Crows or some other scavenger had probably finished off the thing. He wondered for a moment what would happen if a live animal did in fact feast on the carrion of zombies. He remembered the movie *Resident Evil* and how the crows that ate gimps turned into gimps themselves. Freaky shit, but he didn't worry about crows or ravens or seagulls just yet. Seagulls. Gus smirked. What a way to die, being chased down and picked to pieces by a bunch of sea chickens.

He drove through the maze of streets and eventually found the smashed-in storefront of the *Needs* store. He slowed the beast to a stop, facing the hole he'd made the last time, and peered inside from over the steering wheel. Empty, or so it looked, and the surrounding coast appeared clear. Sniffing, he turned the van around with a three-point turn, backing its fat ass up to the opening.

He swung open the rear doors, and the sound of his motorcycle boots hitting pavement stung the air. Visor down, he kept his shotgun pointed forward. He inspected the devastated aisles and deemed them clear. Taking a breath, he proceeded to the swinging door leading into the back. He eased it open with the barrel of the shotgun, fully ready and expecting trouble, only to face a dark and empty storeroom.

"Fuck me," Gus breathed and flipped up his visor. He studied the gloomy interior. There had been a lot of supplies there back in October. Admittedly, he'd dragged his ass in getting back to the shop, but it was still a surprise to find the placed looted.

Someone else was afoot.

The idea sent a surge of hope through him, and he hoped, for a split moment, that it was a woman, an attractive woman who would appreciate having a *man* about. He certainly wouldn't mind having female companionship, but the question of whether she would need him was something else. Gus wasn't the best looking guy, or the brightest, or the hardest working. In fact, even when the world was sane, the women he'd wanted didn't want anything to do with him, and he recalled being flat out rejected so often that he just didn't bother anymore. He often wondered how the hell he'd wound up with Tammy. She could have easily had someone better.

Images and forgotten feelings of hurt and embarrassment flooded his mind, stalling him on the threshold of the shop. He eventually freed himself of the paralysis and got back to the task at hand. Lifting his weapon, he went into stealth mode and moved shotgun-first around the dark room.

Empty.

The person, or persons, had taken everything he'd left behind. The idea didn't bother him too much—other folks had to live, too—but he would have to be on the lookout. Then, he thought, what if they found the liquor shop? Oh, Jesus. He retreated from the storeroom and passed the counter. On instinct, he glanced behind to where the dead gimp had been mashed into the wall.

No gimp.

That put wrinkles into his forehead. He eased around the counter and searched, but the body wasn't there. There wasn't anywhere to go. The thing must not have been dead then, he concluded, just somehow pinned behind the counter. When he'd pulled out, the bastard had probably dragged himself along the floor and out into the open air. Gus studied the ground, but saw no indication of anything crawling away.

Thinking on it more than he should have, he got in the van and closed the doors behind him. He plopped down in the driver's seat and looked ahead, remembering the path he had taken a month ago. The engine started when he turned the key, and he eased away from the *Needs* shop. The road was empty. He knew he had struck a few of them in his escape, but he didn't think he hit them hard enough to outright kill them.

"Aw, fuck it." He eased up to thirty and headed toward another part of the city. He knew of another area where he could do his house picking, a continuation of where he had left off a while ago. His original plan was to move from subdivision to subdivision, mentally checking off the places he'd been to, but sometimes he deviated. Houses were the best stops, and he never went into apartment buildings. Those were too dangerous. Houses could be dangerous as well, but not nearly as much as the potential nests of apartment buildings. Realistically, any building could harbor a number of gimps. Schools, office buildings, and he already knew about hospitals. He wouldn't go back to a hospital unless he was desperate.

The van oozed exhaust as it moved through the sunlit, empty streets. From his driver's window, he spotted gray figures stumbling out from between houses. They shambled in his direction. He turned a corner and saw more of them coming out to fill the road. He drove up over a yellow lawn to avoid where they were thickest, but it was impossible to avoid them all. A thin line of them led by an ashen-fleshed woman wearing a one-piece bathing suit shambled in front of the beast. Her left arm was missing, and her jawless face turned as the van passed. The grill guards split the line of undead, and as he drove through, arms thrashed and thumped against the sides of the van, rattling his nerves a little more. Gus took a breath and wanted a shot of booze.

Turning the steering wheel to the right, he knocked four more zombies on their asses, glimpsing an executive-type guy and one dressed in only a pair of walking shorts. He turned right and then left, giving the van a shot of gas to escape the clingers. Without windows in the rear, he had no way of knowing what was behind him.

He turned the van onto a larger road and wove through the derelict cars. He drove through a series of main streets, passing mom-and-pop shops—how they ever survived among the chain giants amazed him—until he eased the van to a stop in another subdivision. Placing the van in reverse, he backed up to the open front door of a white split-level house. Once the beast was in place, he killed the engine and took a quick look around to ensure the coast was clear.

Gus rattled his way to the back, opting to leave his shotgun behind, and threw open the rear doors. He jumped onto the front steps and glanced inside the house. Seeing and hearing nothing, he entered, closing the door behind him.

Two flights of worn-looking hardwood stairs greeted him on the landing, one heading to a hallway and kitchen above, the other down into the gloom of a basement. Sunlight came in from upstairs, and Gus flipped down his visor. He pulled his bat from his back scabbard, bringing it to guard. Armed and ready, he crept up the stairs, noticing that the air smelled fresh. A good sign.

He stepped into a modern kitchen filled with steel appliances, granite countertops, and a dark wooden finish. *Nice place*, he thought and went to the double-door fridge. He opened it, got a whiff of the remains inside and quickly closed it. He opened the cupboards and found a bag of flour as well as an unopened box of raisins. Going through the rest of the kitchen, he realized that this particular family had grabbed whatever food they could before running. Smart bunch. He moved around the island table in the center of the kitchen and peered into the combination dining and living room, undivided except for a floor of carpeting underneath the sofa furniture. A flat-screen TV interested him for a moment, as did a stereo system with an actual turntable. A picture window covered in drapes gave a gauzy view of the outside.

Retreating to the kitchen, he quickly went through the drawers. Nothing of interest, as he possessed enough cutlery at home. Next, he went to the bedrooms. In the drawers of the master bedroom, he found a flesh-colored dildo hidden underneath some clothes. The sex toy was almost the length of his arm—the things that got left behind. He started to throw the thing back, then reconsidered and tucked it under his arm. Wondering who had lived in the house, he rummaged through the rest of the drawers and closets, and even checked between the mattresses. He pulled out two skin magazines featuring twenty-something co-eds on the cover and a pair of fuzzy handcuffs, which he almost took, but couldn't find the keys. A box on the top shelf held a leather mask with a zipper mouth and eyes, as well as a one-piece bathing suit with the crotch and nipple areas cut out. *Who were these people?* Gus shook his head as he stuffed the mask back into the box and left it on the shelf. He moved into the second bedroom, which appeared to belong to a little girl—pink walls, small bed immaculately made, and a collection of stuffed animals. God help the kid, he thought, with parents into the leather scene and dildos of mass destruction.

Moving on, he found an empty hockey duffel bag in the basement and several pieces of old furniture. A second storage room contained a box full of old paperbacks, military fiction and erotica titles, but the rest of the area lay bare and coated in a layer of dust. He began to wonder if the house had already been looted. He took the duffel bag and books back to the landing, throwing in the dildo, the box of raisins, and the flour. The odd mixture made him smile. What would happen if he added water? He also found eleven rolls of toilet paper, which saved the place from being a total loss. But that was how it went. Sometimes he found something of use, and more times he didn't. He slung the duffel bag over his shoulder, went outside, and crashed into a hissing gimp.

The fright of colliding with the undead woke Gus up. He dropped the bag as the creature swung both arms around him, its yellow-black teeth fastened onto his shoulder for only a second before Gus pushed the thing back. It staggered, off-balance, and hit the front steps with a smack of flesh on wood. Three others hissed, lurching around the open doors of the van and hurrying as fast as their stiff limbs could carry them.

Taking a breath, Gus drew his bat.

Swinging with bad intentions, he crushed the skull of the first zombie, a gray-skinned man dressed in a jeans and a T-shirt. The connection drove the thing off the steps and onto the front lawn. Gus retreated to the open door of the house while two gimps stumbled over their fallen friend. He checked the clearance for the bat. Plenty of room.

The first zombie coming up the stairs got its skull bashed in, the bone shattering like a thick mason jar. As that one crumpled, the next gimp, a woman with her long hair hanging over her face, pawed its way forward. Its hands reached out for him, and he saw that it had no fingers on the right hand. Not even a thumb. Bringing the bat down from overhead, he smashed the gimp on the crown of its head. It collapsed. Gus looked up and saw his first attacker get up, baring its winning smile. It took a moment for him to realize the thing had no lips. Something had chewed them off.

He stepped to the side and swept the dead thing's legs out from under it with his bat. The zombie crashed to the ground, and Gus took two steps to get into position before bludgeoning its head. He straightened up in case there were others. Seeing the area was clear for the moment, he scooped up the bag and plunged into the van, slamming the doors behind him.

"Shit!" He dumped the contents of the bag into a bin. It should never have surprised him. He knew how damn quiet the things could creep along. Gazing down at the treasures collected from the house, he saw something out of the corner of this eye that made him glance toward his windshield.

There, a dozen more of the creatures, spread out like a fucked-up offensive line, shambled toward the van. Gus snarled and gripped his bat. Anger surged through him. Why couldn't he get a break from the things? Why couldn't he house pick in peace?

Stupid . . .

He ignored the inner voice.

Drive away, *it said.*

But he didn't feel like driving away. He'd been driving and running away for the better part of two goddamn years. Fury took hold and his inner voice shut up.

He moved to the back, opened the rear doors, and jumped out. Visor down, he walked with purpose to the front of the van, his rage building.

"You fuckers want something?"

Shambling forward, the mob hissed.

"Yeah, thought so."

He swung the bat, almost taking the head clean off the nearest decomposing gentleman. The impact of bat hitting skull rang briefly in the air, but damn if it didn't feel *good*. He glanced to his right to confirm the position of a large female zombie closing in from that direction, then he tore into the others with vicious strikes. He killed two almost immediately before he heard the clatter of shoes on asphalt. An alarm klaxon went off in his skull an instant before the fat zombie plowed into him from behind.

Runner! His mind shrieked as about two hundred pounds of dead flesh bowled him over. The freshly dead could actually move when they wanted to, unlike the older ones. His helmet protected his head as he bounced off the sparkling road, saving him from an otherwise serious gash. Gus felt the woman on his legs. He sat up just in time to see her mouth, gray and speckled with black sores, open wide and gnaw on his shin protectors. Hands clamped down on his shoulders and helmet, and panic rose in his chest.

They swarmed.

Something grabbed his arm, and he felt fingers gouging into the leather of his gloves, gloves that had no protection on his fingers. Another embraced his head with both arms. Yet another thumped down on his midsection, flattening him. Clawed fingers raked across the leather protecting his guts, pulling on it, attempting to dig through to the tender bits underneath. Teeth snapped furiously over his helmet, and another set of teeth squeaked-smeared across his visor. The owner bit too hard, and some of its black teeth came free of its gums upon connection. They stretched him out, and he saw it then, like he had seen in countless movies where the zombies swarmed their victim by sheer volume, searching with their mouths alone and biting and biting and *biting* until they found flesh. He pulled in a quick breath when something crashed into his balls, robbing him of strength. His limbs suddenly felt as if he were struggling beneath twenty feet of water. He felt invasive fingers twisting at his helmet, trying to solve its riddle. On the other side of the visor, an angry mouth gnawed, giving him a graphic display in a torturous slow motion that part of him *knew* he should do something about, but the agony of his balls held him.

He felt the zipper on his leather jacket give.

Felt the fingers on the hockey vest underneath. More scrabbling on his helmet and inside his thighs.

And he lost it.

Gus bucked, twisted, and turned. He snapped out a boot, breaking the face of the thing on his legs. He yanked his fists from the grips of the dead and punched. He grabbed and snapped the wrists of the man clawing through his leather. He brought his knees up and under him and reached out and placed his hands on the cold asphalt, in between the shoes and boots of the dead. They clawed at his back and his helmet, their hissing and moaning loud in his ears. Dead fingers worn down to bones dragged down his spine. Fists pounded his back.

Propelling himself with both legs, Gus shot upward and through the mob like a supercharged linebacker. He broke free and circled around them, their dead faces tracking him as the ones he'd knocked down climbed to their feet. Fear and rage coursed through his system. His leather coat hung open, the zipper torn apart, and his protective vest bore the scratches of the throng. He ran back to his van, hearing the pursuing *clop clop clop* of the shoe-wearing bitch that had tried to bite off his legs. He jumped in the open rear of the van.

Don't be stupid.

He slammed the doors.

Don't be stupid.

He got the shotgun and groped for a fistful of shells. *Things almost had me. Fucking runner took me down.*

Don't be stupid, countered his inner voice.

Something pounded on the rear doors. The inner voice *pleaded* with him to get behind the wheel, not to go back out there. He wasn't prepared for that kind of fight. He was on bad ground. He should just get behind the wheel and drive away before things *really* got out of hand.

That thought brought on a savage grin. Things were *already* out of hand. And two years' worth of running, hiding behind a very big wall, and eating canned slop well past its expiration date suddenly came to a boil.

He threw open the rear doors and blew the head off the runner. He cocked the gun, ejecting a spent red plastic casing, and blasted a meaty hole in the chest of another, flinging it back. Another pump of the shotgun, and another head exploded in a chunky spray. He shot a fourth and fifth, the skulls bursting in the roar of the shotgun. Finally, he hauled the doors closed again, placed his back against the wall, and reloaded.

Fuckers wanted to play.

He was all up for playing this particular day. He was *all* up for it.

"All right." He went to the front of the van and looked through the side window. His bat was out there, and he wanted it. Badly. He filled his pockets with more red shells, his fury escalating into something terrible. Kicking open the driver's door, he got out and turned to the rear of the van. He finished off the zombie with the hole in its chest, blowing its head away as it struggled to get up. Placing the butt of the shotgun to his shoulder, he took a wide stance and fired four more shots, punishing the mob collected at the rear of the beast. He placed his back to the van and reloaded, his mouth a tight line of concentration as he jammed red shells into the breach. Gimps walked toward him. He chambered a round, placed the butt firmly to his shoulder, and blasted the face from a zombie reaching for him. He moved to the side, pumping and firing. It was impossible to miss his targets at such close range. He entered the street and focused on reloading as well as retrieving his bat.

Right in the middle of the street? *his inner voice screamed.* You're in the middle of the fucking street!

Four gimps closed in on him. Four craniums were blasted open. He reloaded and fired more rounds into the approaching gimps. *More* were coming from the houses, drawn to the noise of battle. Through the gathering mass, another runner charged, barrelling through on legs not yet stiffened by the elements. Its arms rose, and it got within five strides of Gus before he fired, taking away half of its skull with one blast. He inhaled the smell of gunpowder, and that odor brought him back to his senses. He jammed his last shells into the smoking shotgun. The bat lay at his feet, and he scooped it up in a motion that his hips would remind him of later, when the adrenalin left town.

The dead closed in.

Gus grunted furiously, fighting down panic as he retreated. He shrugged aside hands reaching for him and made a run for the van. He reached the driver's door and threw the bat inside. Taking aim, Gus destroyed three more monsters before he emptied the gun, and *again,* he felt a surge of longing to take the butt of the shotgun to the rest of the advancing corpses and bash in as many heads as he could.

Instead, he whirled and climbed aboard the beast. He started the van and rammed four gimps standing in front of it, their forms mashing against the grill guard for an instant before rolling under the wheels. The beast bucked and bounced over the bodies as if they were logs. More zombies came into view, oozing from the sun-bright, yet sepulchre houses, and a chill descended over him.

That was the horror of the things. They simply kept on coming. Not stopping, no matter how bad a shit-kicking they got. It was impossible to throw the fear of God into them. The things had no fear whatsoever. Gus remembered the expression from way back. *No fear.* Nothing. Just a form with teeth and a driving hunger.

His foot hit the gas, and the beast shot across the street. The van swung to the right and narrowly missed a fire hydrant. The near impact reminded him of the almost collision a month ago, and he swore at the red stump of metal. Little fuckers were as ubiquitous as ATMs. The front right tire crashed up and over the flower beds of an overgrown lawn, then roared across driveways until Gus edged it back onto pavement. The right corner of the beast clipped two zombies and sent them flying into a knot of the creatures, bowling the works over like moldy tenpins. Still more filled the road, arms wide as if attempting to corral their dinner.

Gus gave the beast another shot of gas and drove through them.

The van whumped and jumped at each body going under it. Arms and heads careened off the grill guard. One head exploded on contact like a rotten melon, its fragments plastering the windshield. An arm struck the tempered glass almost hard enough to split it. The zombies battered the ribs of the beast as it passed. Gus held on tight to the wheel as he didn't have time to buckle his seat belt. Heads *pick-packed* off the van's metal face and dropped out of sight. More gore dappled the glass, and he had to crane his neck to see where he was driving. He slammed over another wave of dead, jumping in his seat with the multiple impacts as the knot of bodies went under the beast. He felt the wheels spin for a brief, colon-blowing second before finding traction and plunging onward.

More undead blocked the way.

Drawn to the noise, Gus thought, and turned left. The van flew up a driveway and toward a high fence. He stretched his neck to see if he could see anything beyond the barrier and made his decision a second before the van smashed through it. Wood fragments flew as if in a tempest, and the beast crashed into another backyard. The right front tire crushed a plastic fire truck big enough for a toddler. Gus steered the van beside the house, down the driveway, and onto another road. He turned left, thinking he knew how to get out of the area. Ahead, he saw a thick stream of zombies lurching down the street he had just escaped from. He swerved to the right, and the beast ran over only a handful of gimps as it broke through, smacking into one after the other fast enough that the noise sounded like gunfire. The van burst through the last zombie, snap-pirouetting it until it fell and was gone.

Gus drove on, the beast roaring in elated victory as he accelerated. When he reached the city limits, he slowed a bit, holding a hand up in front of his face to check. The thing shook as if he were being cattle-prodded anally. He gripped the wheel and didn't let go until he reached the poorly camouflaged gate of the road leading home.

When he parked the van in the garage, much of the fright had left his system, or so he thought. He didn't bother with unpacking the scant supplies. Going inside his home and locking the door behind him, he went into the kitchen, grabbed a bottle of Captain Morgan, and held it up to the light. The foppish officer on the label smiled at him, coaxing him to do what Gus needed no coaxing for. He took three burning swallows of the rum before taking a breath. The rum bungee-jumped down his throat and poisoned his belly. He bared teeth at the impact, but he didn't put the bottle down and kept those first shots inside.

He moved out the back door and onto the deck, taking violent sips from the bottle. He marched over to the edge, eyes narrowed in anger and frustration and residual fright. He took two more swallows, grimacing at the shots to his body as solid as any fists, and stared murderously at the still bright, indifferent husk that was Annapolis.

Today had been close.

Too goddamn close.

Replaying the events in his head, he swooned at the stupidity of his actions. A fucking bat! He had a spare one in the van, for Christ's sake. The memory of being hit from behind by the runner gimp made him take another furious swig from the bottle. The Captain seemed to wink at him. Gus recalled the opening mouth of a zombie on his visor, so close he couldn't focus on it. The force on his jacket. His jacket! He glanced down, spread apart the flaps where the zipper broke, and felt the vest that had kept the gimps out of his guts. He had never been swarmed before, never come so close to dying, so close to being ripped open.

So close to being eaten. Alive.

Gus screamed, a short powerful blast straight from the gut. With a bark of outrage and spent adrenalin, he flung the Captain out over the railing at the city. Rum fluttered in the sunlight like a lady's dark handkerchief as it spilled from the bottle, then the bottle broke somewhere below. The soft tinkle of breaking glass served as a hypnotist's bell, waking a subject from a deep sleep. Gus didn't feel restful, however, so he plopped his ass down on the nearby lawn chair while holding his bald head in his trembling hands.

The rum did its work after a few minutes, charging into his brain and dousing his anxiety. He lay back on the chair, eyeing the city under bushy brows, waiting for it to make a move. It didn't. Not even a sound. He palm-wiped his face and took a deep breath. He couldn't do it anymore. He couldn't go on like that. He just couldn't.

He stayed like that for a while, feeling the booze soak into his consciousness like a deep penetrating anesthesia. The sun fell and clawed the sky red. He relaxed, the alcohol calming him, making him forget the error of his day. Gnawing on his lower lip, he knew he would have to go back down there. Perhaps the sooner the better. No better way to face the mistakes than to get up and do it again. But not tonight. And not tomorrow. Tomorrow, he expected to be too hung over to move.

Hell, tomorrow he'd be surprised if he rose at all.

With that thought, he got to his feet and went to get a bottle of anything with alcohol in it.

Two days later, the hangover that had kept him glued to his sofa finally dissipated. Gus swore off all booze, but had a drink of rum and Coke by early afternoon, filling the glass half and half, trying hard to ignore how his hands shook as he poured. He shuffled through the house in warm pajamas, knowing he should be doing something, but not sure what. He finally decided to outfit the van again and get back up on the horse. There wasn't much time before the snow came, and he used the thought of being cut off on the mountain for four months to get him moving.

Making his way to the garage, he consulted his mental list of what he needed and scratched off dildo. That made him smile.

Cold air embraced him as he opened the door to the garage and went around to the rear of the van. He opened the doors and pulled out the duffel bag full of the items picked up on the last trip. He looked back to see if he had everything and noticed a spray of holes in one side of the beast.

Gus's jaw dropped.

Someone had shot at him.

He went around to the van's side and ran a hand over the wide cluster of bullet holes. Obviously a shotgun blast, but who would want to fire on him? Someone in the house? Not possible, as he checked it from top to bottom. Someone in another house? That made sense, but why? It was one thing to have to worry about gimps, but to add a shooter to the mix made things worse. Who had he managed to piss off enough for them to take a shot at him? He stood back and thought about when the zombies had crowded in, pounding on the walls of the van as he escaped. Then a thought hit him.

Maybe the shooter had been taking some of the heat off of him.

That put an entirely new spin on things. There might be living people in the subdivision, and he had left them behind to face a mob of gimps he had attracted in the first place. As much as he thought being alone was a good thing, he didn't like leaving behind people who tried to help him. And he had left them down in the city for two whole days while he got drunk, then recovered from a hangover. The notion sank his heart, and he slumped against the van. What were the odds whoever might be down there was still alive after two days?

Scowling, he got ready to find out.

6

The black SUV came from the east, from the direction of the Cape Breton Highlands. It followed the Trans-Canada Highway all the way down to Halifax County, where it eventually hooked up with Highway 101. Having never visited that part of the country before, the driver thought he would take the scenic route and make the best of it. He had all the time in the world to play tourist, and he knew that sometimes, great bits of fun could be had on side excursions. The final destination remained Halifax, and the armory located there, but it didn't concern him if he got there this week or next. He suddenly longed to see the valley and the city of Annapolis.

The landscape meandered by, and as he drove around the occasional derelict car or truck, he admired the colors of the season. He pushed a button on the armrest, and the window came down. A blast of fresh air rushed into the interior, and he took a great whiff, missing the smell of burning leaves. That was one thing he loved about fall in Nova Scotia, that wonderful drifting scent that would cut under one's nose when least expected. No longer, however, he thought with a frown. Maybe even not ever again. Unless he was the one doing the burning.

An Irving roadside service station came into view, with a number of cars and trucks parked around it. He had always enjoyed the meals at the restaurant attached to the station, back when the world still had all of its marbles. He glanced at the fuel gauge and saw that the tank was half empty. *Why not?* he thought, and flicked on his indicator. It was important to him to observe the rules of the road.

He pulled into the parking lot, parallel with the gas pumps, and let the motor run for a moment, craning his neck to see if there was any reaction from inside. He saw none, but knew that really didn't mean anything. Opening the door, he got out of the SUV and stretched. Standing at almost six-five, he thought of himself as a high cross of a man, thanks to his broad shoulders. His frame had been much more powerful two years ago when he maintained a better diet, but lately, he felt his strength ebbing away. Motorcycle boots covered his feet, complementing a pair of faded black jeans and a drab-looking, dark-olive sweater. His black hair, streaked with silver, ended in a fox's tail at the back of his head. The silver in his hair highlighted the silver pricks deep in otherwise black eyes. Shark's eyes, he liked to think. Soulless and hungry looking. Back in the day, his name was Joseph Tenner. He thought of himself as simply Tenner. It possessed a certain *Road Warrior* charm about it.

Tenner gazed at the cloudy morning sky and took another breath. He walked around to the rear of the SUV, depressing a button on his key fob and getting an answering chirp. He opened the rear door and squinted at the station, thinking he should've worn his sunglasses. He reached in and took out twin leather holsters, which he leisurely slipped one arm into and then the other.

From the station came a hissing. Tenner paused in arming himself and placed one hand on an aluminum bat that he sometimes used. The hissing continued, from multiple points, but he didn't see any targets. From the back of the vehicle, he extracted a Glock 18. The older pieces were more for show at one time, as were most of the other weapons in the back of his ride, but they were just as good as anything else out there, based solely on availability. Or in other words, they were the weapons his father had stockpiled in his basement as part of his once very illegal gun collection, complete with ammunition. Tenner had to hand it to dear old Dad. What point was there in having a cache of automatic weapons if you had no ammunition for them? Like a broken pencil—pointless.

The hissing intensified, and he heard the scuffing of footsteps. Moans. He should've worn his sunglasses, but they were up front.

Tenner loaded an extended magazine capable of holding thirty-three rounds into the Glock 18. He flicked the selector switch to semi-automatic, not wanting to blow his load too quickly. He then pulled out the twin of the Glock and loaded it as well. He holstered both pistols, inspecting each magazine.

In the shine of the SUV's body, he could see a shadow lumbering toward him from behind. His peripheral vision picked up movement coming at him from the station itself. It was a veritable mob. Tenner would never have suspected the Irving station to be such a welcoming pit stop for so many motorists.

He looked over his remaining weapons and ammunition in the rear, wondering if there was anything he missed. None he could see. He didn't like using the heavier stuff for such occasions, preferring the more personal devastation of the pistols. Believing he was ready, he turned around and saw the first zombie staggering toward him with its black mouth open. About a dozen others followed.

"Philistines." He wasn't religious, but he liked the sound of the word. He drew both of his pistols and extended his arms.

In three seconds, he unleashed thunder at the zombies, their heads exploding with each measured shot and their bodies dropping in rapid sequence. The last zombie spun with half of its skull missing, and Tenner put a finishing bullet into the brain matter that remained. He then turned to face the zombies coming at him from the station. Tenner stepped away from his SUV, waiting patiently for the zombies to close, shaking out the shock in his arms from firing the Glocks so rapidly. His father would have bawled him out for doing that. His father didn't need much of a reason to bawl him out, which was one of the reasons Tenner had had no problem putting a bullet in the old bastard's head. The old man had already turned into a zombie, but that was beside the point.

One corpse stepped out from behind a sedan, and Tenner took aim. The head shattered when he fired, and Tenner mentally thanked his old man for not only stockpiling the weapons and ammo, but the hollow points as well. Well over two thousand rounds of ammunition. If Tenner didn't know better, he would've thought his father had actually anticipated the rise of the Philistines and prepared accordingly. That, or he just felt nothing killed better than the specialized bullets. Tenner had to admit that having the extended twins in his hands gave him an incredible surge of power. With his boys, he felt there wasn't much on the highway he couldn't handle. And if there was, well, that was just more of a challenge.

Tenner fired a round into the kneecap of one zombie, exploding the joint, while at the same time blowing a huge hole in and out of the body of another. He chastised himself for wasting bullets, but *goddamn* if it didn't feel good to play. He executed both corpses as they tried to rise from the ground, the tops of their heads splattering to the stutter of the Glocks. He took an arm off at the shoulder of one, spinning the zombie about like a top before stopping its whirl by firing a round into its ear. He blasted the heads off three in quick succession before dropping to a knee, sighting another target, and blowing out one zombie's pelvic region. He turned from left to right, killing the undead with the focused calmness of one used to playing first-person video games. He took the heads off two zombies with the gun in his right hand, while putting down the pelvis-shot zombie crawling towards him with his left. Three more had their faces shot off and wholly destroyed. A boy-sized zombie came around the corner of a car, not ten feet away from where he knelt, and Tenner took his time lining up the smaller cranium before bursting it with one squeeze of the trigger.

Then there were no more.

He got to his feet and surveyed the dead. The place had gotten much quieter. He shook out his arms, feeling the after-ache of firing so many rounds, and got to his feet. Carnage. Raw and unimpeded by anyone's law, that was what he liked about the world of today, the ability to unleash hell and muzzle it as he saw fit. Jesus Christ and balls of holy hand grenades, but it was awe-inspiring. And satisfying—better than a cold beer after a ten kilometer hike, that was for sure. Tenner wanted the dead to rise again so he'd have just cause to blow the fuck out of them once more.

They did not, however. *Well, fuck 'em,* Tenner thought and went among the cars, searching. Nothing made a grab for him as he reached the Irving station's open door and looked inside. The shelves had already been picked clean of supplies, not that he had expected to find anything. It was becoming harder to scavenge anything of use. He suspected that, unless he found the armory in Halifax, his days with the twins were numbered.

He entered the station and walked to the men's room. There, he holstered his pistols and took a leak, peeing in the sink, across the wall and broken urinal, and making a loop. Once finished, he tried the water and got not even a trickle. He flick-dried his hands, knowing they weren't wet in the least, but not giving a shit. Next, he went through the restaurant area, ignoring the dry human remains littering the floor. The kitchen area was empty, as was the dining area. Nothing to scavenge anywhere. Unfortunate. Food might become a concern, as it was running low. Tenner thought it too bad that he couldn't eat one of the zombies. That would make things bearable instead of foraging from town to town.

Having made the stop, he figured he might as well get some gas. He walked back to his SUV and hauled out a twenty-liter red plastic gas container, a metal stake and mallet, a funnel, and two large plastic bowls. He went to the nearest car, a Dodge sedan, and got under it. He located the plastic tank and got the bowls into position to catch the falling gas. Tenner worked quietly, looking around occasionally, though he knew he'd hear anyone before he saw them. He punched a hole in the tank and let the gas flow into a bowl. Gasoline. Twenty years after peak oil, and the world still thirsted for it. Well, he mused, not anymore. It was probably the most abundant resource on the planet. Every derelict car and truck was a mini-deposit of regular or unleaded. He repeated the tapping process for six more cars until he filled the gas container. He used the container to top off the tank of the SUV, then filled the container again. Once finished, he lugged it back to the rear of his ride, grimacing at the weight. He secured the fuel in back, scanned the highway left and right, and sized up the Irving station.

Quiet. Too damn quiet. The natives were obviously planning something. Chuckling, he removed his leather holsters. He hauled out a box of nine-millimeter shells, the hollow tip kind, and took the time to reload each of his pistols' long magazines before placing them back into their toolboxes. Ordinarily, he would clean them at the end of an encounter, but being the only guy around was making him feel relaxed. He would do it tonight, just before sleep.

Checking on the gas container and guns once more and ensuring all was secured for transport, Tenner closed the rear door and walked around to the driver's side. He reached up and patted the plastic carrier on top, where he stowed a few extra goodies. He got behind the wheel and started up the engine.

Ahead lay the carcass of one of the Philistines. Headless and staining the asphalt with brain matter.

A bad place to lie down, Tenner thought, and shifted into drive.

He slowly drove over the unmoving body, relishing the soft squish and bump as it went underneath his wheels.

7

Gus replaced his motorcycle jacket with his spare, thankful for the practice of keeping at least two of everything when he could, and hosed the dead matter off the van and grill guard. That was one thing he didn't like doing, cleaning up after hitting some of the fuckers. He didn't throw the damaged jacket away, thinking perhaps he could repair it somehow later.

There would be no mistakes this time, he thought while arming himself with shots of Crown Royal. The freak-out from before was an isolated incident. Or so he hoped.

Gus drove down the highway toward Annapolis. The late morning sun glowed in a cloudless sky, but its heat didn't reach the city. He drove through the outskirts, spotting a gimp every now and again, and thinking it strange to see so much activity. Their movements on the whole struck him as tidal, being in one area one day, and drifting to another en masse, driven by whatever mystery animated them in the first place. Smells and sounds attracted them, but sight couldn't be possible. Not with some of the undead he'd seen with their faces chewed off. Whatever the reason, more of them were wandering the streets of Annapolis than before, and that made him nervous.

Perhaps there was someone alive there. Someone who had shot at his van.

He proceeded at a speed of forty and kept his visor up to see better. He found the turnoff for the subdivision he had almost died in two days ago and slowed to thirty, looking for signs of the living.

What he saw made his jaw drop.

The zombies he'd put down were gone, all gone. Whatever fluids had remained in their husks stained and marked the places where the creatures died, but the bodies had disappeared. A feeling of unease swelled within him. He exhaled in wary amazement, feeling his breath reflect off his helmet and heat his face. Where had they gone? He eased his foot onto the brake and stopped the van, taking in the sight before him. The door of the house he had visited remained open. He stretched to see, making the leather seat creak, then sat back and just listened. There was no sound but the dull buzz of silence. He lowered the window and stuck out his head. The area seemed clear, and the fresh air chilled his face.

Raising the window, Gus mulled things over. He backed up to the open door of the house. Loaded shotgun in hand, he opened the rear door and jumped to the porch. Cautiously, with his shotgun held firmly against his shoulder, he entered the house. He paused on the threshold, listening, but heard nothing. Fear began to take hold, and for a moment, he wished he had a bottle of something to drive it away. He struggled with going back into the house or simply bolting back to his fortress, forever leaving the seemingly haunted place. Perhaps the dead had become able to get up and move around without heads? That thought made his jaw drop. If that was possible, what other way was there to stop the things? Dismemberment? Fire?

Taking a breath, Gus flexed his fingers on the pump of his weapon and proceeded down the stairs, focusing on the corners just ahead. He moved right, then left, swinging the shotgun in each direction. He quickly established the basement area as clear and went upstairs, waiting to hear a *thump* of something moving. A squeaky floorboard, something dragging along the floor, or *something*.

Gus snaked into the living room, his shotgun sashaying from side to side. He sized up the room though the sights of the weapon, then crept into the kitchen. Clearing that, he moved into the bedrooms, all the while waiting for a gimp or some other unknown fright to pounce. He expected the worst, and even when he inspected the closets of the house, not finding anything did nothing to release his tension in the least. And Christ, did he want a drink.

He retreated back to the van, still wary. The thought of how soldiers in combat situations ever coped with the constant alertness, of being ever aware of their surroundings in the field, was beyond him. All he wanted to do was get home and do shots. *Many* shots.

With a sense of relief, he boarded his van and got behind the driver's seat. The road, houses, light poles, and fire hydrants were all forlorn-looking in the growing sun. Gus sensed the not-rightness of the scene, and it bothered him, bothered him enough for him to want to get the hell out of there and back to his bat cave. He pulled out of the driveway and turned back the way he had come. In the distance, a zombie pulled across a front lawn, the dark body leaving a crease in the tall yellow grass. Behind that one, three others emerged from around the corner of the house.

Gus picked up speed. The zombie crawling along the lawn moved quickly, like an energized snail, dragging one leg that appeared broken. Only four of them, Gus thought, and decided to crush the nearest one under the front tires of the van.

Gus pushed on the gas.

The gimp crawling on the ground looked up and clawed at the air.

And Gus's eyes widened.

8

"You ready?" Teddy looked at them, squinting because of the sunlight coming in through the windshield.

"Yeah," Lea answered from the passenger's seat, strangling her aluminum bat with both hands. Her eyes were wide and eager, like a bungee jumper about to take the plunge.

Scott nodded with a souped-up kind of jerk that spoke of nerves and adrenalin. He held his shotgun with the barrel pointed to the ceiling of the minivan.

Teddy grinned at him. "You look like you're about to shit yourself."

"Yeah." Scott's eyes flicked to the window. His scruffy face hitched up on one side in a sinus-clearing snort.

"Remember to breathe out there, okay?"

"Fuck off, Teddy."

Teddy grinned again and held up his hardwood nightstick to inspect the surface. Bats and clubs were better than shotguns in his opinion. The only thing you had to worry about with them was getting in close enough to use it. A shotgun was fine when you had ammo, but Teddy knew Scott only had two shots left in that boomstick of his. Then Scott would have to use his medieval-looking, spiked horseman's pick that he had gotten from the museum. Teddy didn't like the pick. Originally a cavalry weapon, the thing was heavy, made of metal, and had a hammer head on one side and a single, slightly curved spike on the other. Teddy thought it was great for puncturing skulls, but after that, Scott really had to wrench hard to free it for another swing. The guy still held onto the century-old weapon, finding comfort in the weight of the thing. Teddy thought it was simply too slow. Give him a bat any day . . . if he didn't have a gun on hand, that is.

"Awright." Teddy put his hand on the door handle. "Get it done."

He burst from the side of the blue Dodge minivan, while the others jumped out of their own doors. They ran for a large green two-story house, only twenty feet away. The three of them wore plain clothes under puffy winter coats. Lea's ponytail flopped as she zigzagged, and Teddy had the image of her bouncing up and down on top of him. Those thoughts always seemed to happen in the morning and whenever he saw her without her coat. It hadn't happened yet, but it would soon. She didn't seem too hot on Scott, who was something of a bruiser, which made Teddy the only ride left in town.

They clustered around the front door of the home. Lea got a hand on the knob while Scott stood behind her with his back to the house, keeping a lookout with his pump shotgun and his horseman's pick slung across his back with a loop of rope. The door opened without any problem.

"Go, go!" Teddy urged, pushing Lea on her lower back and urging her inside. He went in right behind her. Scott followed and closed the door a moment later, pulling a curtain aside to keep an eye on the minivan.

Teddy held up a hand, and they listened for movement. After a moment, Teddy rapped the wall twice. To the right lay a hallway and open living room. To the left was a kitchen and a pair of sliding doors leading to the backyard. A set of bare wooden stairs in the living room ran up to the second floor and down into a basement level.

Teddy rapped the wall a second time. "Nothing," he finally said.

"Could be downstairs," Lea suggested.

"Could be," Teddy agreed, wondering how her breasts would feel in his bare hands. Shaking the image out of his head, he moved ahead of her and peered down. He rapped the wall there and stood poised for action. When none came, he edged around and looked up toward the second floor. "Nothing here. They would've come running if there were. I'll check downstairs."

He descended and checked around. He went back up minutes later.

"What's down there?" Lea asked.

"Den, laundry, and extra bedroom. Anything move up here?"

"No."

"Scott?" Teddy asked.

"All clear," Scott said from where he waited on the porch.

"Okay, let's check upstairs," Teddy said, holding his nightstick in one hand. "Watch my back."

They moved up the stairs cautiously and stepped into a reading area with a large wooden shelving unit pressed against the wall. Paperbacks and hard covers filled the five shelves, and a cozy reading chair and foot rest stood nearby.

"Looks good," Teddy commented. "Love to read."

"Me too. Wonder what's there?"

"Go ahead, I'll check the bedroom."

"I'll come with you," Lea said, and Teddy hoped she would. Often.

They slipped inside the master bedroom. A dark blue comforter with matching pillows covered a king-sized bed. A fan hung motionless overhead. A chest of drawers rested against one wall, and a flat-screen TV on a dresser faced the bed. To the right lay the open door to a bathroom.

Teddy looked in. "They have a big tub."

Lea moved into the doorway, close enough that he could smell her. He didn't know how she did it, but she always managed to smell fresh.

"It is a big one," Lea said, eyeing the creamy white tiling.

"Almost big enough for two," Teddy threw out there and got a funny look from her. He seized up, bracing for whatever reaction might come. They had been together for a month, the three of them having met, oddly enough, on the same day in the business section of city, but it was the first time he had dared crossed the line.

To his shocked relief, Lea smiled. "We'll have to try it to see."

Teddy could only nod like a dummy.

"Hey." Lea pointed to the window. "Look over there."

Teddy gazed out of the window toward a neighboring house. He went to the window and looked out across the fenced backyard, complete with a swing set. On the other side stood the house facing the next road over. Teddy never liked city planning, didn't like the way houses crowded in on a person from all sides. Looking over the fence, they were at an angle to see straight into the other house's living room through a curtained sliding door.

"What?"

"That curtain just got shoved back. I saw it just now." Lea stood beside him, closer than before.

"Just now?"

"Yes, just now."

"Hmm." Teddy kept his eyes on the curtain, but it didn't move. "Want to check it out?"

Lea seemed to mull that over. "Couldn't be a zombie. They don't care about curtains."

"Agreed. So what do you want to do?"

"Let's check it out."

Teddy studied the backyard. A fixed gate in the fence separated the two houses. The owners had probably been good friends or even family. They moved back downstairs and went to the sliding door.

"Scotty," Ted called from the kitchen area.

The man appeared with shotgun at the ready.

"Lea spotted something in the next house over, so we're going to check it out."

"Spotted what?"

"Something pulled a curtain across the window."

"A curtain?" Scotty's face screwed up in disbelief.

"Yeah, you coming?" Lea asked, standing at the sliding door.

"I guess," Scotty said, not sounding confident in the least. It didn't bother Teddy. Scotty worried about everything.

"All right. Let's go. Ready?"

Scotty lumbered over to where he and Lea poised to bolt. Lea nodded, and Teddy unlocked the door and slid it open.

"Go," Teddy whispered and launched himself out of the doorway, staying hunched over. All three bunched up at the gate in the fence, and Teddy opened it without a squeak. Inside the other backyard, they quietly and quickly gained the steps to the new house's deck and paused at the sliding window.

"Where to?" Lea asked.

Teddy tried the door. It opened easily with a hushed rumble. He pulled back the curtain and went in, the others following in turn. They entered a dining room with a modern kitchen to the right. Just past the table was an open living room, complete with a brown sofa, matching chairs, a fireplace, and a widescreen TV. An open stairway led up and down, in the same fashion as the previous home. They spread out in the kitchen, and Teddy strained to listen, but heard nothing.

He looked at Lea and shook his head. Lea shook her head back. Scotty pulled the sliding door closed and stood ready with his shotgun. Hooking the curtain with a finger, Scotty peeked outside.

"You stay here," Teddy ordered Scott before motioning for Lea to follow him. They moved to the right and found an empty bathroom and bedroom for a teenage boy.

"Nothing," Lea whispered.

Upstairs, something creaked.

They both froze. Teddy pointed to the ceiling, and Lea nodded. He listened, but the sound didn't repeat. From the sliding door, Scott stared at both of them with a look of unease. Teddy shrugged, and a *clump* sounded overhead, the sound of a heavy boot coming down on the floor.

Stepping lightly, Teddy backed up, following the direction of the sound and keeping his eyes on the ceiling. He held his nightstick at the ready. Across from him, Lea did the same, lifting her bat.

Clump.

They froze. Scott divided his attention from the outside to the ceiling. Teddy lifted his shotgun, asking if he should be ready to shoot or not. Scott waved him off. He knew Teddy had an itchy trigger finger. It was better to save the sh—

Clump.

Then, the soft squeal of planks pressing against each other.

Clump.

Teddy heard the sound of something being slowly pushed, as if bumped, followed by another *clump,* moving across the ceiling.

Teddy backed up, his eyes fixed upward. He clacked his bat against the wall to get the zombie's attention.

An answering *clump,* followed two long seconds later by another.

Adjusting his grip on the nightstick, he slipped into the living room and faced the stairway. Lea flanked him with her bat held across her midsection. He pointed to the landing above and the shadow drawing bigger on the wall beyond it. He heard another step. The thing was wearing boots of some sort. It drew closer to the edge of the wall, walking very slowly, and both Ted and Lea held their breaths, waiting to see what the horror was and anticipating the worse.

Once before, they had entered a house where they heard the squeaking of a rocking chair and eventually confronted the undead grandmother, still in her pink house coat. The creature had rocked and grinned at them with white dentures half hanging out of a mouth festered with black sores.

The one above moved slowly, but then a tip of something came into view, at hip level, and withdrew.

"C'mon out, you bastard," Teddy whispered.

"Excuse me?" a voice said, and a face timidly peeked around the corner.

Lea let out her breath, and Teddy's relief made him smile.

"Hey," Teddy said. "Thought you were a zombie, man."

"Really?" the face came into view, partially in shadows. "I thought *you* guys were zombies. Christ. I think I shit myself."

Lea giggled.

"What's happening?" Scotty asked from his position at the door.

"It's okay, man," Teddy assured him. "Just another scavenger. Whew."

"Don't shoot me, okay? I have a gun, see? My name's Tenner." The man moved onto the landing and held up what looked to be an impressive sidearm with something long sticking out of the grip.

"Not gonna shoot you," Teddy said, watching Tenner come halfway down the steps and look in the direction of Scotty at the sliding door. "Man, I'm just glad—"

With frightening quickness, Tenner shot Scotty in the back, blowing him face first into the glass door. The sound of the shot exploded in the narrow confines of the house, and Teddy was momentarily paralyzed by the scene. More than enough time for Tenner—who had a wild-looking ponytail—to swing the gun back at Teddy and shoot out his knee. Lea screamed and turned to run. A bullet caught her heel, splitting her boot and separating the pad of hardened flesh from the bone. She fell face first into the sofa.

Teddy groaned in agony and clasped his ruined knee. Tenner stepped over to him and aimed the gun at his face. Teeth clenched and tears streaming from his eyes, Teddy moaned loud enough to cause his attacker to frown.

"You weren't careful enough, man." The gun didn't waver. "Can never be too careful."

A motorcycle boot broke Teddy's jaw and knocked him unconscious.

The girl screamed. Tenner stood over the first guy's body long enough to be satisfied that he was out, while keeping his gun on the girl. Finally satisfied, he stepped away from the unmoving man and moved closer to her, levelling the gun at her face.

"Oh, my," Tenner said. "You're a sexy one."

She swung her bat at his knees, but he knew it couldn't have much power behind it with her stuck sitting on the sofa. He easily hopped away from the blow. "Now, now. Relax. I don't want to shoot you again."

"Fuck you!"

"I can do this the hard way or the easy way. It's your choice."

"Fuck *you*!" she screamed again.

He shook his head and sprang forward. She swung the bat again, and he caught it with one hand and punched her in the face with the other, once to split her lips, a second to break her jaw, and then a third time to blacken one of her eyes. She didn't make any noise after the second punch.

Satisfied his guests were subdued, he went back to the one he had shot in the knee and kicked his face, just in case he was napping. He pointed a finger at the woman on the couch and kissed the air as he moved past her and went to the sliding door. The third guy lay in a widening pool of blood. Two out of three, Tenner thought. Not bad for a morning's work. Rolling up the sleeves of his sweatshirt, he dragged both the woman and the man he'd shot in the leg down into the basement. Tenner had discovered earlier that the previous owner of the house had been something of a carpenter. There were plenty of wooden support beams in the guy's underground workshop.

In the basement, he put duct tape over their wounds. Then, he used it to tape their ankles and wrists together. He tapped a long spike of a nail into one beam, then turned and put another nail into a second beam. He lifted the man onto the first beam, and then the woman to the other, hooking their taped wrists on the nails. After adding more duct tape to their ankles and wrists, Tenner stood back and admired his work. Both of them looked like offerings one might see in a jungle movie, where the hero or heroine gets tied to a pole by god-fearing natives, facing the jungle where *something* would emerge.

Thinking about old movies, he went out to his SUV and got his knives. They were special ceremonial knives he'd once bought online for top dollar, shiny and curved with skinning edges, molded handles, and spiked metal bands to protect his fingers.

Tenner hadn't worked on a living person in a while, and he suspected he was somewhat rusty. He wanted to save the woman for later, but he knew he wouldn't be able to keep his hands—or his knives—off of her. Shrugging, he gave in. Living people were increasingly hard to come by in the new world, but it was a world where someone like Tenner could hunt without fear of reprisal. The one nice thing was that he didn't have to rely on chemicals like ether to subdue his victims. He could be brutally direct, provided he could find living people. Before the collapse of the world and the dead rising, Tenner had taken the lives of eleven people across the country. He'd planned to hit Nova Scotia last before taking a ferry from Yarmouth and going down into Maine. Or Boston. Wherever the ferries went. And have a travelling slit show right down to the Mexican border.

He'd read on some very select forums online that a *lot* of fun could be had in Mexico.

The world turning upside down had ended all of that. Not that it mattered. Tenner liked the new world just fine.

The woman woke up as he removed her sweater with a knife. She screamed when he went to work on her bra.

Somewhere in his night, Scott heard the screams. He heard Lea cry out repeatedly, and he struggled to wake up. Then he heard Teddy scream, screams like something a dying animal might make. Those sounds stayed with him as the tide pulled him back, deep into unconsciousness, protecting him like a dark cloak being drawn over his head. Scott opened his eyes.

It was dark. His face was on the floor. His back wailed, and he turned his head, feeling something sticky against his cheek. Taking a breath, he lowered his head back to the floor with a grimace and listened. Quiet. Too quiet. His back throbbed. He stayed prone for a while before rolling over, which was a bad idea all-around. When his back hit the floor, a web of pain rippled out from one point, and Scott thought he remembered being hit with a hammer of some sort. That was the last thing he could recall. No, wait . . . he remembered the screams, those terrible pleading screams that started off as human, but became frayed, like vocal chords under extreme duress, and finally snapping, if such a thing were possible.

Taking in shallow, but steady breaths, he studied the shadows of the ceiling. He strained, but heard only the wind outside, and the occasional creak of the house. No footsteps, no snoring.

Gritting his teeth, he pulled himself up from the sticky floor, and with his limited night vision, he saw the dark white of the linoleum covered by a messy black circle. Puzzled, he reached around and probed his hurting back. He felt holes and a sting that was more like a stab, and drew away fingers coated in black. *Holy shit.* He'd been shot! He hadn't been hit by a hammer; he'd been plugged! Blown away!

Groaning, he got both knees under him while grabbing a nearby countertop. With a push, he got to his feet and flopped over the counter, suddenly dizzy. He took deep breaths and listened to the house. Whoever had shot him might very well still be around. He spotted the dark rod of his shotgun at his feet. Gritting his teeth, he bent over and picked up the weapon, all in one slow motion and thanking Christ that he got it right the first time because he knew there was no fucking way of going down there again. Not in his current world of hurt.

He looked into the kitchen area—empty. He looked toward the living room, saw the pale glow of moonlight outside, and shambled over to the stairs. The stairs. The guy had been coming down the steps.

My name's Tenner. He'd heard that much before being shot in the back. *Shot in the back.* His train of thought drew him up short. He staggered to the nearby sofa and lay down his shotgun. He unslung the horseman's pick from his back and brought it up close to his eyes. In the gloom, there was light enough to see where the bullet had hit the metal shaft of the weapon. He dropped the thing onto the sofa and prodded his right side, just under the arm. There was a bloody hole in his coat there, no doubt to match the one in his back. The bullet must have hit the metal shaft, not square on, but enough to deflect it to one side, where it cut through the meat of his back at an angle and popped out the front. He took a breath. It hurt, and he wiped his mouth. Blood covered his palm and gave him a fright. Then, he realized he had been lying in a pool of his own blood for hours. He bent over and wiped his face on the upholstery of the sofa, then coughed into his hand. It hurt, but after a palm wipe and intense study, he knew his lung hadn't been pierced. He might have broken a rib or two, but he'd broken one of those when he was a kid, and knew there wasn't anything he could do about it.

Retrieving his shotgun, he walked over to the stairs. He shambled upward, leaning heavily against the wall for support. Three quarters of the way up, he decided that either Tenner was stone deaf or wasn't upstairs any longer. He reached the top and went around to the bedroom, reading area, and bathroom. All empty. That left the basement.

The basement. The very word sent a chill through him. The basement had always been one of those places in houses that scared him, more so than an attic. People were buried in the ground, and Scott believed that existing below the earth, even, he thought with a shudder, *sleeping* in basement bedrooms, somehow violated some mystic rule that only the dead knew, but were more than willing to let the living in on the secret. Still, Teddy and Lea were probably down there, and he owed it to them to save them.

If they were alive, which he didn't think they were.

Scott eased his way back down, and made his way around to the steps leading to the basement. He couldn't see anything below. *As black as the grave*, was his clichéd thought, but it still gave him a feeling of dread going down there. He knew it was going to be bad. His heart told him *not* to go down there. Told him they were both dead.

Aiming his shotgun, he took the first step. Then another. Then a third, grimacing at the wood's squeal.

On the fourth step, his foot became entangled with something, and his feet went out from under him. His head hit the edge of the steps, and the impact yanked his consciousness back from his eyes and plunged him into that same black well.

The smell roused him.

Scott opened his eyes to daylight shining in from a window and winced. Realizing he had landed on his back and slid down the steps, he gingerly moved his arms and his legs. His right ankle screamed. It probably wasn't broken, but it sure as hell wasn't happy. He looked around the room and gasped at what he saw hanging from the support beams in the basement. His two companions, stripped of clothing and gutted, their flesh as pale as pearl. Bloody innards pooled at their feet like a macabre heap of sausage skins and coffee grounds. He looked away, not wanting to see any further details, not wanting to see their faces. The smell grew more powerful in his nose and mouth, and he tried to limit breathing in air fouled by decomposing tissue, shit, urine, and whatever else. Making a face, he retrieved his shotgun which had, thankfully, not fallen far from him. On the floor in a pool of blood lay Teddy's night-stick, which Scott thought was most likely what had tripped him. He took a painful breath and hopped onto his one good foot. He got halfway up the steps before having to stop.

Then, he heard the gunshots.

The noise made him jerk his head up, and he looked wonderingly at the top of the steps. Was it Tenner? Setting his jaw, he climbed. More shots rang out. Had the undead caught up with the killer? *A killer!* Scott shook his head as he struggled upward. Of all the sick bastards to survive the end of the world.

He heard another barrage of heavy gunfire as he reached the top of the steps. He knelt on the carpet and crawled over to the drape-covered picture window. Hooking a corner of the curtain, he peeked out at a swarm of undead gathering in the street. They walked toward the house next door, and he spotted a van parked in front of it. A man, decked out in leather and wearing a motorcycle helmet, got aboard the battered vehicle. Undead crowded around it like flies to shit.

Anger flooded Scott's senses. He yanked open a smaller window set in the larger frame and punched the barrel of the shotgun through the screen mesh. Ready to exact revenge, he aimed for the driver's window, trying to steady himself, but a second later, the van lurched forward. It grill-butted a bunch of zombies and plowed onward, bursting through several more as it sped off down the street. The sounds of walking corpses being hit filled the air. Then the driver did a crazy thing. He turned and crashed through a fence. Even through the glass, Scott heard the impact and the ferocious roar of the engine as it cut through to the road behind the row of houses. The van came back, gaining speed, and Scott knew he would have an almost impossible shot. He shouldn't even waste the shell, but then he thought of Teddy and Lea hanging in the basement.

Tracking the speeding van as it flashed through the gaps between houses, he saw it appear for a second at the mouth of the street, framed in his mind's eye, and he squeezed the trigger. The blast knocked him on his back and almost caused him to black out from the pain. He struggled back up to a sitting position and gazed out the window. The van was gone.

The undead remained in the street.

Fright engulfed him as he pulled the window closed and lay flat on his back, breathing rapidly. He thought about closing the curtains entirely, but he was afraid they might see the activity. Then, he remembered the smell from below, and how he had opened the window.

Whump.

The front door.

He clutched at his shotgun, knowing he had one more shell in the weapon and hoping to fuck he didn't have to use it. Getting to his knees, he made the painfully slow crawl toward the steps. He couldn't go down into the basement. Not with *them* down there. He made it to the stairs and headed up.

Whump. Whump-whump.

Shadows against the window. How long before they came through the glass? The door? He pawed his way up the stairs, pushing his shotgun ahead, blood pounding in his ears until he came to the landing. The reading area on his left, the bedroom on his right. The sound of a door opening below made him jerk around in fright, splayed out on the landing like a turtle caught on a narrow beach.

Hissing.

He moved toward the bedroom. Somehow resisting the urge to charge that last room, he crawled to it as quietly as possible. Below, the hissing seemed to multiply. *They were in the house.* Scott got his ass into the bedroom and closed the door with a grimace. He lay on the brown carpet and looked to the right. A bathroom lit by a skylight. He crawled in there. Gasping, he lugged his damaged ankle inside and closed the door as quietly as possible.

They can smell, *his mind told him.* They can smell you.

He glanced around the bathroom and finally snaked his way toward the gleaming white tub in the back, next to the toilet. He hauled himself up, flipped his legs over, and sat down in the body-length bathtub. Breathing hard from pain and exertion, he faced the closed door. Thumping came from below, and he wasn't sure exactly where they were, but they were under him. He aimed the shotgun at the door, then thought better of it and reversed it, tucking the barrel against his neck and wedging the shoulder stock between his legs. If they came through, he would have a second, maybe two, before—

More noise beyond the door. Scott's senses zeroed in on the dark wood, and he wished, prayed, *bargained* that nothing would come up the stairs. He placed the barrel of the gun underneath his chin. *Defcon 1,* he thought blackly, and took care placing his thumb on the trigger guard. The clumping below seemed closer, and he wondered just how many were down there. He had no chance, none at all. The undead flooded a place once they caught the smell of meat.

A crash and a loud moan. More scuffling. Another crash, perhaps a window.

Scott's thumb drifted towards the trigger until the edge of his fingernail was all that kept him in this world. He squeezed his eyes closed, not wanting to see what might burst through the door. He willed the creatures below to leave. He fought down an urge to moan in terror as his mind played dark movies in his brain, delighting in pointing out how the next few seconds could possibly go down.

A loud rumble came from below, and he opened his eyes. It sounded like . . .

His mouth parted in horrified realization. *The smell.* They smelled Teddy's and Lea's bodies in the basement and one—or more—had fallen down the steps. The sounds of more bodies thumping their way into the basement reached him, and he eased his thumb off the trigger. He had a few more moments of life, thanks to his companions below. He had never thought of Teddy and Lea as friends, having only met them on the road, but they were protecting him, diverting the zombies. He pictured the scene in the basement, the decomposing bodies hung like meat slabs in a freezer, and a throng of undead stumbling upon them. He shook his head, not wanting to think anymore. He didn't want to think about that first bite, didn't want to see where the undead would start eating, the abdominal cavity or the pooled guts on the floor. Or even the faces, his traitorous mind suddenly added, thinking of lips and noses.

And above all, he didn't want to hear the sounds. He clenched his eyes and jaw shut as he turned and pressed his forehead against the cool metal of the shotgun's barrel.

They had left him alone.

The day stretched on. He sat with his sprained ankle balanced on the rim of the tub and tried to make himself as comfortable as possible. After the first hour, he shifted to relive the subtle aches in his body, but he dared not get out, dared not even breathe, for fear of attracting the attention of the guests below. The shotgun stayed in the tub with him, ready to blow his head off if necessary.

Somewhere in the third hour, he *had* to move. He placed the shotgun across the seat of the toilet and, grabbing the tub's edges, pulled himself up, his triceps burning from the effort. Easing his body out of the tub quietly proved to be difficult with his gunshot wound and bad ankle, but he managed. He grasped the stock of the shotgun and took it off the can. It dragged loudly against the porcelain, and he bared his teeth and froze, listening and picturing the zombies below stopping in mid-chew, their decaying features coated in Teddy's and Lea's blood, to gaze up at the ceiling.

Nothing happened, however, and he eventually got the gun onto the floor beside him. There was a mat underneath him, and he got it out, rolled it up, and positioned it behind his head. His attention strayed to the door every so often. He sometimes froze and simply listened, hoping he would hear nothing that would give him nightmares later.

The sun drooped and fell, the skylight marking its descent and eventually draping the bathroom in darkness. The temperature dropped, and he shivered despite wearing a thick coat. In the swelling gloom, against the gleam of black marble tiling and creamy porcelain, Scott waited for that dreaded *thump* against the door. The undead could smell, but could they follow a scent like a dog? Was their sense that strong?

Sometime during the night, the sound of a struggle below jarred Scott from a semi-doze. The coldness of the room made him shiver again. He listened, blinking away sleep. More noise, muffled by the door and carpet, but growing stronger. Getting closer.

It faded, however, and Scott let out his breath as he sensed whatever it was heading into the kitchen. *Maybe looking for a drink*, his mind joked morbidly. Nothing like a beer to wash down a burger, his mind went on, or a greasy slab of pizza. Even a chicken leg. His eyes suddenly teared up at the images his mind was throwing at him. He would not scream out, though he suddenly felt the very real and very strong urge to do so. He hitched a sob, a muted thing, and sniffed wetly. Then, he steeled himself and took another settling breath. He felt the throb of his wounds and the exhaustion of his body. He wanted to sleep, but knowing they were still below him, he couldn't relax. In the end, he moved to position himself on his belly, taking his rolled mat with him as a pillow, and faced the door. He stopped once, sounds from below making him pause until he thought it was safe to continue. When he got himself around and on his belly, he laid the shotgun at his side. He placed his head against the mat-pillow and hoped he wouldn't snore if he fell asleep.

During that long torturous night, where squeaks of wood and soft bumps caused him to tense and stare at the door, he eventually drifted off.

And slept.

A loud crash woke him, and his fingers scrambled on the black marble tiling before finally locating the shotgun. He heard soft shuffling below, and still on his belly, he placed an ear to the tile and listened. Things moved, bumping into walls. Sometimes the makers of the noise paused, as if sensing something, before moving on.

At the quietest time in the day, in the afternoon, Scott eyed the toilet. He sat up and slowly edged his way to the flush box. He was thirsty, and wondered if there might have been anything in the container. His ankle still bothered him, but he managed to wedge himself into the space between the toilet and the tub and lift the cover. He forced himself up and peeked in.

Dry as a bone.

All of that effort for nothing. Disappointed, he replaced the cover and lay back down. He thought of starving, or dying of thirst. He wouldn't allow it, however, not while he still had the one shell left. He would risk going to Hell rather than suffer through a slow death from thirst. God would understand.

The day wore on, and he tried to sleep, cat naps that weren't restful, but more like something in the gray between being awake and death itself. He periodically heard movement below, but it didn't bother him as much as before.

He opened his eyes and thought that the day had moved on, just from the shadow from the skylight. His stomach rumbled. He got onto the toilet and voided, grateful that the owners of the house had left an almost full roll of toilet paper. He couldn't flush, and it smelled, but there was nothing he could do about it. Mentally shrugging, he lay back down and waited.

For what, he didn't know.

All the next day, Scott lived in perpetual dread of the undead discovering him. The previous night had been terrible, as he couldn't completely rest. Every time he was about to fall asleep, a noise from downstairs would hook him back to consciousness, and he would spend the next hour listening, trying to pinpoint where the sound had come from. He didn't feel the need to pee anymore, and that made him suspect something was wrong. The smell from the toilet didn't help his situation either, and he wondered how long it would take for his shit to dry up and become odourless. He had no idea about such things. Back in the real world, he had been a baker, and the toilets flushed. If he had known he would later be trapped in an upstairs bathroom with his own shit while the dead walked below and feasted on the last two people he knew in the world . . . well, he sure as Christ would have watched extra episodes of the Discovery Channel to brush up on the subject.

Sometime in the afternoon, he believed that a long time of quiet had passed. The idea came to him to try to make a run for it. Bleary-eyed, he sat up and tried standing on his ankle. It crackled with pain as he increased the weight on it. At the same time, something moved below and seemed to be coming up the stairs. The noise culminated in a loud crashing, and then silence. The commotion was more than enough to freak him out, and he put a hand on his shotgun, ready to exit the world with one squeeze of the trigger. The noise retreated to another area of the house, and Scott eased off the trigger. His mind teased him with the image of being on a wide piece of wood siding, floating somewhere in the South Pacific, with sharks circling relentlessly, just waiting for an ankle to slip and dip into the warm water. And he knew then, he just *knew*, he was going to die.

His eyes teared up, and he buried his face into his winter coat to weep . . . for fear of the dead hearing him.

Scott heard a zombie on the steps.

He had woken up to a steady *clumping* on the steps, a slow, irregular beat, as if the thing had downed a bottle of booze and really had to concentrate on where to place the next step. Scott counted off four steps before he heard a more sinister noise, like someone leaning against the wall in a coat and dragging its zipper along the surface. And the low whining buzz drew closer. He got into a sitting position, placed the barrel of the weapon underneath his chin, and squeezed his eyes closed. The noise came closer, and something nudged the surface of the bathroom door, testing it. Scott inhaled deeply, knowing it would be the last breath he would take on God's sunny earth. His thumb found the trigger, and his nail hooked on the guard, just a fraction of metal separating him and the unknown.

A heavy blow came to the door, forcing Scott to open his eyes. Another crash, and he saw the door bulge inward just a fraction. Another strike, spiking his fear to new heights.

Scott moaned. He felt the hard rim of the open barrel pressing into the softness under his chin. He swallowed. Another slam against the door was followed by that sobering hiss he knew so well, but *fuck* if he couldn't pull the trigger. How much strength did a person have to have to do that one little simple movement? One quick squeeze and he would be off, and that would be that. He eyed the turning door handle, a curved lever and not the traditional knob, and Scott knew he hadn't locked it. The lever turned down, then snapped back up, as if the thing on the other side had lost its grip. That was Scott's chance, and he swore he would pull the trigger *now,* and yet goddammit, he couldn't, even as the door handle went down and opened with a click loud enough for him to defecate himself if he had a full load in the pipes. The door swung open, and Scott moaned again and shook his head as a zombie that had to be four hundred pounds shambled into the doorway and fixed him with empty eye sockets filled with balls of worms.

The thing hissed, and Scott heard himself *whimper* of all things, but he could *not* bring himself to pull the trigger. He let out his breath in a burst of snot and tears and, red-eyed, stared at the fat dead man taking that one uncertain step toward him, followed by another. It crossed the black tile in slow shuffles that left grease stains on the clean surface. The smell from the thing made him gag, a putrid stench of meat that had been in the sun for far too long. A fleshy gray hand came up, and Scott saw that there was a hole the size of a golf ball in the palm, and the bones were coated black. That one hand reached for him. The face of the undead had half of its cheek chewed away to expose a row of teeth, making it appear to be smirking at him.

Something in Scott locked in place at that grinning corpse, before a greater sense took over, and he tilted the shotgun forward and blew the zombie's head from its shoulders. The blast flung its reeking bulk backward to land with a splash on the floor.

Scott got to his feet. He had very little time. Moving around the headless corpse, he hopped out of the bathroom, leaning hard against the walls and taking the shotgun with him even though the thing was empty. He held onto the railing as he hopped heavily down the stairs. Sounds of hissing came from the basement, but he ignored them. He rounded the corner, found the front entryway, and slammed off balance against the door. His back and ankle cried out in pain, and Scott grabbed for the knob, yanking the door open with a grunt. Sunlight blazed in. He hopped down the steps on momentum alone before collapsing on the yellow lawn. His shotgun flew from his hand. Hisses cut the air behind him, closer than he thought possible.

Then, he heard the engine. There on the road, a van drove down the street toward him, while the hissing grew louder.

Scott gasped and raised his hand.

9

That's no fucking gimp! The thought ripped through Gus's mind, and he turned the wheel right at the figure lying on the yellow grass. He lined up the wheels of the beast at the last instant so that the vehicle went over the person and crashed into the three undead cocksuckers at the guy's heels. The grill guard knocked them back ten feet, sending them to land in broken heaps.

Flipping his visor down, Gus swung open his door and jumped out. He ran over to the three deadheads just getting to their knees and caved in their skulls with his bat. He turned around and saw that the street was clear. It wouldn't stay that way for long. He flipped the visor back up and went around to the side of the van. Dropping to his hands and knees, he peered under it and locked eyes with a very frightened-looking young man.

"You okay?" Gus asked.

"Yeah." The guy smiled.

"C'mere." Gus offered his hand, and the man took it. Gus pulled him out from under the van. "Get up and get in the van."

The guy on the ground rolled onto his back and winced. "My ankle's fucked up."

Gus bent over and, grasping the guy's arm, heaved the hurt man to his feet. Together, they struggled around the front of the van. Gus got the door open and pushed his soon-to-be passenger inside.

"My gun's over there." The man pointed. Gus turned and spotted a shotgun, a twelve gauge, just like his own. He scooped up the weapon and hurried back to the van. As expected, zombies emerged from between houses and shambled toward them. Gus didn't give them another moment's thought. He had gotten what he came for. He climbed aboard, tossed the extra shotgun in the back, buckled in, and shoved the beast into drive . The van smashed into three approaching corpses as it barrelled away from the house and into the street. He paused only for the moment it took to change gears, then they sped off toward the main drag.

"Buckled in?" Gus asked, leaning over the steering wheel.

A *snick*, then, "Yeah."

"What's your name?"

"Scott."

"I'm Gus." He glanced over once, then twice. The dude was staring at him. "What're you looking at?"

The other man squinted in discomfort for a moment. "Nothing."

Gus frowned before turning his attention back to the road.

The van turned onto the main street and began the drive home. Gus eased off the gas a little and glanced over at Scott—bulky and tall, thinning blond hair with a shit-load of stubble, maybe a week's worth. The guy had a fat face, which puzzled Gus.

"What's up with the foot?"

"Fell down some stairs."

"In that house?"

"Yeah."

"Anyone with you?"

"Yeah." Scott's face became set then, and Gus didn't have to ask any other questions on the matter.

"Where we going?" Scott asked after a bit.

"Back to my place." Gus looked out the side window. "You can't do much like you are. You're lucky. I thought you were one of them."

"Yeah."

Hearing the weariness in the man's voice, Gus looked over at and saw Scott press his head against the headrest. Scott's eyes opened and closed slowly, as if his system was being hit by a heavy sedative.

"You relax," Gus said over the growl of the engine. "It's a twenty minute drive back to the house. Okay?"

Scott's head had already slumped forward by the time Gus had finished speaking. Gus didn't mind. The man was buckled in. Just as long as he didn't snore.

"Don't worry," Gus added, and focused on the road.

Scott woke up in a bed, lying on his stomach with his cheek mashed into a pillow. He tried to roll over, but he felt pain when he pulled to his left. He realized then that he was stripped to the waist and bandaged. He lay underneath a thick comforter. He eyed the room, and from what he could see, the place was nice. A glass of water sat on a night table. He sat up, wincing at the tug in his ankle. He pulled back the blanket and gazed down to see that his ankle was heavily bandaged. Not bad, he thought, and inspected the cloth wraps looped around his chest. He took a deep breath, and it hurt, but considering where he was, he could bear it.

"Hey!" He reached for the glass of water and drank it all.

The door opened, and Gus walked in. Light gleamed off his bald head. "What?"

Scott eyed Gus uncertainly. "Where are we?"

"At my house. Interested in knowing how long you slept?"

"How long?"

"Two days. I got your boots off and bandaged up your foot there, and your bullet holes. I disinfected them with some peroxide. Best I could do with what I got."

Scott placed the glass back on the table. "Thanks. Where'd the water come from?"

"Got a well."

"A well?"

"Yeah, a fuckin' well." Gus frowned. "Why's that a shock?"

"How do you . . . ?" Scott shrugged.

"Get the water up?"

"Yeah."

"Got an electric pump, too." Gus leaned against the door frame. "I'm pretty much self-contained here."

"Jesus, I'll say."

"It ain't perfect, by any means. Solar panels on the roof take in energy and save it in a battery or some such bunk. I don't understand it really, and I expect the whole damn works of it will die on me this coming winter. But it's working now, and it operates the pump that draws up water from the well. Gotta cistern on the mountainside, too. Collects rainwater, or so I think."

"Oh." Scott arched his eyebrows in surprise.

"Yeah, but if you need to use the can, you use that bucket." Gus indicated a five gallon plastic bucket near the bed, a roll of toilet paper beside it. "You fill that, give a holler, and I'll empty it. We don't use the toilets in the house; that's rule one. There's an outhouse out front. But I figure by the time you can use that, you'll be ready to leave anyway."

Scott nodded. He supposed he would.

"Regardless, you're here now. If you need anything, give a shout. I got books, but I'm not moving the TV up here."

"You have a TV?"

"Bet your ass I have a TV. Only one of a few things you can do up here. Flat-screen bastard as wide as your ass. Home entertainment system, too."

"Jesus Christ."

"Oh, yeah," Gus said. "Got a full digital library of just about anything you want to see. Sports, old TV sitcoms, horror movies, comedies, action, you name it. Even got a bunch of foreign flicks down there."

"How many people are here?" Scott asked.

Gus picked something off his black sweatshirt. "Just you and me."

"That's it?"

"Yep. Only you out there?" Gus asked.

"Just me now," Scott said and rubbed at his growing beard.

"Hmm." Gus looked down at the floor for a moment. "Were you the guy who shot my van?"

"Huh?"

Gus looked at him. "Were you the guy who shot my van?"

Scott thought about it. "Were you driving around that same area a couple of days ago?"

"Yep. I was. House picking."

"Then I probably shot at you."

Gus nodded. "You got my attention."

Scott grimaced. "Thought you were someone else, man."

"Oh, yeah? Who?"

"Didn't see his face. He called himself Tenner. He . . . he killed the two people with me."

"He killed two people?"

"Yeah."

"Why?"

"Don't know. I was at the back door when it happened. All I heard was them talking, and then I got punched in the back. I came to in a pool of my own blood, man. I had this war pick-hammer thingy I took from a museum slung over my back. The guy shot me, and the bullet went off the metal bar of the thing."

"Lucky for you."

"Yeah. The two folks I was with, he got them into the basement. Taped them up with duct tape and cut them. Sick fuck . . ."

"And he left you?"

"I figure he thought I was dead. When I woke up . . . the house was empty. And I heard your van out there. I spent two nights in that house's upstairs bathroom with zombies stomping around downstairs. No water. Nothing. Then one of them caught a whiff of me or finally decided to check out the upstairs, and that was that. The game was on. I . . . I was this close to getting it." He held up his hand with two fingers pinched almost together. "I even kept the one shell in my gun to blow off my own head."

Gus listened with a pensive expression.

"But when the thing came into the bathroom . . ." Scott shook his head. "I couldn't pull the trigger. I couldn't. That bastard was maybe two or three steps away from me when I shot him. After that, I got the hell out of there. I knew there were others. If you hadn't come by . . . well, anyway, thanks, man."

The silence grew, and Gus finally broke it by straightening up and leaving his spot in the doorway. Scott remained in bed, the images swirling through his head of just how close he had come to dying, to being eaten by something dead but still running around. He collapsed back on the mattress and watched his hands shake until he made fists. He hadn't had any nightmares, but he figured they would be coming, and they'd be dingers when they did.

Gus returned with two bottles. Pursing his lips, he walked over and held out both of them. One was a bottle of Crown Royal whiskey, the other, Captain Morgan dark rum.

Scott looked up at his host in puzzlement.

"Take one," Gus offered.

"What?"

"You drink, don't you?"

"Well, yeah, a little . . ."

"Then, take one. It'll help. Sure as hell can't hurt."

Hands still shaking, Scott hesitantly took the whiskey.

"Good choice," Gus said, and removed the cap from the bottle of rum. He gestured for Scott to do the same.

Gus waited until the man had the whiskey opened, then he dipped his head in a somber fashion and held out the bottle. "Cheers."

Blinking, Scott clinked the whiskey bottle off the rum one. "Cheers." He watched as Gus took a heavy sip from his bottle, drinking it straight down. He regarded his own bottle, saw the contents tremble somewhat, and took a drink.

Scott cringed and bared his teeth at the fire going down his throat. "God . . . damn." He coughed. "That's some hard shit."

"You'll get used to it," Gus said. "That's one of the other things to do around here besides watch TV."

"Is it?" Scott sputtered, still recovering from the initial shot.

"Oh, fuck yeah. If I get really bored, I do two of these together."

Scott chuckled. "Well, thanks." He held out the bottle.

"What are you, dry or something?" Gus frowned. "That's yours. This is mine. Think of it as medicine for the nerves." With that, Gus took another blast from the rum.

"Jesus, you really like this shit, don't you?"

"Yep."

Scott took another shot, and felt the burn race to his gut.

From the doorway, Gus nodded with approval. "Feel hungry?"

"Yeah."

"You keep on sipping that, and I'll cook something up."

"You can cook?"

"Well, heat something up in the kitchen. For you, I got a can of Irish stew."

"Holy shit, that sounds great!"

"Yeah, well, relax then, and I'll get started on that." Gus turned and left.

Scott studied his surroundings. A wooden chest of drawers sat at the foot of the queen-sized bed, and two night tables were on either side. The place was dusty; he could see the motes floating in the air as they crossed in front of the only window, which was mostly boarded up except for perhaps half a foot at the very top. The sky seemed overcast, but Scott's mood was improving. Scratching at his chin, he took another drink of whisky and grimaced.

Gus was right after all. He got used to it.

10

Later that day, Gus gave two sweaters to Scott and helped the injured man to his feet. Scott draped his arm around Gus's shoulders, and they made slow, but steady time toward the outside. The hard-looking newcomer was a head taller than Gus, and much heavier as well, and they stopped once in the living room to take a breather.

"We can do this tomorrow," Scott said.

"What? Nah, what else you have to do?"

Scott shrugged. "That's true."

"Just a few minutes outside. Get some fresh air into ya."

"Thanks, man."

"You said that already."

"I mean, thanks for this. Helping me outside."

Having nothing to say to that, Gus merely grunted. "Gonna have ta see if we can get you some crutches or something. You're too damn heavy to lug around all the time."

He helped the bigger man onto the deck and past the pool, to the pair of lawn chairs facing the valley full of city.

"Watch out for the glass," Scott said.

"What? Oh, yeah. Meant to clean that up. Here." Gus lowered him onto one of the chairs and stepped back to lean against the railing.

"Whoa," Scott said, taking in the sight.

"Somethin', ain't it?"

"It is."

"Hold on." Gus walked into the kitchen. There was still a good three hours left to the day, and he figured he would clean up that mess of glass. He grabbed a broom and dust pan, and the two bottles of alcohol, and went back to the deck. He placed the booze on the table between the chairs and dusted the broken glass over the edge of the deck. He should've done that long before he had a guest. What would the man think?

"Break a bottle out here?" Scott asked.

"Huh? Yeah," Gus said, giving the broom a toss in the direction of the house. With a huff, he landed on the other chair and picked up his bottle of rum. "Cleaning's done for the day." He took a slug from his bottle. "What do you think?" he asked, gesturing toward Annapolis.

"Great view."

"It is great. Best damn house I ever had."

"Was it yours from before?"

Gus shook his head. "Shit, no. I couldn't afford a place like this. I couldn't afford one of the *closets* in a place like this. No, I found this place maybe five or six days after everything went tits up. Someone had money to do this place, but it wasn't me. I just got lucky."

"Where do you think the owners went?" Scott asked and finally took a sip of his bottle.

"Don't know. Not really important now, is it?"

"I just want to know if you killed them or not."

The statement stopped Gus in his mental tracks, and he thought about what he would say next. After all, from Scott's viewpoint, especially after surviving a very close shave, Gus might be just another crazy fattening him up for the kill.

"I didn't kill anyone not already dead," Gus responded. "I ain't got no problem puttin' a bullet or a shell into the head of one of those fuckers down there. A living person, though, is a whole 'nother ball of wax. I ain't killed anyone for this. God as my witness. Okay? Besides, what kinda sick fuck would I be to bandage you up, feed you, and get you drunk before killin' you?"

Scott smiled. "Pretty sick."

"Pretty fuckin' sick. Damn right."

They clicked bottles and drank. The sun hung above, pausing before skidding down the arc of the sky.

"What did you do before the fall?" Scott asked.

Gus snorted and rubbed his head. He should've brought a toque out with him. "I was a house painter."

That revelation put a smile on Scott's face. "No way."

"Yeah. A house painter. Hard to believe?"

"Figure you to be Special Forces or something. Joint Task Force Five or some shit."

Gus scoffed. "Just 'cause I ran over a few deadheads?"

"And saved my ass."

"Yeah, well, no, I'm just a house painter. Back in the day, I swore when I died I'd want to be buried in latex."

"Why latex?"

"Jesus, you ask a lot of questions."

"Sorry, man." Scott's head tilted to one side. "I'm nosy. Sorry."

"S'okay. Not used to it, that's all. Sorry if I sound, y'know, curt, sometimes." Gus shrugged and made his shoulders crack. "Yeah, latex. 'Cause it's so easy to use. That's why."

"I was a baker. In a donut place."

"Really?"

"Yeah." Scott nodded. "I used to work in Saint John. Small outlet. Had the night shift."

"How was that job?"

"Shitty. Well . . . it wasn't so bad. Got to bring home the leftovers after my shift. The ones I wanted, anyway."

"All those doughnuts and muffins." Gus shook his head. "Man, that sounds good."

"That's what everyone thinks. It is good until you get sick of it. I did everything except the doughnuts. Cookies, pies. All good. I was good at it, too. A decent job. Lonely, though, at times. Night shift and all. Yeah."

"All gone now," Gus said and pursed his lips.

"Yeah. All gone."

Gus gazed out over the cityscape and felt November's light breath chill his face.

"You ever find out how it happened?" Scott asked.

"The zombies?"

"Yeah."

Gus took another drink. "No. Don't know if anyone knows. You?"

"No."

"TV said it was a virus before everything went off air. Something mashed together with Ebola or Sars or Avian flu or something like that. Never for certain. Some folks said it was a leak of some biochemical weapon. Some sorta weaponized agent. I don't know. You're asking the guy on the lowest rung here."

"Same here."

"The worst were the religious fucks. Jesus, they were fucking dancing in the streets they were so goddamn happy that, finally, the world was ending on the day they said it would. Or the month, I guess."

"You see that old fucker on TV? The old rich one that wanted to seal himself in the bunker?"

"With the fifty pieces of ass?" Gus chuckled. "Fuck me. The old bastard must of thought it was his lucky day. Going to do his job to repopulate the earth."

"The women went down into the bunker with him."

"Yeah, well, he was rich and crazy, and evidently hornier than everyone on the eastern seaboard put together."

Scott smiled. "Think they'll make it?"

"Don't know," Gus admitted. "TV went off the air around that time."

"Oh yeah, that's right. Forgot."

"I like to think the old codger got his rocks off at least once or twice before something took the door off his holy bunker. 'Repopulate the earth for the Lord!'" Gus shook his head. "My ass. Y'know the sad thing about that, besides the women going down there with him, were the followers who donated money to that pious bastard over the years, just so he could build shit like that bunker and call it the church of whatever the hell that was."

"I forgot that one, too."

"Same guy was on TV years earlier calling for forgiveness because he lost a couple of million at the horse races," Gus said, lifting his bottle for emphasis.

"Never heard of that one."

"Oh yeah, he did that. That's what he did. Bet the farm, lost it all, and went on national TV asking the congregation to help him out. And the sad thing, the piss *poor* sad thing, is they helped him out. And he went ahead so many years later, built an ultra-modern 'church,' which just happened to be set into the side of a mountain, all self-contained and only big enough and with supplies enough for fifty of the hottest worshippers, all no older than thirty, I heard, who submitted applications and photos online, complete with health records. Joke's on him, though. A man's sperm starts to degenerate as he gets older, increasing the risk of mental problems with the youngsters."

Gus took another shot of booze, and pointed at the horizon. "Holy bunker, my ass. And that's only a fragment of the shit. Y'know, I did hear a conspiracy theory that it wasn't an airborne virus at all. It was some sorta chemical reaction that turned people after eating their favorite preserved snacks. MSG and MC-nine some shit-or-other, combined with some other additive that made people crave more. I heard they were coming out with the obesity laws just before it all went down. All a farce, I think."

"Why's that?"

"The continent's food supply is controlled by all of what, six or seven mega-corporations? That export all over the world? And if they don't export, they sure as shit got, what do you call 'em . . . affiliates? Subsidiaries? Over there to sell their *enhanced* products for years. They've been polluting the grub for God knows how long with their ultra-preservatives filled with ingredients a Yale graduate would have a hard time pronouncing. Personally, I think it was already in the food supply and just needed time to go off."

"Scary shit, man."

"Yeah, scary shit." Gus took another drink and looked toward the city. "Scary shit."

"I always thought the military would push them back," Scott said. "We heard there was a division fighting in Quebec, but nothing ever got into New Brunswick. I think some folks went down to the States, but were never heard from again. There's just nothing. Not even a radio signal. Like being in a void."

"Sometimes," Gus began, "I sit out here and drink and hear things. Screams. Gunshots. But only, uh . . . sporadic. Then, nothing. The wind takes it away, or the situation was taken care of. But you're pretty much the first person I've seen and talked to for a very long time. Maybe two years now."

"Hard to believe you survived this long up here."

"Not too hard. Defensively, I'm pretty much set, I think. I got a trench I want to dig out front there, in front of the outer wall. And a few more things I'll dig. Pits and such."

"You ever watch zombie flicks?" Scott asked, looking at him with eyes that were sly slits.

"Yeah. All the time now. Why?"

"You have to count on those things getting up here."

Gus took a shot of rum. "I know. I do. That's why I'm doing the outer defenses. Try to make it as secure as possible."

"Ever get any up this far?"

"Not often. And always in singles. Never a pack. I don't know what drives them up here, but yeah, sometimes I get them. One morning, I woke up to the sound of one wailing away at the outer wall. I took care of him quick, but I was shaking for the rest of the day. Figured it came up through the woods, bypassing the road gate altogether. Another time, I opened the road gate, and one was right there, looking like it had run a marathon. Scared the shit outta me. I put it down and dragged it off to the other side, and that was that. They come around every now and again. They seem to keep to the towns and cities, though."

Scott nodded.

"You have a family?" Gus asked.

"Had one. A wife and a little girl. They're gone now. Dead. Parents passed on long ago. My sister's dead. You?"

"Girlfriend got the bug or was bit. I saw her in a mob coming down a street. Cop shot her in the head just before the crowd overran the street blockades. Got two brothers out west, but I don't know what happened to them. Probably never will."

"This talk's getting depressing."

"So it is."

"The guy I used to hang around with, he used to ask, why did they have to turn into things that ate people?"

"Good question."

"Yeah."

They drank until the evening turned red, until their senses became screwed, and the conversation got weird.

"Y'know something," Gus slurred, holding onto his bottle of Captain Morgan by the neck. "I've been up here for practically two fuckin' years. Two fuckin' years. Nobody to talk to. This's been good for me. Really good. Thanks for droppin' by." He broke into a giggle then, which Scott joined.

"You talk a lot," Scott said.

"Do I?"

"Yeah, I mean . . ." Scott shook his head. "Movies I watched always has the guy all grim and silent and moody like. You haven't shut up since we met."

They both chuckled.

"Sorry, man."

"No, no, it's okay. I guess I'd be . . . Nah, I wouldn't. I'd be the quiet one. Hell, I *am* the quiet one. When I was with the others, I was, anyway."

"Hmm. Well, you're here now."

"Don't know how long I can stay, though," Scott said, still nursing his whiskey.

"Huh? Why? You just got here."

"Yeah, but . . ."

"But what? C'mon now, I saved your ass down there."

"Yeah, I know, and I appreciate everything, but . . ."

Gus looked over at his drinking partner and gestured *what?*

"That fucker is still out there."

"Who? Oh, okay, I get it."

"Yeah," Scott said quietly and took a sip of whiskey. He shivered, and Gus didn't know if it was from the booze or the dropping temperature.

"I'm gonna find him. Before he hurts anyone else. And make him pay."

"Make him pay," Gus repeated. "You sound like Charles Bronson."

"Who?"

"Action star from the seventies. Starred in a flick called *Death Wish*."

"Never heard of it."

"I hadn't either, but whoever owned this place from . . . from before had a whole library of movies on digital."

"Yeah? That's cool, man. So why are we out here gettin' smashed when we could be in there watchin' movies? It's startin' to freeze out here."

Gus suppressed a rising lump of gas in his throat. "It's peaceful out here, man. Look." He swept his arm toward the darkening city.

"It's peaceful cuz everyone's fuckin' frozen to something. Even the dead are fuckin' frozen to something. Shit, if I were a dead-head right now, I'd be sayin', '*Christ,* it's fuckin' cold out here.'"

Gus laughed.

"It's cold out here," Scott directed at Gus with a smile.

"You're sayin' it's cold?"

"I think I can use my toes as piano keys."

"Oh. That's not kosher. All right. Gimme that." Gus held out his hand for the bottle of whiskey.

Scott hesitated. "I'm kinda attached to this brand now."

"I can see that, but gimme anyway."

"What are you gonna do?"

"Don't worry. I won't lose it."

"You won't, eh?"

"You talk a lot for a freezin' guy. A *quiet* freezin' guy."

Scott shrugged and handed over the Crown Royal bottle, which Gus took and immediately threw over the railing.

"Whoops," Gus said as straight-faced as he could under the circumstances. "Got some bad news for ya."

"You lost my bottle?"

"Yeah." Gus shrugged. "Slipped outta my hands. Sorry."

"I see. I see you managed to hold on to the rum there."

Gus regarded his bottle for moment, startled, and baseball-pitched that one over the railing.

"Lost that one too, eh?" Scott asked sardonically.

"Yep."

"I'd call that a drinking problem."

"Don't worry about it." Gus helped the man up. Scott slung an arm around his shoulders. "I got lots in the house."

"How much you got?" Scott asked.

"Gobs 'n' gobs."

"Not sure if that's a good thing."

"If it isn't, I don't wanna know the bad."

"What if you run out?"

"Just go get more."

"More? Where?"

Gus stopped and wheeled around, taking a hopping Scott with him. He pointed to Annapolis. "Down there. Don't worry about it. When you get all mended up, I'll show you if you want."

"Not so keen on that idea."

"The booze helps."

They continued their banter all the way back into the house. Gus helped the wounded man get down the steps to the den below. He deposited him in the recliner and went to get more booze. He brought back two new bottles of Crown Royal and Captain Morgan. He then queued up a movie from the terabyte unit to watch on the wide-screen TV.

Death Wish.

11

Scott woke up with a black blanket thrown over him and his half-empty bottle of Crown Royal in his lap. He smacked his lips and grimaced, feeling the gummy residue from a night of heavy drinking. His bladder urged him to take immediate action. The den was dark, lit only by a shaft of light from the stairs behind him, and he sniffed dry, cold air. He'd passed out in the recliner, which he thought wasn't a bad thing since the chair kept his foot somewhat elevated. He remembered reading somewhere that keeping a twisted ankle elevated was a good thing. He arched his back in a stretch and looked around the dark room. *Death Wish.* There was something about a rape in the story, but he couldn't recall exactly. They had watched that movie and then *Death Wish 2.* Gus had even suggested watching the 2025 remakes of them, but Scott didn't need to see them. Instead, they'd opted on, of all things, some travel documentaries called *Rick Steves' Europe.* For the rest of the evening, they had watched images of a Europe they would never see and didn't even have any idea if it still existed. They marvelled at old world destinations of Venice, which had been completely given in to the sea in 2022, and Sicily, drawing sounds of wonder from two very drunk men.

Scott didn't know exactly when he'd passed out, only that he did, and that he woke up in the recliner in a dark room, facing a dark TV screen.

"Gus?" He looked around. No Gus. "Hey, Gus!"

Then, he spotted a plastic water jug on the floor next to the recliner. He leaned over the armrest and picked up the jug, which had a note stuck on it. The jug was full of water, and he downed a third of it before stopping to gasp for air. The ink on the note had smeared, and the paragraph left there was unreadable except for "or so," at the very end, along with Gus's signature.

"Or so," Scott said to himself, and again felt the need to pee. Gus hadn't thought of that, he realized, and he would have to climb the steps to get to his room's bucket.

Taking the jug with him, Scott got out of the recliner, left the booze in the chair, and hopped over to the stairs. He paused there, composing himself for the more difficult part, and began hopping up each step. He almost lost his balance twice, and by the time he reached the main level, his left leg burned with exertion, while his chest ached. Each hop made him feel as if he were on the edge of pissing himself, and the sound of water sloshing around in the jug didn't help. He went through the house, leaning heavily on walls until he made it back to his room and the bucket. If he had any reservations about using it, they went out in a sigh and a hissing splash of urine. He finished up, tapped and zipped, and lay down on the bed. He took another deep drink of water before capping the jug and placing it beside the bed.

He fell asleep immediately.

The sound of someone moving through the house woke him up again, and he pulled himself up to a sitting position.

"Gus?"

The clatter got closer until Gus's leather-covered frame filled the doorway. He carried two wooden crutches with him, which he tossed onto the bed.

"There you go," he said and turned to leave.

"Wait!" Scott blurted.

Gus paused in the doorway.

"You got these for me? I mean, thanks, man! Where'd you get them?"

For a moment, he didn't think Gus was going to answer. The man appeared to space out before shaking his head. "Hospital."

"You have any trouble?"

Another spaced-out look. "Yeah," Gus finally muttered.

The expression on his face silenced any further questioning from Scott, and he listened to the receding footsteps and banging of a door. Scott looked at the crutches and picked them up off the bed. They were about an inch shorter than what he needed, so he took a moment to adjust them. He tested them out, fitting the sponge padding into his armpits, and got moving.

These are great, he thought, although he was still a little uncomfortable around the back and rib area where he had been shot. But he wouldn't be restricted to the bed anymore, and his mobility had just improved. He swung himself out into the hall and crutched down to the living room. No Gus. He spotted the sliding door to the deck out front. Getting to the window, Scott looked out and saw Gus sitting in a lawn chair, facing the city. Gus raised a bottle to his lips and took a drink of what Scott knew to be rum. *Man likes to drink,* he thought, and considered going out to join him, but he didn't. Something stopped him.

Hospital was what Gus had said, with an exhaustion that sounded both mental as well as physical.

Scott watched him for a bit. A solitary figure set against a drop of gray and black under the cold glare of November, singed around the edges by late fall.

In the end, Scott turned away, leaving the man to his internal sorting of things. He didn't know the guy, and a few good deeds didn't mean anything. He stood on the crutches, his body somewhat scrunched up, bad leg lifted off the floor and bum ankle wrapped in thick bandages. Scott made his way back to his room and lay down on the bed. He thought of his old life, baking on the nightshift and sleeping half the day away while the world lived on. It had been a lonely existence, but he had gotten used to it. He'd gotten used to the new world, too, and felt it more in tune with wild animals in nature, where every day was a fight for survival. Although he had to admit getting blasted by whiskey was probably a little bit better. And the house certainly was.

Scott studied the high wood beams of the ceiling and relaxed further. How often had he been able to relax out there with Teddy and Lea? Even when it wasn't his shift, he'd slept with one eye open. With the wall beyond and the location of the house, he felt safe, and that was important. He knew he had been living on something of a wire in the last two years or so. It was bad when people were turning into dead things in the beginning, and there was simply no explanation given. It had affected him more than he let on, as every person he met could potentially be a carrier for the disease, or whatever it was that turned folks.

Civilization had begun breaking down in late 2026 like some great beast harpooned from multiple directions and bleeding profusely. Scott barricaded himself in his apartment for weeks, having already stockpiled a good supply of preserved food. He lasted maybe three weeks in his place before something found out he was up there on the fifth floor and came to investigate. Those were the beginning of the running times for him, where he lived like a rat, scurrying from place to place, eventually making it to a cabin in the hills, away from it all.

He'd stayed there as long as he could, foraging from nearby communities, doing that for long time until he met up with Teddy, and then Lea. *Strength in numbers*, Teddy had said. But Scott thought there was strength in being alone, too.

The set-up Gus had was good. The best Scott had come across. He only wondered if, being alone in all that time, Gus still had all of his marbles or was suffering from some form of cabin fever. Scott hoped for the full marbles. He didn't want to think about Gus being nuts, but he would be on guard, just in case. There *was* strength in numbers, and he had to admit if Gus hadn't come along when he did, his fate would have been decided. He would've been one of those poor bastards walking around rotting in the summer and freezing in the winter.

Scott closed his eyes. He suddenly wanted a shot of whiskey, but he'd left the bottle downstairs. Weariness seeped into his frame. It was something, to truly relax, to truly let down your guard and not think about what was outside.

If only for a short time.

A loud banging woke Scott up. He tensed, listening in wide-eyed fright.

"You fucker! You lousy, cheap-assed cocksucker! Fuck. *Fuck!* Jesus!"

Scott looked around for a weapon, but saw nothing except his crutches.

"Goddammit!" came the voice.

It became quiet then, and Scott heard the muted grumblings of someone that sounded like Gus, but he wasn't certain, then the clanging of metal.

Footsteps approached. Louder, coming down the hallway. Scott tensed. They slowed as they got closer to the open doorway before finally stopping.

A bald head came around the door, and that simple silent appearance scared the living shit out of Scott.

Gus shook his head. "Sorry, man. Guess you heard all that, huh?"

"What're you doing out there?" Scott demanded.

"Aw, cooking up some grub there. Beans and wieners. I'm pretty much shitfaced from earlier. Rule one. Don't cook while shitfaced. You might knock the whole damn works off the stove and onto the floor. Anyway, sorry for wakin' you up. I heard you snorin'."

"I snore?"

Gus's bearded face looked somber. "You sound like a fucked-up chainsaw." He smiled and rubbed his bald head. "You hungry?"

"For beans and wieners?"

"Well, I'll eat those. I scraped them up off the floor. Can't throw that shit out, man. It's all food, right? But I got another can of it if you want some."

"Yeah, please."

"All right. That smell botherin' you?"

"Huh?"

"That." Gus pointed at the bucket. "The piss bucket. You want me to empty that?"

Scott just noticed the pungent odor. "Maybe later."

"If I had sawdust, that would take the smell away, but I don't. Sorry."

"Hey, don't apologize. I'm just glad I have a bucket here." A grin came out with his words, and Scott didn't want to think about the alternative.

Gus stifled a belch and raised a hand. "You're a guest. No problem. I'll get them beans and wieners on for ya." He disappeared from the doorway as abruptly as he had appeared.

Scott lay back down and waited for about twenty minutes before deciding to get up. It was getting dark outside. He grabbed his crutches and swung his way into the hallway. As he came into the kitchen, he saw Gus pouring the beans and wieners into a white plastic bowl, right beside its twin.

"There ya are," Gus said and swayed a bit. Scott noted the bottle of Captain Morgan rum, almost empty on the island counter. "You know what's worse than knocking shit onto the floor?"

"No, what?"

"Cleaning it up. I got plenty of paper towels, but it wasn't—oh, s'cuse me—absorbing the shit. I was spreadin' it out like pizza sauce. Finally . . . finally changed tactics and scooped what I could into the bowl. That one's yours, by the by."

Scott leaned over the island table, took up a spoon and starting eating, blowing on each scoop before devouring it. "Tastes good," he managed to get out.

"I'll get you something to drink." Gus went to the fridge and poured a glass of water.

"Thanks," Scott said with his mouth full. He nodded at the bottle. "A little early, ain't it?"

Gus looked at the rum and smiled tightly. "Any time's good these days." With that, he ate his food in silence until it was gone.

For Scott, it was the first can of B&W he'd had since it all began, and while a little stale, they tasted just fine. God bless whatever chemicals preserved them.

The sun drooped lower, and the shadows grew in the house. Gus cleaned up the dinner dishes and placed them to one side.

"You wash those?" Scott asked.

"Sometimes. Only for special company. Usually use paper if I have them or just straight from the can. I'm not picky. Let's go into the living room here."

Gus grabbed his bottle and moved out of the kitchen and into the living room. He plopped down onto the sofa and gestured for Scott to take the recliner.

"Want another bottle?" Gus asked.

"I'm fine. Too hung over from last night."

"You get over it. I did. Do. Sometimes." Gus cackled, baring faded white teeth. He patted his flat belly and took another shot of rum. "I was never a drinker. Came into it. Can you blame me?"

Scott eased into the recliner and sighed. He shook his head.

"That's what I figured," Gus said. "Hardly touched the stuff. Now, it's bottled comfort. You read at all?"

"A little."

"We got books here, too. Mostly horror fiction, but the owner seemed to like a bit of everything. Some point in time, I'd like to get to the city library. There's another one at the university, but that's a scary place to visit now, like any place that had a high population. Ah, well. Some good reads here all the same. Ever read any King?"

"Who?"

"Stephen King?"

"No, not really."

"I think all of his books are here. You'll see, anyway. I never asked you before, where you from? Saint John?"

"Yeah. Saint John."

"Like it there?"

"Back in the day, yeah, it was fine. Not now, though."

Gus drank some of his rum. He studied the bottle. "I'll have to get another one of these soon. Anytime you want anything, just let me know. I've got lots down below. I gotta get you a Speed Stick as well. And a toothbrush."

"You have those?"

"Got lots. Raided a drugstore a while back and took what I could from the shelves. That included a shitload of deodorant, shampoo, toothpaste, dental floss, you name it. Stored it all over the house."

"Jesus, you're a packrat."

"I prefer the word *survivor*," Gus said with satisfaction, staring in the direction of the dead fireplace.

Scott thought about something for a while, and decided to ask his question. "Why are you doing this for me?"

"Huh?"

"All of this? Why you doing it all?"

"You worried about something?"

"Maybe."

Gus smiled. "Then don't. I don't have any secret plans."

"All right, then, why again?" Scott had to know. He had seen too many things on the road, people reduced to base savagery before, during, and after the collapse.

Gus took his time answering, taking a long drink. "I've been up here a long time. Got to a point where I felt like talking to myself at times, like Will Smith in *I am Legend*, there."

"That a movie?"

"Yeah, old bad movie—it's in the library below—but, anyway, as sad as it sounds, man, you're someone to talk to. I haven't talked to anyone besides the walls, the TV, myself, and the dead outside."

Scott nodded. Two years in relative seclusion. Cabin fever of a different kind. "I hear ya."

That brightened Gus. "Good. You ready for that drink now?"

12

A week later, Scott felt better about staying at the house. His sense of being fortunate grew with his contact with Gus. The man was a peculiar one. He drank constantly, *smiles* as he would refer to them, but he had plenty remaining downstairs. Gus had taken him down to one of the storerooms to see what exactly he had, and the revelation nearly blew him away.

"Where the hell'd you get all of this?" he asked, gazing at the shelves and boxes of stored goods, bathroom supplies, household cleaners, and alcohol.

Gus shrugged. "Around."

Gus later told him that he squirreled away everything he found in shops and stores, even after the looting. And he occasionally found small convenience stores that had been missed. Gas was the easiest, as Scott already knew. All one had to do was check the derelicts on the roads and drill a hole into the tanks. Gus figured he had close to ten extra gas containers in the garage, all full. And there were the mountain bikes, as well, that he used in a pinch. Gus informed him that he took what he could from the houses in Annapolis. House picking. Some contained vast stores of supplies, while others didn't, but he tried to be systematic in his search.

"Winter's comin' up, though," Gus said. "And once that comes, getting down into the city will get that much harder, if not dangerous."

Scott didn't question the mountain man.

During the days, he would use the crutches to get around the house. His gunshot wound healed slowly, and he had to be careful moving or he could cause it to bleed again, but staying in the house for hours on end was difficult to do when he knew from Gus that there were a good three acres of land cordoned off by the stone wall. Three acres of relative undead-free freedom. So, he explored the grounds on his crutches. He saw how the solar panels that gave them electricity were situated on the south side of the house to maximize efficiency. He found the wind generator high on the mountainside that didn't move at all as Gus wasn't sure if it would attract attention. Gus had even taken him to the shed behind the garage and shown him the batteries for the solar panels, twenty units the size and shape of car batteries arranged neatly on the floor and a shelf, connected to a panel and generator of unknown purpose.

"All I know is that the sun shines, and I have power," Gus said, and that was good enough for Scott. He didn't ask too many questions if he could help it. He didn't want to bother the man that would carry out his bucket of excrement to the outhouse for dumping and sanitizing.

In the second week, Gus took inventory and made a list of things he needed. On the following Monday, he suited up and left Scott alone in the house while he drove down to Annapolis to see what could be found. While he was gone, Scott amused himself with reading one of the many paperbacks in the house.

The feeling of comfort hadn't left Scott, and he luxuriated in it while he had the chance. Gus made it back to the house before nightfall and went straight to the deck with bottle in hand, where he stayed well after the sun went down. Scott didn't approach him during that time for fear of disturbing some private ritual he was unaware of. He found him in a better mood the next day, and when he asked about it, Gus told him it was the job, and the dangers that went with it.

In the fourth week, seeing Gus after another run into Annapolis, Scott discerned a distinct pattern. Gus would drive into the city and be gone for most of the day. He'd return just before sundown and go off to some part of the house, usually outside, and drink heavily from his basement supply. He'd pass out, regain consciousness the next day, and spend the day moving about as though shot through the guts, something Scott thought funny when he heard the groans and curses. Gus would be fully recovered on the day after, and he would then unload whatever he had scavenged from the suburbs, as well as inspect the van's condition. Then, he'd take a day of rest before heading back down to the city again for more house picking.

In the middle of the fifth week, Scott removed his bandage and tentatively took his first step in the living room without the support of crutches. His ankle was sore, but thankfully, the sprain wasn't as bad it could have been. He knew there were three different kinds of sprains, ranging from mild to severe, and he supposed he was lucky enough not to have a severe one.

"How's it feel?" Gus asked.

"Still hurts." Scott took another a step. "Stiff. I'll have to bandage it again."

"But you're up and around, so that's good."

"I am." He beamed. He looked at his bare foot and wiggled the toes. "Might bandage it again anyway, while I'm moving around."

"Think you can drive with that thing?"

He met Gus's eyes. "I think so. What's up?"

"Depends." Gus sat on the sofa and regarded him. "How long you figure on staying here?"

"Good question." He'd thought about that as well. Some nights, he'd woken up from the nightmare of finding Teddy and Lea in the basement, but they weren't dead. Tenner was there, chewing their flesh off, and Scott was slipping on the steps just at the worst time. Sometimes, he woke up feeling Tenner's bloody breath on his face. "I've thought about it."

"Same here, and I've got a deal for you."

"Let's hear it."

Gus nodded. "You can stay here for the winter, if you like. If you want to go, we'll get you set up for that, too. But the snow will be here by the end of December, and it'll be down for three to four months. That's a long time. You can stay here, but if you do, I'd like you to come along and ride shotgun with me. Until you feel strong enough on your feet to do more. Work with me in the house picking, and you're more than welcome to stay. How's that sound?"

It sounded fine. "And I can leave whenever?"

"If you really want to, man, I'm not stopping you. You drink too damn much."

Scott frowned and smiled at the same time. "I do not."

"You're like a fucking fish. An *alcoholic* fish, I might add."

"I am . . . ?" He saw the amused glint in Gus's eye. "I get you. You're an evil bastard, you know that?"

Gus looked at his feet, his thick mossy beard covering his expression, but Scott suspected the man was smiling. "You got a deal," Scott finally said. "I'll stick around. For a while."

"Fair enough, then."

"Fair enough."

They cleaned and oiled their shotguns in silence. Gus got up at one point and placed a box of red shells in the middle of the dining room table, and they loaded each weapon with five shots apiece. Gus brought in a leather jacket for Scott, but he didn't have a neck protector or another pair of leather pants.

"I used to be a hundred pounds overweight," Gus disclosed when he brought out the jacket. "This should be okay for you. Wear your sweaters underneath tomorrow to bulk yourself up. We'll have to keep an eye out for anything that's your size. Sports equipment has lots of padding."

"What about the fire department?"

"What about it?"

"They have thick coats there. Might be worth a look."

"Just might. Well, never thought of that before. Shit. Good idea. If we pass it," Gus added.

"Fair enough."

"Get a good night's sleep, 'cause I guarantee you'll be drinking to forget in the evening when we get back."

"*If* we get back."

"No, *when* we get back. At least, I'm coming back. You can decide if you're sticking around down there or not. No negative thinking in this dojo. Got it?"

Scott nodded reluctantly, but didn't feel very certain.

"Listen," Gus aimed at him. "I'm serious. Positive thinking on this. Take no risks. No stupid chances, and we'll be back in no time tomorrow. Most of the runners are gone by now, or the night chills them so they can't break for us. All that leaves is the rest of whatever's left of Annapolis's population to deal with, and they move mighty slow."

"How big is, or was, the population here?"

"I don't know. Don't matter. See?"

Scott sensed an untruth there, but he didn't want to press the matter. "How many shells do we have?"

"Figure a thousand or so. I grabbed whatever boxes I could from the gun and rod shop. Plus backup. A lot of that shit got taken right away."

Scott rubbed his thickening beard. "Any smaller guns?"

"You mean like pistols?"

"Yeah."

"Nah. I wish. That'd be cool." Gus grinned.

"It would. Did you ever get to the cop station to check?"

"I did, but all the good stuff was taken. Place was balder than a waxed snatch."

"So this is all we got."

"And the bats," Gus informed him, stretching his neck. "Don't forget the bats. The shotguns are great, but a good bat . . . well, that's magic. Does wonders. Just make sure you got your helmet visor down. Don't need to accidently swallow a piece of scalp."

Scott made a face. "That's gross, man."

"It's a gross world."

Gus took Scott into the garage and formally introduced him to the beast. He pointed out the reversed gear labelling, where *Drive* was really *Reverse* and vice versa. He showed him the racks on the ceiling for the guns, the storage bins, and the spare mountain bike hanging on the wall.

"There's only one, though," Scott pointed out.

"You're only here for a short time though, right?" Gus asked, smirking under his beard. "Besides, only room for the one, with the bins and everything. Can only take so much on safari."

"What do I do if the van breaks down?"

"Can you run?"

"Smartass."

"Speed walk?"

"Smartass."

Gus clapped him on the shoulder and walked away, enjoying the fact that Scott was starting to loosen up around him.

"But *really* . . ." Scott said.

They turned in shortly after prepping the van. Gus thought Scott looked a little nervous, but he didn't let it bother him. He'd only be driving the first time out anyway, and Gus had made it clear his role would be that of driving. He wouldn't go into the street, wouldn't go into any houses, and essentially wouldn't step out of the vehicle. He'd have Gus's back once he was inside. If Gus fired the shotgun while in the house, he'd come check on him. If Scott laid on the beast's horn, that was the sign for Gus to get the hell out of Dodge. Simple plans made by simple men in difficult times. They retired to their respective rooms around ten, and Gus left two full bottles of Jack Daniels on the table.

To celebrate their joyous return.

13

The beast rumbled toward town the next morning, the sun making the night's frost twinkle on the highway. They drove on the familiar road that Gus always followed into Annapolis. They were suited up and ready for the day. Gus had on all of his equipment: knee and elbow pads, neck brace, chest protector under the jacket, and helmet. He made note to see if he could find any extra pads for Scott, thinking it might be easier to pick some up at Home Hardware or Walmart. That kind of padding might not have been looted. Gus had extras back at the house, but didn't see a need for the driver to wear them just yet.

"See anything strange out there?" Gus asked.

Scott glanced over at him, looking uncertain. "Huh?"

"Notice anything?" Gus asked again, his words muffled only slightly from the motorcycle helmet. Gus knew the man was concentrating hard on driving, but he didn't want the guy to have a goddamn aneurysm over it.

"I'm driving here," Scott grated.

"I can see that, but do you see anything out there?"

Scott squinted at the road ahead as if he were memorizing every inch, and finally shook his head. They passed the semi that had been driven through a roadside billboard. The cars were starting to thicken on the road.

Scott's lack of perception disappointed Gus. "Slow down and get ready to stop."

"Stop?"

"Yeah, we need to fill up those three gas containers back there."

"Where?"

"I'll tell you. Just slow down."

The beast slowed.

"Okay, right here," Gus said.

Scott halted the van in the middle of the highway among cars coated in frost. The sun made everything sparkle in grandiose fashion.

"I'll do this," Gus said as he moved to the back of the van. He got out an aluminum bat and scabbard which he threw over his shoulder, a red gas container, large plastic bowl, and a handheld rechargeable drill. He also grabbed a stretched-out coat hanger, a funnel, and a fistful of rags. "You see if you can pick up on anything interesting about those cars."

Scott frowned. "But I—"

Gus closed the door on his words. The morning freshness smacked him in his face, and he took a moment to just breathe. He smelled the exhaust and walked away from the van with a frown. His boots scuffed on the asphalt and his bare fingers, the only part of him uncovered, felt the biting chill on the air. November would soon be over, and he was only a little done. With Scott, however, it would be much easier to house pick and loot in general.

Loot, loot! his mind yelled, making him smile. He walked by three cars with their sides dented, knowing that Scott's eyes watched him and had his back. It was rare for gimps to be in or between the cars, and it wasn't the first time he had taken gasoline, but with that second set of eyes on him, he felt safer.

He stopped at an old hybrid Toyota that seemed to be still intact and untouched. He glanced inside the car to ensure it was indeed empty. Then, he opened the door and checked for keys. Some cars had them, as the beast had had her keys left in the ignition, much to Gus's relief. No keys, but it was just as well. He didn't want a sedan. He preferred SUVs or pickup trucks. He did, however, want the gas if there was any left in the tank.

Looking around out of habit, he reached down and popped the lever opening the tank's cover. A second later, he stuffed the long rag down into the tank with the help of the coat hanger, then withdrew it, soaked.

He took off the scabbard and got under the car. He put the bowls in place and made a small hole with the drill. Gasoline pissed down into the bowl. Gus filled one bowl, and while the other filled, he emptied the first into the container with the funnel. Gas splashed into the bottom and for a moment, Gus thought of peeing in a cup for any number of urinary tests. Glancing back at the beast, he waved and gestured for Scott to pull closer.

A moment later, the van huffed to his side.

The sedan held only enough to fill the container less than a quarter full. Before moving on to the next car, a pickup, Gus took the bat and bashed in the side of the car's driver's door, denting it just enough to mark it. He looked back to Scott, who shook his head.

That's right, *Gus said to himself.* Gotta mark the cars somehow.

The sun shining overhead, Gus moved to the next vehicle—a Dodge Ram—and repeated the process, using the dry end of the rag. The pickup wasn't in bad shape, but the keys were missing, and damn if he knew how to hotwire one of the 2025 models. He would ask Scott once he had the chance. He got the container up to half full with the gas from the pickup before denting the driver's side, and lugging the can to the next car, a Lexus.

Scott and the beast followed.

Gus filled the first container after the tenth car, another sedan, before carrying it back to the van. Five of the vehicles were electric models, and those he left untouched. Opening the rear door of the van, he hefted the gas inside and stowed it away.

"So you dent all the car doors?" Scott asked.

"Yep."

"The ones on the other side aren't checked."

"I'll do them next time. Don't you worry."

"A lot of fuel out there," Scott commented, looking out his driver's window.

"Yeah, but it'll be all gone sooner or later. Either we'll get it or someone else. See that black SUV up ahead there?"

"Yeah."

"Hope that one has its keys. Hey, you know how to hotwire a car?"

"No, sorry," Scott answered with a shake of his head.

"S'okay. No trouble. Need more rags."

Thirty-one cars, SUVs, and pickups later, Gus loaded the last of the containers on board and stowed them away. He closed the rear door with a slam and got into his seat.

"Not bad, usually have contact with a few gimps after bangin' in the doors," Gus commented.

"Maybe it's gettin' too cold?"

"It's gettin' there."

"You call 'em gimps, eh?"

"Yeah. What do you call 'em?"

"Dead fuckers."

That made Gus chuckle. "They are that."

"Lea used to call them deadheads."

"That sounds familiar."

"I think it was an old band or something or other, I dunno."

"Deadheads," Gus tried the word. Liked it. "Dead fuckers has a ring, too."

"I think so. Hey, do I have to wear this helmet?"

"Don't have to, I guess. You're in the van. But it'd be pretty shitty luck all around if you take that off and later down the line a single deadhead comes through the windshield and chomps your ear off."

"They'd have to get though the beard." Scott smiled.

"Your fuckin' beard ain't growin' out of your ear, man."

Scott's smile dissolved into a frown.

"I'm just shittin' ya, okay? Don't take it personal," Gus assured him.

"No problem," Scott said, and after a moment added, "shithead."

Gus grinned.

Carefully putting the van in gear, Scott eased back onto the road.

"Too bad about those SUVs back there," Scott said, keeping his eyes on the road and the van at a steady forty.

"Happens. I haven't checked all of these cars, and I'm sure someone will have left their keys or have a spare set hidden inside. Just finding them is the thing. Couldn't do it alone, but with you, all sorts of things are possible."

Scott rubbed at his eye. "Into town, then?"

"Take us in, Scotty."

Gus noted that the reference was lost on his companion. Probably before his time.

The beast turned into the sun, and the rays made them both squint until they lowered their visors. On either side, the houses began to thicken. In the distance, dark towers loomed like hives in the morning light.

"Y'know something?" Gus said.

"What?"

"This place, way back when it was only a bunch of towns and most of the farmland hadn't been bought up, you'd get the smell of fertilizer coming from the farms. That sweet stink of pig shit, or whatever the hell the farmers used on the soil, would waft down through the entire fucking length of the valley and cause most everyone to gag. Stink. Christ, you'd think Ottawa itself dropped its drawers and shat on someone's front lawn."

"You smell that now?" Scott's brow scrunched.

Gus shook his head. "Nah, I . . . I just miss it."

Scott nodded and glanced at the dashboard clock. "It's nine."

"Is it?"

"Yeah."

"Worried about the time?"

Scott's head tilted a little. "A bit."

"Don't, then. We'll be outta here before mid-afternoon. Gives us plenty of time to get back before nightfall."

"That's about five-thirty now," Scott observed, sounding worried.

"A little later, I didn't adjust the clock back from daylight saving."

"Why?"

"Only me. I know when it's going to get dark. Daylight saving's only for the shop owners. And you can see where they are," Gus finished with mild sarcasm.

They passed empty sidewalks and deserted houses with smashed windows. The front lawns, tall and yellow, were bent over like canes and glistened with melted frost. Trees stood bare and harsh, their bases hidden in the dead wet leaves. Old cable lines sagged from houses to the poles.

"There." Scott pointed.

"What? You see something?"

"In the driveway. A Dee."

"Dee?"

"Dee for dead. Dead fucker."

"Drive on, then. I've picked these houses."

"Roger that," Scott said.

"We're going to a new subdivision. That place where I ran over you is picked clean," Gus told him.

"Yeah, you did run over me, didn't you?" Scott tugged on his beard.

"In the best possible way, I figure. Anyway, time to get to a new area. I think there's a fire department around there, too. Might just be able to find some of that stuff you were talking about."

"Sounds good."

"If anything," Gus continued, "we can grab it and save it for another time. I got spares of most things back at the house. Problem is going to be finding places to stash it all."

"Worry about that when it happens."

"Yeah."

They drove along a two-lane strip which Gus knew ran the length of the valley. More deserted vehicles crowded the road and even the sidewalks, forcing them to slow down, but the driving was clear going in some places. Rotting debris lay everywhere, black and soggy. Gus looked out his side window, gazing up at the high elms and watching the sun through their bare, upraised limbs. More battered and deserted houses lined both sides of the street. A school with the charred bodies of two school buses on the parking lot passed his field of vision.

"You ever miss the old days?" Gus asked over the growl of the engine.

"You have to ask?"

Gus took his time before answering. "No. I guess not."

The road turned into small dips and rises, just steep enough to feel it in the stomach. Just ahead, on the left, stood what Gus knew to be the fire station, behind a series of posts whose signs had been ripped down. The two-story concrete building had a pair of dented red bay doors. A third smaller door for the offices and dormitory was located to the left of them. A pickup had crashed into one corner of the building, wrecking its front. Gus wondered what the hell had been on the driver's mind to jump the curb on that side and lose control. Despite the crash, the station looked very much intact. Like most other places in the city, the unchecked grass rose up to almost thigh level.

Scott looked at Gus. "Drive right to the door?"

"Yeah, but back 'er up."

Nodding, Scott did just that. He rolled down his window and stuck his head out. The beast did a ninety degree turn and stopped perhaps a meter away from the office door. The engine died with a flick of Scott's wrist.

In the stillness, Gus took a breath and stared ahead. Scott glanced over at him and waited.

"Okay," Gus finally said. "You wait here, and I'll be back shortly."

He got up from his seat, holstered his bat across his back, and took the loaded shotgun down from the rack. He stuffed the pockets of his leather jacket full of red shells. Once ready, he went to the rear of the van.

"Be careful, man," Scott called.

Gus paused at the rear. It had been a very long time since anyone had told him to be careful. It was nice to hear. He opened the rear door, and jumped to the pavement. He closed the door and looked through the windows of the fire station door. Office area. Counters. Lots of debris and dark. Several of the windows on the far side had been curtained. Gus didn't like that. He brought up his shotgun and held it with one hand while turning the knob.

The door opened, and a zombie filled the crack as smoothly as a target popping up on a firing range, jolting Gus from his head all the way to his ankles. The thing moaned as it pawed at Gus's visor, and then its chest exploded, and it flew backward. Before he could control himself, Gus stepped into the office, pumped another shell into the shotgun's chamber, and destroyed the creature's head. A second monster rose from behind a red counter, still wearing the filthy remains of a white uniform. Gus blew its head off with one shot. Two more undead shuffled from the hallway, lifting their arms and pointing, as if accusing him of living. He took his time with those. Checking the corners to make sure nothing else was in the area, he took aim at the corpses and fired twice, dropping both gimps in their tracks, the ejector of his weapon spitting out the spent red plastic casings.

Scowling, Gus rapidly reloaded, looking about for any further trouble. His breathing was loud in his ears. Once he pushed the fourth shell into his shotgun, he chambered a round and brought it to shoulder level. Realizing he was trembling slightly, he eased back outside and saw Scott sticking his head out of the driver's window.

"You okay?" Scott asked, perhaps louder than he should have.

Gus raised his hand in reply and went back in.

He had a choice of going left or right. He chose left and gingerly opened the door to the dark apparatus bays where two gleaming red fire trucks waited. Gus slipped carefully into the bay, noting the open lockers at the far end. He moved up and down one truck and then the other, searching for gimps. Stooping and checking underneath the machines, he returned to the lockers and the coats hanging from metal hooks. Gus reached out and touched one of the black Nomex coats, feeling the grainy texture of the material. A yellow horizontal stripe covered the front and back of the coat, with additional yellow rings around the sleeves. He picked up what looked to be ninja masks, marvelled at them for a moment, and dropped them back on a bench. Stepping back, he counted twenty lockers, complete with boots, coats, and pants, as well as multiple gear racks containing rolled-up hoses and other equipment. There was no way he could take all of what he wanted, and he still hadn't checked out the rest of the station. He declared the bay clear in his mind, looking around and not seeing the fire pole or hole in the ceiling he thought might exist. Times had changed for the station, he figured.

Gus walked back to the office area and proceeded past the counter and desks, ignoring the smell of the corpses on the floor. He went down a hall draped with paper notifications and moved into a common area, complete with large table and chairs. Opposite the table lay a worn brown sofa set, complete with plush chairs. A map of Annapolis hung on the wall, major routes and roads all highlighted and clearly marked. For a moment, he didn't understand why the trucks were still in the bay along with the equipment, but then he realized why. In the final days, people were turning into gimps so fast, the fighters simply couldn't respond to all of the calls and gave up.

Adjusting the shotgun stock against his shoulder, Gus moved into a sleeping quarters area where two small rooms contained a single cot each. He then found a kitchen and refrigerator. He opened the fridge and winced at the prunish, green-black sludge that was once some manner of vegetable. A milk carton and four cans of cola remained on the upper shelf, but nothing else edible. He left it all and moved out of the kitchen. Readying himself for something wholly unpleasant, he went into the women's and men's washrooms, but found them all empty. Another closed door revealed the supply closet, and Gus smiled at an untouched tower of individually wrapped toilet paper. *Anal gold*, he thought.

Shotgun forward, he went up a set of stairs.

Squeak.

He stopped on the second step, the noise making him cringe as if he'd been goosed. He looked up and saw that the staircase turned to the left. Panel wood covered the walls, making it dark, and numerous historic pictures of the station hung along its length, showing happier times in both Kodak color and ancient-looking black and white.

Nothing appeared on the stairs.

Gus took another step.

Squark.

Squueee.

Jesus Christ, Gus swore mentally. It sounded like mice farting. Nothing moved from above, however, and sensing it was okay, he climbed the steps faster. The wood squealed as he went up, pissing him off enough that he hoped there was something at the top to shoot.

No such luck, however, as he entered a cozy living area stuffed with more historical items. Old bronze fire extinguishers hung from the walls, as did old firemen hats, gloves, and posters. Signs of various colors with street names and a poster of the movie *Backdraft* hung over a beaten sofa. The place had a comfortable clubhouse feel to it, and Gus could imagine the men and women serving in the station retiring up there for a moment to unwind and shoot the shit. Some old paperbacks filled a small two-shelf bookcase, but Gus left them there, seeing the name Jackie Collins on the top cover.

As far as he could tell, the place was clear.

They would have to work fast.

14

It was too goddamn quiet outside.

The sound of his own impatient breathing was driving Scott nuts. Not only did he expect to see a mob of deadheads rounding the corner, he found himself looking out his open window to check if anything was creeping up on him. Like that fucker Tenner. Scott shook his head and wished he'd paid more attention to what was happening behind him in the house when he had been shot. Never again would he be taken in such a way, he swore, never fucking again. His fingers did an irregular drum roll on the steering wheel, and he checked his window again. It was the shooting, he knew, that had him going. Gus blowing the hell out of the dead inside had shaken up his nerves, and he was struggling with bringing them back down. He reached up and adjusted his motorcycle helmet, a black one with lightning bolts streaking down both sides. He looked both ways on the street, the asphalt shining in the sun, and didn't see anything approaching. Sunlight came into the van at an angle, making him squint. He took another deep breath and willed himself to calm down, but *what the fuck was taking the man so long?* Did it take fifteen minutes to clear a building? Was he in trouble? He ached to sound the horn on the beast, just for the grounding comfort it would bring him. Where the hell was Gus? Should he go in? No, he told himself, that wasn't the plan. That *wasn't* the plan.

Then he saw them.

Stark and morbid in the glare of the day, the dead staggered up the road from the left, shuffling along as if each step might shatter a leg. Their clothes were black, stained, and filthy. He could clearly see their dark flesh, and soon would see their unseeing eyes. One of them wore once-dorky summer shorts and a T-shirt, oblivious to the change in the weather. Another looked to be a barefoot young woman in a mini-skirt, her long gray legs covered with black sores. Children stumbled into the picture, and

Scott winced as if shot once more. He hated the children the worst. Hated putting them down. They creeped the hell out of him. He counted eight corpses, perhaps fifty meters away and closing. Scott had his shotgun hung in a rack nearby. He looked out his side window and almost knocked foreheads with Gus as he appeared.

"Jesus Christ!" Scott burst out.

"Sorry, man," Gus replied, his shotgun lowered. "You got me, too."

"Oh, Jesus Christ. I think I shit myself. Jesus Christ. I just shit myself. I know I did."

"Calm down."

In reply, Scott jabbed a flat hand out of his window in the direction of the gathering dead. Gus flipped up his visor. The putrid smell of rotting flesh crept in, and Scott actually gagged.

"Keep it down!" Gus whispered harshly. "Don't you puke."

"I ain't gonna puke, but Christ, the smell." Scott placed his helmet-covered forehead against the steering wheel and took deep breaths.

"We can't stay here now," Gus said. "Start it up."

Nodding weakly, Scott turned the key as Gus hurried around the front of the van. The dead shifted toward them, a shambling tide of wrecked flesh. At least forty were in sight, and Scott choked as he rolled up his window.

Gus jumped into the van, throwing his bat and scabbard into one of the open bins before going back and securing the rear door. He returned to his seat and fastened his belt, electing to keep a hold of his shotgun.

The beast growled as a shot of gas went through its system.

"Where the fuck do they come from?" Scott asked.

"I think they just walk and walk and walk," Gus said, watching as the road filled. "Get us out of here. Go right. We can find another subdivision."

The undead tide closed in as the van pulled away from the fire station with a lurch. Scott took his foot off the gas, cursing himself for stomping on the metal. Beside him, Gus pointed the shotgun toward the roof, as his free hand came forward and rested against the dash.

"Don't drive us into the curb!" Gus yelled.

Scott yanked the wheel, sending the van into a fishtail. He got the machine under control and raced away from the crowd of zombies. "How many people lived in Annapolis?"

"More than we have shells. More than we can kill with our bats."

"What kinda answer is that? Two hundred thousand? Three?"

Gus shook his head. "Only a hundred thousand. Feel better?"

Scott shook his head.

"We'll come back later, when the area's died down. Drive straight here. I'll tell you when to turn."

"We headin' back to the house?"

Gus shook his head. "No, too early. A waste of time to go back now. Like I said, we'll find another place. Turn down here."

Scott did so.

"Hey," Gus said, grimacing. "I think you did shit yourself."

Scott looked over, blinking, before turning his attention to his crotch. "Aww shit."

"You can't do anything about it now."

"I gotta clean myself up."

"Wait 'til I clear a house."

"I can feel it, awww, *man*!"

Gus rolled down a window. "Christ, what'd you eat anyway?"

Scott felt himself blushing.

"Scott's a dirty boy." Gus said in a teasing voice.

Scott broke out laughing. Gus erupted into a belly chuckle, too, which quickly escalated into tears of laughter. Scott roared, actually slowing and stopping the beast. His helmet met the upper curve of the steering wheel.

"Oh, God," Scott panted between high peals of laughter. "I can feel it *squishin'* between my ass cheeks! Like I'm sittin' in rotten Jell-O."

That crack took Gus away on a fresh gust of laughter, doubling him over in his seat.

The hooting eventually died away to head-shaking chuckles.

"Man," Gus said hoarsely. "I . . . I haven't laughed like that in fuckin' three years at least."

"Me either." Turning his attention to the street, Scott noted that they were on a main shopping drag. "Okay, get serious now," Gus said.

That only brought another bubble of giggles from Scott.

"We gotta get out of here. They're probably hearing us right now."

"Sure as fuck can smell us," Scott threw out.

"Drive straight. I'll tell you where to go. Nothing here. S'all been picked over."

"All of it?"

"All of it."

Under control, Scott eased the beast back up to speed.

They continued on past the shopping district and took a series of turns until the larger buildings fell away to a series of houses. Gus directed Scott to take another left, and the beast turned into a new subdivision built on the side of a hill in the neighborhood once known as Kentville, before the towns had amalgamated.

At Gus's instruction, Scott brought the van to a stop and backed into the driveway of a two-story white house. A small front lawn sprouted an uncontrolled frizz of tall yellow grass, half-hiding several faded lawn gnomes. Gus hopped out of the rear of the van, armed as always, and moved to the front door. He saw the hiding gnomes, their chipped faces bright and merry. *Happy little fuckers, aren't ya?* he thought as he moved over a concrete walkway that the elements had split in places. He stopped at the door and tried the knob. Locked. He stepped back, inspecting the windows and seeing none broken. Gus didn't like breaking into houses, on the very slim chance there were people living in there. He hadn't encountered anyone in his picking process, figuring he'd allowed enough time to pass that folks had either run for the hills, died, or become one with the gimps. He didn't want to smash out the side window next to the door to unlock it, as he might want to lock it later. Still, he relented, he had shitty-assed Scott stewing in his own beef stroganoff, and he certainly didn't want to think about how that felt.

He broke the glass with one pop of his shotgun butt, the crinkling sound making him cringe. He reached over the jagged ends, and felt around inside for the lock. A moment later, he opened the door, revealing dark wood flooring and a welcoming area that branched off to the left and right. A musty smell permeated throughout, which told him that none of the windows in the place had been opened in a long time. A staircase to the right went up to a landing with an open door, and then went left. Bright wallpaper covered the walls, and one look around informed him that the owners had money. Shotgun at the ready, he moved quickly through the downstairs, then proceeded up. The three bedrooms had been left neat and clean, as if the people had thought to return at a later date. Gus found a large flat-screen TV in the master bedroom and went into the adjoining bathroom that had a window facing the street. Oak cabinets and walk-in closets were half-full of clothes. Old-people clothes, Gus thought, while the other bedrooms were filled with other items: desks, school textbooks, paperbacks, laptops, and other things that didn't attract his attention while in house-checking mode. It was a house where the people had children who had grown up and moved away.

Gus left the upstairs and cautiously took the wooden steps down to the basement. A long row of paperbacks lined the wall and a pile of hockey sticks and equipment were piled up in a corner. Gus tried the light switch, knowing it wouldn't work. He stared into the dark below and rapped his hand against the wall, once, twice, before easing back and waiting with shotgun poised.

Nothing came.

As it was much too dark down there for him to explore, he decided that the house was pretty much clear, and went out to get Scott. At least Scott could clean himself up and maybe even find some clothes that fit.

Exiting the house, Gus saw that the street was still clear, and that made him happy. He didn't like to rush when picking.

"C'mon in," Gus told Scott. "It's cleared."

"No trouble?"

Gus shook his head.

"Took long enough," Scott grated. "Almost thought you were purposely taking your time in there."

"And let you wallow in your own shit?" Gus shook his head. "Don't know you well enough for that. C'mon in. The van'll be fine. Clean yourself up. There are clothes inside. You might be lucky."

As it turned out, Scott wasn't fortunate enough to find anything his size, but he did locate a pair of black pants with a leather belt and some long johns. He found plenty of old towels, too, and even a four-liter bottle of water, which he took to the washroom to clean himself.

Gus moved into the kitchen and went through the cupboards. He didn't find much. He took the sealed bottles of condiments, pepper, salt, even cinnamon, and popped them into his duffel bag. He also tossed in some paper towels and eight rolls of toilet paper. He found a bottle of vinegar and more household cleaning products under the sink. When Scott appeared holding a plastic-bagged pair of jeans in his fist, he helped carry stuff out to the van.

"What about the furniture?" Scott asked as he brought out a pile of well-kept paperbacks.

"Leave it. The furniture at the house is fine."

"There's an exercise machine in that room off the laundry room."

"You really want to exercise?"

"What about the old DVDs?"

"Already checked. Got them on digital on one of the terabytes."

"Hey, they got a bunch of board games here."

"Which ones?"

They took what they wanted and left with one bin full of mostly non-edible goods. Sitting again behind the wheel, Scott positioned the van in the driveway of the next house.

Gus entered and searched. He remerged minutes later with more toilet tissue, some clothes that looked as though they might fit Scott, and some cans of sausage. There was a CD collection of 70s rock music, which Gus carried back to the van and stowed as if he'd located a holy relic. He found some towels and two bottles of Glenfiddich scotch along with three bottles of Bailey's Irish Cream in a closet. Gus tucked them in the bin, wrapped and covered with the plush towels. He next came out with hockey sticks and a set of hard plastic balls. After stowing those, he leaped into the rear of the van and gave the okay to drive to the next house.

They continued along the street, picking the houses clean, until Gus noticed Scott's increasing nervousness about the dropping sun and decided to give the signal to get out of there. The time was a little after four according to the clock in the dashboard when Gus finished storing his shotgun and plopped down in the passenger seat. The welcoming heat of the interior made him sigh.

"You know something?" Gus asked as Scott drove the van back onto the main road.

"What?"

"I got into nine houses today."

"That a record?"

"Given the time, no, but it was good knowing you were out here watching things." Gus nodded. "Gave me a sense of security."

"Despite me shittin' myself?"

"Ah, don't worry about that. I shit my own self once, trying to get away from a fucked-up nurse."

"What?" Scott's helmet turned in his direction.

"Yeah."

"What happened?"

"Ah, I'll tell you about it another time. But I did come close to buyin' the farm. Lucky to be alive."

"A nurse?"

"Yeah."

"Shit. You shoot her?"

"What? No, I didn't shoot her. Shooting the dead's one thing, but I couldn't shoot the living. Drive on, there, Chico," Gus said, relaxing for the first time. He felt good with Scott around. "Take us home."

15

Gus initiated Scott to the welcome-back-alive shot he customarily took once inside the garage, and when the burns of the shots got down, they unloaded the van. Afterward, they retired to their rooms and rejoined in the kitchen a few minutes later, both changed into sweatpants and sweaters.

"You find it warm in here?" Scott asked, walking to the island in the middle of the kitchen.

Gus pointed to the living room. "You can't see it from here, but just inside the wall, there's a solar panel for heating. Heats most of the place. This area gets toasty now, but it'll be fine in the winter."

"This place is amazing."

"It is." Gus nodded, rubbing his hand on his black fisherman's sweater. He turned to the cupboards and took down two cans of Chunky soup. "Chicken okay?"

"That's fine, man."

"Go get us some booze."

Scott limped as he walked to the dining table and picked up the two waiting bottles of Jack Daniels on the table. He brought them back to the island and held one out to Gus. They opened the bottles and clicked the necks together.

"Other than the incident at the fire station, a job well done today," Gus announced.

"Yeah, it was." Scott grinned, and both of them took a burning shot.

After he finished grimacing, Scott coughed. "Gotta wash my jeans, though."

"They still in the bag?"

"Yeah."

"I'll get you some water tomorrow to do the job. A scrub bucket, too."

"What about the washer and dryer in the mud room?"

"That works, but takes power. Gotta be conservative."

"Right."

Gus took another shot from the bottle of Jack and started preparing supper. He emptied the contents of the two cans into two different pots and heated them on the stove.

"Didn't want to use the same pot?" Scott asked, holding his bottle by the neck.

"Well, y'see," Gus said as he stirred both with different spoons. "I kinda half believe that one story about the infection coming from the food supply. I never worried about it when it was myself. Man's gotta eat. Now there's two of us. If it is in the food—and I don't think it is—and one of us eats it, at least the other will have a chance."

He could tell from the sudden sour expression on Scott's face that he might have said too much. "Don't worry about it," he added, trying to reassure the man. "Just eat and drink."

After finishing their supper, they left the pots, bowls, and spoons in the sink and went down into the den. Gus turned on a single shaded lamp, but kept some candles nearby in case it started to flicker. He then plopped down on the sofa, while Scott took the recliner.

"Here's shit in your eye." Gus smirked and downed a shot.

"Just hope I don't have nightmares tonight."

Gus held up his bottle. "This should help. Can't hurt."

Scott studied the label of his own bottle. "Medicine."

"Better than Buckley's Mixture."

"Ew. I remember that shit. Tasted horrible."

"It did," Gus agreed. "But it worked."

"Didn't the president of the company say that in the commercials?"

"He did. Smart man." Gus took another shot of the whiskey. "This stuff's going down too easy these days. We'll have to get to the liquor shop and pick more up."

"There's still some there?"

"Oh, yeah. A whole warehouse full. I don't understand it myself. No one went there at all for supplies."

"Booze isn't high on a person's list, I guess."

"Guess so. Hey, you notice anything down there today?"

"No. What?" Scott stretched out in the recliner, filling its frame and gingerly lifting his healed foot.

"How's the foot?"

"Getting there. Still sore. So what about today?"

Gus took a moment before answering, as he didn't really know what to make of it all. "I don't know how accurate this is, but . . . we were into nine houses today. You asked if that was a record. It's not, but I didn't find any corpses in any of those houses. And there weren't any dead walking around that subdivision."

Scott's brow scrunched and his eyes flicked to Gus'.

"Next time we head down there, just keep that in mind. I might be wrong. Probably *am* wrong, but I have a feeling that the gimps are thinning out."

"You think so?"

"Maybe." Gus shrugged and stroked his beard. "They're like storm systems, y'know? Sometimes they're thicker in areas than others. Like where I ran over you. That area was thick with 'em."

"Were you shooting them?"

"I was. Yeah. Maybe that's it . . . But there's something else."

"Spit it out."

"That same area where I found you, well, I shot up a few of them. Left them in the streets to rot. But when I went back, they were gone."

Scott's face became drawn and pensive in the shaded light.

"Not a fuckin' trace of anything. And I looked. I mean, I left them out in the streets, and they don't decompose that fast. They were completely gone. Like the might have got up and walked away."

"Oh, shit."

"Yeah."

"So you think we can't shoot them anymore?"

"I don't know what to think. All I know is that I shot some deadheads, and they weren't there a few days later."

"Christ," Scott said quietly.

"All will be revealed in the days ahead, I figure."

"All will be revealed," Scott repeated, nodding. "Jesus, though, that's a creepy thought."

Gus shook his head. "Let's not worry about that, then. Let's just focus on the rest of the month and gettin' things done before the snow comes."

"And it's coming."

"Yeah. It's comin'. But we'll be okay. We'll be ready."

"What's on the schedule for tomorrow?"

"You should be worried about what happens tonight." Gus held up his bottle. "I wanna see yours half empty."

Scott winced. "We're goin' back into the city?"

"If we get up in time. And depends on how hung over you are."

"You don't get hangovers?"

As an answer, Gus chugged about a quarter of the bottle. He lowered it with a gasp. "I do, but I'm learnin' to not give a shit. Now then, I saw you lug in a game of Scrabble. I'm here to tell you, there ain't nothin' more amusin' than tryin' to spell big words when you're fuckin' sloshed."

16

Fall had almost spent the days of November, and the trees of the valley shrugged off the remainder of their foliage, letting it fall to the ground. Tall, wild grass completed turning yellow, and frost glazed it in the mornings. The air became crisp, fresh, and seemingly free of the smell of decaying flesh. One of the nicer things about winter in the new world.

The van backed up to the fire station in a growl of exhaust. The streets were clear of zombies, and Scott let Gus know that it had been two days since they were last in Annapolis. The drinking had been bad, quite bad for Scott, Gus knew, as the man informed him the day after their drunken Scrabble marathon. Gus also knew there was no sense in worrying about winter when one was hung over, so he declared they'd take some time off and rest up. Annapolis wasn't going anywhere. They had spent it playing both Scrabble and Monopoly, drinking lightly, but still drinking, and watching old episodes of *Breaking Bad*. The recovery days were over, however, and Gus had gotten up that morning feeling as though there was a mission in his bones.

Scott remained in the driver's seat with his lightning bolt helmet on, keeping an eye on the street, while Gus readied his shotgun and made his way to the rear. Flipping down his visor, he unlocked the doors and threw them open. The heels of his boots hit the pavement, and he hurried for the open door of the office. Gus stopped at the threshold and peered inside the area. Shadows clung to the walls like spiders webs. Sometimes, the dead wandered back into a previously cleared building, so he entered with caution.

And gagged. The smell of the putrefying dead halted him in his tracks, and Gus realized that the cold had probably dampened the smell. If it were summer, he'd have been puking in the doorway from the stench. Holding his breath in intervals, he continued and quickly established the fire station was empty. He went back to the van and got Scott to enter the station's bay with him.

"Find two of everything that fits you," Gus said.

"We got room at the house for all of this?"

"We'll make room if we have to. Just get two of everything."

They took off their jackets and tried on the black-and-yellow striped coats until finding their sizes. They took four of the ninja masks, as well as two sets of fire-retardant Nomex pants, gloves, and steel-toed boots, which reminded Gus of old science fiction movies. They loaded up three fire extinguishers and two crowbars, as well as a pair of first-aid kits. They left what they didn't need or understand how to use and were back at the van within twenty minutes.

"Stuff's heavy," Scott muttered as he loaded.

"Damn right it's heavy. And think of the shit we ain't takin'. They carry around a lot of gear."

He paused at the rear doors and looked back at the station.

"What's up?" Scott asked.

"Forgot something. Start up the beast."

Dumping his shotgun in the back, Gus drew his aluminum bat from the scabbard and returned to the station's common area. He faced the map that outlined all of the streets of Annapolis behind a thin sheen of glass. Whoever had hung the thing had nailed its wooden frame in place. Gus tsked and took a samurai pose before smashing the glass with two quick swings of his bat.

A few nails weren't going to stop vandals if they *really* wanted it.

After a few moments of wrestling it loose, Gus rolled up the map and retreated to the van with it. He stopped once and peered in at the great fire machines filling the apparatus bay, and wished he could drive one of them away. It wasn't practical, however, and gave them one last lingering look before leaving.

They rumbled away in the van, seeking to continue their house picking from the other day.

"You know, we should be checking garages, too," Scott said. "There might be another van or something in one of them."

"A brother to the beast? Existing in this town?" Gus's helmet cocked to one side. "Is such a thing possible?"

"One never—Oh . . . shit . . ."

Gus saw what had made Scott cuss and leaned forward in his seat.

Just ahead, filling the entire breadth of the road, stood a wall of corpses. Bodies of all sizes and heights shambled along on bare feet and broken ankles. Some crawled like filthy fat carpets. Gray-faced children missing limbs wore summer clothing. Undead that appeared almost skeletal, with bare heads bearing the brunt of the sun's glare, turned in the direction of the slowing van. As the cold sun beat down upon the mob that spanned from one row of houses to the other, Scott slowed the van and stopped a good thirty meters from the line. The dead on the outer edge of the horde wavered and turned like a dark audience of headbangers left thrashing for far too long.

Then, five of the corpses rushed the van.

"Runners," Gus yelled. "Back up!"

Scott shifted into reverse.

One of the runners stumbled and fell face down onto the cold asphalt, a sneaker flying into the air. The runner behind it tripped over the flailing arm of the fallen dead and likewise crashed.

The other three charged.

"Scott . . ." Gus put his hand on his seatbelt. If he had to, he would get his shotgun.

The beast swung around in a wild ninety-degree turn. Scott fumbled with the gears, got a lower one that made the engine groan.

Ten meters.

The three runners came on, their arms held straight out as if looking for hugs. Gus could see their gray-black features, the empty holes of their eye sockets. One didn't have a jawbone, and its upper incisors hung down like nails worn to nubs.

Scott pushed the gear into *Reverse* and turned back the way they had come. A startling barrage of flesh beat upon the rear of the van, pounding out a mad bongo tune. Scott pressed down on the accelerator, and the beast shot forward, quickly getting up to forty.

"Do a fishtail!" Gus said.

"What?"

"Do it!"

Bending low over the steering wheel, Scott jerked it left, then right. His shoulder slammed against his door, and his helmet bounced off the glass. The connection startled him, but he maintained control of the vehicle.

Gus rolled down his window and stuck out his head, looking behind them. A moment later, he pulled back in and put up the window. "You just lost one unwanted hitchhiker."

"Yeah?"

"Bastard was hangin' on to something back there. It happens sometimes." Gus pointed to the upcoming intersection. "Take a right here. We might be able to drive around them."

Scott looked to Gus, the worry clear around his eyes as his helmet covered the rest. "We're not goin' into that subdivision, are we?"

"Through that tide?" Gus shook his head. "We go around it and find another place. Another street. There's plenty. But shit, that pack back there blows my theory out of the water. I thought—hoped—they were thinning out."

"Ain't nothin' thin about that goddamn convention."

Gus rubbed a gloved hand over his helmet and adjusted it. "Turn here. I know this city. I know where we are."

Following Gus's directions, Scott drove the van to another part of the city. They crossed what was once the tidal flats lined with dikes, and proceeded into the neighborhood of Port Williams. They didn't see any more dead, and avoided the main roads. The beast finally slowed and stopped on a side street lined with huge naked elms, behind which hundred-year-old houses squatted and waited to be visited. Some of the dwellings were newer and had plastic siding stuck to their ribs, while the older models were in bad need of a paint job. Scott backed the van into the driveway of the first house and killed the engine.

Gus looked out of his window and saw the state of decay the place was in. The front lawn had grown up into a yellow jungle while the white house looked as if it had been blasted by sand. Bare gray wood, ancient-looking under the sun, peeked out under the rotting white coat. Chips and long ragged strips hung off the soffit and fascia like droopy, cured flesh. The place needed a complete scraping and a solid coat of primer, followed by at least two coats of paint. It would have been a huge contract to paint such a house, Gus knew, back in the old days. That put a smile on his face. The old days were only a few years ago.

"We'll do the whole street if there's time," Gus said and got up, moving into the back.

"Is this a three-story house?" Scott asked.

"Looks like two, but they probably have an attic. Wouldn't want to be up there in the summer. Or the winter for that matter." Gus slung his bat scabbard over his back, then took down the shotgun. He grabbed a fistful of shells and filled both of his pockets.

"Looks like a gas station down the street there."

"Dry," Gus said, slapping down his visor. "I was there about a year ago. Long looted, but I'm wondering about the houses."

Taking the shotgun to the back of the van, Gus opened the door and jumped out. He closed the door softly behind him and walked down a short crushed-gravel driveway. The door to the house was on the left, but Gus pointed the shotgun toward the garden in the back, just past another elm with a lonely swing hanging from one of its lower limbs. The cold wind broke on his leather and helmet, but something about the white reeds wilted in the garden drew his attention. Checking the corner of the house, Gus warily moved forward, edging past the swing. The garden appeared like something washed up on a shore somewhere. Dead stalks formed a white weave over the earth, but Gus spotted a few wasted bulbs still attached. Looking around, he knelt and picked up one of the bulbs for closer study.

Garlic. He squished it between his fingers. Someone grew their own garlic behind the house and probably a little something more, but Gus wasn't an expert on produce. The valley was a farming hub right up until the end, and those who had the property to do so had possessed little gardens behind their houses. Gus got to his feet and tossed the dead plant back into its bed. He turned around and looked up at the house. A wind rose up and buffeted him, and the high windows seemed like dead eyes gazing off toward the Bay of Fundy. Gus didn't like the chill that passed through him, and wasn't certain if it was the wind or his own fear.

"Fuckin' gimps." He trekked to the door. He turned the old-fashioned brass knob of the wood and glass door and found it locked. The keyhole was another throwback to older times, but Gus wasn't interested in remembering them. He ran his bare fingers over glass with edges freckled with paint, and peered in. A short hallway led to another closed door, as well as a staircase on the right. Not seeing any other way, Gus put his plastic-padded elbow through the glass with a tinkle and reached in. He felt wood against the door. Grunting, Gus put his helmeted head through the broken window and saw a piece of two-by-four nailed both into the floor and the door, creating a brace.

Frowning, Gus used the butt of his shotgun to clear the glass fragments from the window. He returned to the van, his thoughts dark and his craw boiling for some unknown reason. He knocked on the rear door before opening it. "It's me," he said, climbing into the back.

Scott looked back. "Problem?"

"Someone placed a brace against the front door on the inside," Gus said, pulling out one of the crowbars.

"Someone might be still in there."

Gus grunted and got back out of the van. That might be the case, he thought as he closed the doors, but then he remembered the untended garden in the back, and his mood soured even more.

He carefully climbed in through the window and landed off balance. He righted himself and noted the shotgun's short barrel pointed at his foot. Gus felt more bad juju. He got those feelings at times and had learned to pay attention to the foreshadowing. It wasn't only fear building through him, though. It was irritation. If he got filled enough with it, he knew the shit would turn into anger.

His mouth becoming a tight line, Gus channelled that irritation into applying the crowbar and ripping out the brace. He turned the knob and let the door swing inward with an almost embarrassed squeal. *Yeah, that's right, fucker. I chopped down your mother, too.*

Moving toward a closed door, Gus leaned over the stair railing and glanced upward to the second floor. Eggshell paint covered the hallway, and the heavy stale air and something else filled his senses, like old smoke from rotten lungs. He turned the knob on the door and found it also locked. Placing his shotgun down, he tore into the door with the crowbar, inserting one end into the crack and wrenching it back. As if he had pulled back the lips on a dead dog, the wood around the bolt snarled and splintered. Gus pried the door open, destroying the old lock, and swung open the door.

That familiar smell assaulted his senses, making him wish he had an air filter of some sort. Or that ninja mask he had gotten from the fire station. The stench backed his head up on his shoulders, and he dropped the crowbar in favor of the shotgun. Taking a breath, he steadied himself, while the fresh air from the door circulated inside. The entry area still stank to low hell.

All right, Gus thought, placing the butt of the weapon to his shoulder. *Where are you?*

Edging into what he assumed to be a lower apartment, he turned and faced a faded kitchen. Light oozed from boarded-up windows. Then, he heard it.

Squeaking. A gum-aching sound repeating again and again to a slow, but persistent beat.

His fingers flexed on the trigger guard and the pump of his weapon. He slid up his visor and took a step into the kitchen, walking on stained linoleum. Blood, he figured. The smell of dead flesh almost overpowered him, but he pressed on. Ignoring the counter on his right and the small table on his left, both covered in tarnished kitchen utensils, he faced the room ahead, a living room, one wall filled with a brown sofa covered in patches of piss-stained newspaper. The room appeared gloomy and cloaked in shadows, as the large picture window had been boarded up from the outside, allowing only narrow slivers of daylight to enter. He took two more steps; a toaster's side reflected his swelling reflection.

Squeaaak . . . Squeaaak. Like an old swing swaying from log rafters. *Squeaaak. Squeaaak.*

Thump.

Gus froze in his tracks and looked at the ceiling. A spider's web of cracks spread across its painted surface, as if something had thrown itself at the floor above in an effort to break through.

Squeaaaak. Squeaaa . . .

Irritation got the fuck out of Dodge, replaced with incoming fright. Gus blinked, divided between the nerve-grating noise ahead, and the—

Thump.

Accompanied by the sound of a short drag of something heavy across the floor above.

Squeeeeee.

Gus looked back to the eerie living room, the greater part of it shielded from his vision. He haltingly took another step forward.

Thump. From above, right over his head.

He took another step forward, his mind screaming at him to *get the fuck out of the apartment. Get the fuck out.* He wasn't being stupid; he was well over the border of squirrel shit crazy for inching to his left, expanding his field of vision until he saw the tip of a black boot come into sight, the toe moving back and forth.

Squeak . . . squueeeee.

Thump, and that raspy dead weight drag of something unwilling, moving over Gus's head, and back the way he had come . . . in the direction of the stairs. Fright quickened his breath, and he glanced back at the moving black boot. He moved another step forward, fingers flexing on the trigger guard. *Squeeak.* The boot rose up to a white pants cuff, splashed with black.

Thump thump thump. Gus whirled at the noise, pointing the barrel at the ceiling and waiting to see if the way he had come would fill with the dead. The grim light softening the threshold and open doorway was momentarily fluttered by darkness. Something was coming. Something was coming for *him.*

Squeak.

Gus knew he was cut off. He looked ahead and back, wondering where the first corpse would appear. He angled further to his left. He saw the boot place itself, very precisely, onto the floor. There was no other leg. The pants cuff rose to a knee and a gray hand came into view, its last two fingers missing and meaty stumps bare and white. The remaining fingers flexed like a spider's legs. Gus heard something come around the hallway behind him, dragging itself along the wall. A groan of wood perked his attention, and he moved further in to see dark splashes over a white-shirted torso. The black flesh of one side of a face came into view, the lips eroded over black gums housing the dull gleam of gold. The robin's egg of a single eye turned in Gus's direction and, as he watched in mounting terror, the thing in the rocking chair *pushed* itself up and stood on one leg, the empty pant leg rolling off the seat like a bloated ribbon of dead skin. Breath hissed from a chest that did not move, and that gold-toothed mouth actually *clicked* open.

It released its hands from the armrests of the rocker and collapsed to the stained carpet with a clatter. The noise distracted Gus from the two runners bursting into the apartment behind him. He heard the patter of their shoeless feet and turned in time to see jaws opening and black orbs rolling in their eye sockets. Gus fired and punched a toaster-sized hole in the first zombie, throwing it back against the kitchen sink. The second undead crashed into him and bit into his visor. The putrid smell of the decomposing flesh swamped Gus and almost made him swoon. His shotgun pinned against his chest, he angled it under the zombie's working jaw and exploded the top of the dead fucker's head, flowering the ceiling in a nasty soup of decayed gore and brain matter. Particles freckled Gus's visor, and the touch of it sent a *Shit* through his mind. The blast knocked him backward, and he careened off the door-frame, landing flat on his back—the aluminum bat nearly breaking his spine—halfway in the living room. The wind flew from his lungs. Gus wheezed, desperately clawing oxygen back into his body while the black hand of the one-legged gentleman with the gold-toothed grin reached for him with two missing fingers. The hand closed in on Gus's visor and gave him the rare treat of seeing how the splintered stumps bled dry over time. Shards of dead skin hung from the bitten-off bones, and just beyond, the white-eyed fucker's teeth *clicked* open another degree.

Gus felt as if he were in a vacuum, sucking in air moving in the other direction and not filling his begging lungs, but possibly drawing in the mess splashed on his visor and the horror of that made him roll away from the hand. He felt fingers graze his shoulders, pointed things like old spikes, and he swung an arm, hitting something, but not knowing what. His ears exploded with the *THUMP, THUMP, THUMP* from somewhere above. He looked up from where he lay on his stomach and saw that his fist had taken the gold-toothed jaw off the old bastard's face, but *still* it crawled toward him.

Air finally went back into Gus's aching lungs. He coughed, felt his eyes water, and pistoned his boot heel out and into the face of the zombie slinking toward him. Then, fingers gripped his helmet and hooked the thing up over his eyes, blinding him.

A train whistle of a howl blasted his ears, and Gus ripped the helmet from his head. A corpse with a huge hole in its stomach attacked, wasted guts jiggling like old rubber from the edges of its wound. Gus flailed out with both arms and knocked the thing away to land on top of the old man. Coughing as though he'd just infected himself with a super strain of influenza, Gus found his boomstick on the threshold of the doorway. He snatched it up as more shadows appeared in the kitchen, a woman chained to a chair, dragging it toward him with an expression of dead glee on her frightening features. Gus whirled and roared as he pumped the shotgun and blew off the heads of the two creatures at his feet with one shell. A ridge of gold teeth jumped onto the carpet. He pumped another shell into the chamber, the ejector of his shotgun spitting out an empty red piece of plastic. In one fluid movement, where the mind and body act as a single instrument, he brought up the barrel and unleashed a blast square into the ghoulish white smile of the dead woman behind him, disintegrating her skull from the chin up.

He fell back against the doorway, breathing hard and suddenly buckling over and throwing up. He heaved twice more, retching as if his eyes would fucking explode onto the carpet before him. Shotgun blasts rocked his world then, sounding days away and yet right in his eardrums. He wanted to get clean. He wanted dearly to scrub his face and any other body part that had come into contact with the dead things. He didn't know if he'd swallowed anything or not. His eyes filled with water, and he didn't know if it was from the force of his voiding or if something had entered them. His hands shook as if holding on to train tracks while a locomotive thundered down upon him. He wept. He heaved again and blew snot out of his nose, knowing the complete experience that had just occurred in a fish bowl of seconds had broken his mind and yanked on his nerves. A shadow rushed him, and he tried to raise his shotgun, but his fingers felt boneless. He blinked and saw only a black thing bearing down on him.

And then blackness swallowed him.

17

Tenner had come across the man in a small nameless town on the road to Halifax. He had pulled over to inspect another service station, an Esso, when he heard a clatter from the roof and a human voice yell out to him. Pleasantries were exchanged, and Tenner informed the man that he was on his way to Halifax, and by all *means*, he was more than welcome to join him.

Five minutes later, the guy—in his fifties, bald-headed, and with a huge overbite—ran from the station, dressed in faded denims and a dark winter coat that puffed him up. The old guy practically cried at seeing another human being. The man couldn't believe Tenner drove a hybrid SUV, and overall damn near pissed himself with joy.

His name was Lou, he informed Tenner with a broad smile missing two front teeth. He was a mechanic.

The fact that he was a mechanic saved his ass for a day. Tenner had him inspect the Pathfinder and give it the thumbs up, and even let him cook dinner in the back of the service station. Old Lou was sampling the soup he had cooked when Tenner grabbed him in a chokehold from behind and squeezed all consciousness from him. Old Lou had woken up bound and gagged. Tenner had been more than happy to have a new toy, even if it would only be for a little while.

Tenner stood on the roof of the service station and gazed through telescopic sights down at the rusty drum filled with rocks to keep it in place. Rough rope bound old Lou to the drum, looping around his bare upper chest. Cement blocks lashed to his legs kept them stretched out before him, and in old Lou's weakened condition, he was helpless—the poor bastard had been on the cusp of starvation and eating roots when Tenner found him. Tenner zeroed in on Lou's hands, inspecting the spikes he had driven through the backs of each, nailing him to the drum. The wounds still dribbled blood.

That was just great, Tenner thought. More sauce for the goose. Or geese. Or whatever the fuck might happen along. He wasn't picky. He simply wanted something to shoot.

Old Lou's pain-wracked wails came from where he sat square in the middle of the highway, three-quarters of a kilometre away from the service station. The distance had been a bastard to figure on because Tenner just wasn't certain of the range of his weapon. He hefted the rifle to his shoulder again and moved its bipod-mounted barrel onto the ledge of the roof. Tenner peeked through the scope once more, smirking as he looked over old Lou's screaming form.

Nothing thus far.

Tenner sighed, folded his arms, and dropped his head onto them. Minutes later, old Lou stopped screaming. Tenner checked and saw that the highway remained empty. A few houses were far up one end, but if there were any undead around, old Lou's blood would certainly bring them around. He glanced down at the ten magazines of twenty shots apiece and smiled contentedly. He had to thank dear old Dad again. A rush of wind grazed his back, chilling him despite the thick black winter coat he wore with a fur-lined hood. His ponytail pulled a little when he moved his head. Tenner studied his gloves for a moment, thinking about the stitches in the material, when Lou screamed again.

Tenner pulled the bipod and rifle back and squinted through the scope. A zombie moved up the highway, walking as if it wore a bloated colostomy bag. Tenner got into position and placed the targeting lines of the scope right on the approaching zombie's right arm. He scrunched his brow in concentration. Old Lou's pleading for help—only just heard to begin with—was periodically drowned out by the wind. *Wind . . .* he'd have to figure that into the shot and adjust accordingly.

Tenner sighted the zombie. The wind was blowing past him so it shouldn't affect the shot. His finger left the guard and touched the trigger.

Squeezed.

The creature's face blossomed violently, and the thing dropped to the pavement. Grinning, Tenner swerved the rifle back on old Lou and saw that the man wasn't in the best of shape—even though he'd just been saved. That struck Tenner as odd. He then saw the cause for old Lou's distress. Zombies. Perhaps a hundred, maybe even two, moving out from houses and from the forest, coming down the road.

"Shit," Tenner swore with irritation. He had about two hundred rounds with him, but he wondered if that would be enough. "Gonna be close, Lou, old buddy. Gonna be close."

Tenner was more than happy to give it a go. He loved old video games. Loved old shooters where the player stared down the barrel of a rifle to blast away at whole armies of animated fiends. His scenario was just a tad more realistic, a drop more visceral, and far too much fun. He had to shoot straight and accurately, else he'd lose old Lou to the advancing mob. That wouldn't be kosher. Lou was important in Tenner's new world. He possessed a valuable skill set. Losing him wouldn't be a good thing, which gave even more excitement to the upcoming game. Tenner set the stock of the Bushmaster rifle to his shoulder, telling himself he'd have to be perfect.

The writhing, moaning wall approached old Lou's position, or at least Tenner expected they would be moaning. Stinking, as well, but he had no worries of that where he was situated. He eyed the mass as they closed the distance, the scope powerful enough to spot bodies and individuals, but not quite features. There was always the option of allowing them closer, but Tenner thought not, and drew a bead on the first corpse.

Drumming his legs and cursing the day he had met that conniving bastard, Lou sat with his legs immobilized to the cinderblocks and his hands nailed to the drum behind him. His hands ached dearly, and he knew the chances were exceptionally high that if he got out his predicament, he'd probably have to hack both of them off to save himself from infection. He listened to the wind blowing and felt its cutting breath on his cheeks, freezing him. He'd never been colder. He couldn't see what was behind him, but he slowly became aware of a creeping tide rising above the horizon of asphalt. He knew what they were, and he struggled again against his bonds. He pulled hard enough on his hands that he passed out from the pain.

The sounds of gunshots revived him. The mob of lurching dead people marched on. Lou's senses cleared, and he shook his head. Focusing on the approaching wall of corpses, he estimated they were about a hundred and twenty meters out, a little more than a football field, and still much too close for Lou. Fear dried out his mouth and throat, and his legs kicked weakly.

At that moment, a zombie's head exploded, and he heard the distant crack of the rifle. The dead collapsed and disappeared in the creeping tide.

Another zombie stumbled and fell, and Lou heard another far off report. He looked left and right, spotting only an empty field of tall yellow grass and a curtain of stark trees. The shots came from over the field, from the direction of the service station.

What the hell was happening? Lou thought as he watched the steady march of the dead eating up the distance with every step.

With the wind blowing past his hood, Tenner quickly emptied the first twenty-round magazine into the ranks of the unliving. Some he missed. Some he nailed dead on, exploding their skulls with a soundless poof. Others he missed, but hit something else instead as they were packed so tightly together—a shoulder here, a neck there. It didn't really matter to Tenner. When the first mag finished, he ejected it and quickly inserted the next full one. He primed the weapon, took sight, and noted that the mass was about ninety meters away. He shot the head of a fellow in blue coveralls, and perfectly exploded the brainpan of what looked to be a priest. He fired and hit what could've been a pro basketball player, blowing the head clean from its neck.

Grinning, he took five to ten seconds in between shots to line up the next one. He focused on the dead leading the pack, closest to old Lou, who was either praising him or cursing him to low Hell. The second mag went dry, and Tenner reached for the third. The zombies kept pressing ahead, despite the thirty or so he'd put down. Gritting his teeth, Tenner made seventeen more kills, his rate of fire unconsciously speeding up, chipping away at the lead dead people like a hammer against rotten marble. He burned through the fourth and fifth clips, dropping another thirty or so at the eighty-meter mark. The pack seemed to be thinning out. He sniffed as he loaded up the sixth mag and noted old Lou hollering something lost in the wind. Whatever. Tenner couldn't be distracted, and he ignored the growing ache in his shoulder from the Bushmaster's repeated kicking. He wondered if he would have a misfire or experience some other malfunction as he took another head from the shoulders of a Mountie, the head spraying apart in spectacular fashion.

Seventy meters. Tenner took a breath and loaded the eighth magazine much slower. He pinched the ridge of bone between his eyes and snorted. Taking sight on the crowd, about three dozen unliving walkers left, he squeezed off a round and missed entirely. His second shot spun his target about like a ballerina before it fell. His shoulder ached like hell, and he massaged it, allowing the remaining bunch to close within fifty meters.

Tenner took aim and put down ten more dead before the spent mag popped out. He loaded in the ninth with a curse, realizing the game wasn't so much fun anymore. He would carry on, however; he owed that much to old Lou.

Crack. An undead little girl flopped over.

Crack. A man with a jean jacket hanging off his left arm staggered back. Tenner sighted again and blew out the back of his head.

Crack. A woman wearing no pants dropped to her knees and fell over.

And on and on. Until he emptied the ninth. Tenner ejected the mag and simply dropped his head to his arms. The wind blew over him, but his coat kept him warm. There were seven or eight of the undead left. Closing in on old Lou. Tenner believed they were about thirty meters out. Lou's screams sounded very far away. He had to give it to the zombies. They were relentless. Fearless. Even as others were dropping dead around them, they marched on without any concern for their personal safety. Of course, Tenner knew they would. Over time, he had made a gruesome study of the things. He was fairly certain they went by smell, perhaps sound if they had ears or their hearing canals were unblocked. And even sight. He sort of doubted the last one, as he'd seen too many of them with a milky film glazing their pupils. The thing that amazed him the most was their single-minded focus on feeding, and utter fearlessness of finally dying. He wondered if they were really dead at times, wondered if they were somehow distantly aware of their condition and welcomed final death. He didn't know. Maybe he would one day.

Sighing, Tenner loaded his rifle again, wondering how hot the barrel was. He charged his weapon and fixed his eye to the scope.

Eight zombies left.

He sighted a woman wearing a uniform. Tenner shot her though the temple, shearing off the entire frontal part of her cranium and hooking her off her feet.

He heard the tinkle of the spent shell being ejected and looked to see a pile of brass next to him. *Jesus.*

Twenty meters. Tenner shot a man in a dress suit, ripping his head clean off his shoulders. He shifted quickly and popped the top off of a skull with a reflexive jerk of his trigger. Tenner shook his arm to loosen it up, wondering what had happened there. Old Lou, he figured, was probably scared shitless. Tenner knew he would be if their positions were reversed.

Crack. A bearded man spun around and almost gracefully dropped to the pavement.

Ten meters.

Crack, crack. Two more put down, their heads exploding like tough fruit gone bad.

Five meters. Two left.

Tenner sighted on the shambling form of a little old lady in a flowery dress. A larger male hung at her heels. The scope shifted, and he saw old Lou, white-faced and howling like a broken fire alarm. For an older guy, he shook and screamed and shuddered against the drum, primal instinct taking over now, and Tenner remembered a time when he was a boy and found a rabbit with two broken legs on the side of the highway. A car had smashed it while it was crossing and left it to die. That rabbit, however, had life enough in it to bawl like a child, terrified so much it actually tried to escape on its broken legs when it saw Tenner approaching.

Tenner had never heard anything so pure, and yet so heartbreaking, since.

He imagined Lou sounded something like that rabbit.

Through the scope, Tenner watched. His finger tensed on the trigger for a second, as the granny zombie closed the last few feet and gripped Lou's face with its decayed hands. Old Lou's eyes looked ready to just about pop out of his skull. The granny bent over, just as the second zombie stepped up behind her. She bared her barren gums, worn down to raw bone, and started to gnaw through old Lou's scalp.

The larger zombie started in on Lou's shoulder, biting into the meat with enough gusto to remind Tenner of eating a jelly donut. The male still had some teeth. He sighed and watched for a bit more, listening to Lou's screams peter out. Tenner lost the game in the end. He figured old Lou had defecated himself right in the last few seconds.

And Tenner hated the smell of shit more than he needed a mechanic.

18

Scott wanted to shoot the dead thing reaching for Gus, but he didn't. Instead, he rushed into the room and kicked the thing square in the bare back. His boot crunched through the gray-black flesh, and for a single insane moment, he stood there with a zombie on the end of his leg. The gruesome thing reared up and tried to turn. Unable to free himself, Scott stumbled backward, and the deadhead fell with him. Panting, Scott scrambled to his feet as the Dee seemed to understand that it was facing the floor. It looked up, and Scott blasted the skull, dropping the corpse in the kitchen.

"Gus!" He stepped over the carcasses to get to his companion, who was shrivelled up in the doorway with his hands to his face. "Gus!"

Scott pulled the hands down, and Gus stared at him blankly. Black and gray matter speckled Gus's face as if he had stood behind a screen door when the shithouse exploded.

"Swallowed some," Gus whispered, his eyes frightened. "I . . . swallowed some."

"Oh, Jesus." Scott heard moaning from above. "Oh, Jesus," he repeated. He had killed two of the things on the staircase on the way in, but the house was turning out to be a goddamn nest. He pulled Gus to his feet and leaned him against the door-frame. Scott searched the area, yanking open two drawers in the kitchen before finding a red-and-white checked table cloth. He grabbed it and went back to Gus.

"Close your eyes and mouth!"

Gus blinked at him.

"CLOSE YOUR FUCKIN' EYES AND MOUTH!"

Gus obeyed, and Scott tried to spit onto the end of the table cloth, but no spit would come. Muttering, he frantically dry-wiped Gus's face, cleaning it as best as he could while the moaning grew louder. He looked over his shoulder. The daylight spilling into the room from the hallway darkened.

Snarling, Scott left the cloth in Gus's hands and reloaded his shotgun, shoving four shells into the breach. He brought the weapon to his shoulder and waited. Three Dees wandered into the doorway. Scott shot them all and reloaded. He heard a single voice of one corpse closing the distance to the doorway, rustling as it dragged itself forward. Its shadow grew against the wall. Just before entering, it paused, creeping Scott out. Could the thing be thinking?

"Hey!" Scott yelled, and the dead thing, its head a hideous flesh-patched skull with its eyes eaten out, practically wrapped its huge bulbous form around the corner. A walking blob of a corpse, perhaps three hundred kilograms of reeking, rotting flesh, rubbed its rolls of fat against the narrow entryway as it came in. The sight and smell made Scott gag. The thing paused then, seemingly hearing him, then shuffled forward, its mouth hanging open.

Scott blew off its head. The headless corpse crumpled in the doorway, and he realized with dawning horror that the immense bulk of the thing blocked their escape.

"Well, Jesus Christ." He rushed to the fat man's form and leaned over to see how much room remained to crawl over the dead. The idea suddenly revolted him as he looked at the black sores covering the gruesome flesh. "Fuck that." Scott backed up.

More hissing and moaning came from outside.

"Oh, Jesus," Scott swore again, and went to a boarded window in the kitchen. He peeked out through the cracks and spied figures lurching past the van toward the open door of the house. "Oh, Jesus." He looked back at Gus and then rushed into the living room. There was a picture window boarded up on the outside. The glass on the inside could potentially be dangerous enough. Then, Scott saw the old rocking chair. His features twisting into a scowl, he took two steps, uprooted it from the carpeted floor, and flung it into the glass. The picture window shattered with a clap and large shards tinkled to the floor. Scott stomped on the rocking chair, snapping off an armrest. He raked the length of wood around the edges of the frame, clearing it as best as he could in the time he thought he had. Realizing he was moaning, he fought down his fear and sized up the wood. Narrow planks stretched over a large window.

"I swallowed some," he heard Gus mutter again and again. "I swallowed some, I swallowed some, I *know* I swallowed some . . ."

Scott returned and pulled him to his feet. He saw with growing horror that there were fragments of flesh in Gus's beard. "Oh, fuck." Had Gus ever been that pale before? How long did it take to change if someone ingested a piece of the dead? Oh, *fuck!* What if he was changing right fucking *now*? Oh, Jesus *fucking Christ*.

His breath coming hard, Scott listened to the growing sounds of visitors outside, some banging against the side of the house as they approached the doorway. He could hear shuffling in the hallway again. Taking a deep breath, Scott righted Gus and shoved his shotgun into his arms. "Hold this!"

Scott took five steps back from the window and bared teeth.

Then, he charged.

He was a big man, standing at six five. In his younger days, he had been a hockey player. A forward, and legend had it that if Scott Harris was coming down the ice, the last place on God's frozen earth you wanted to be was in front of him. The last two years had taken away a lot of his fat and bulk, and even some of his muscle, but he was still a big man. Perhaps all of a hundred and twenty kilograms.

That weight crashed through the planks covering the picture window like a wrecking ball with a full desperate head of steam behind it. Scott fell to his knees on the other side and rolled over to stare at a zombie who was probably the neighbor, a tall, lanky individual with a rotten straw moustache. Scott kicked the thing's legs out from under it and jumped up as it fell to the ground. Roaring, Scott stomped on its head, hearing the chalky, vase-breaking clatter of shattering skull. Scott looked around and spied several dead fuckers walking in the street, drawn to the commotion.

He went back in through the jagged hole he'd made and saw that Gus had dropped his shotgun. Suddenly furious, Scott picked up the weapon, spun Gus around to face the wall, and jammed the weapon into his bat scabbard, barrel first.

"We're going!" Scott shouted.

"My helmet." Gus pointed. Scott bent over and picked the thing up. He held it out, grew impatient, and stuffed the protective device over Gus's head, wrenching it into position hard.

"Come on!" He dragged a torpid Gus toward the hole and pushed him through it. A zombie closed in on Gus, but Scott cracked the wooden stock of his shotgun across its dead features, knocking it to the ground. He fired a shell into its head, the ejector flinging away the spent cartridge.

Knowing that he had only seconds before the gathering mob zeroed in on him, he manhandled the smaller man toward the van. Scott opened the passenger door and got Gus into the seat.

"Buckle up!" he shouted and spun around the front. He ran into a little dead girl, no higher than his waist, with long hair that seemed glued to her pasty white scalp. Part of her jaw was missing, but she still had teeth. Scott bowled her over and left her in the dust. He reached the driver's side and saw that the dozen or so deadheads going into the house were turning their direction. He lunged into the driver's seat and started the beast. The machine cranked into gear and lurched forward, crushing the back and head of the rising little girl. The van pushed through five more of the gathering dead, probably not killing them, but knocking them away and breaking bones.

Scott turned the wheel and drove back the way they had come, leaving the pack behind them. He took the next right and drove fast down the streets. Houses flashed by. Scott turned left, looking for the street that would take them back to the main highway and the house. An intersection came up, and he went right, knowing that was the direction of out of town.

"Gus, where are we?" he asked, daring a look in the other man's direction. Gus bounced in his seat, staring ahead and unresponsive. Scott saw that he hadn't buckled up, and that the shotgun was pointed downward in the scabbard, into the seat. He didn't know if he should worry or not, but if he hit something hard enough . . . visions of Gus blowing his own ass off filled his head.

"Gus!"

Gus leaned back in his seat as if trying to avoid something, his eyes fixed ahead.

Scott looked back at the road.

Well, *shit*.

A wall of zombies scores deep curtained off the street. Scott jammed on the brakes in time, but the beast's nose still bashed the foremost ranks of the wall of deadheads. One reached up and clawed at the windshield. Others pawed at the side windows. More closed in on the sides, rattling the walls of the beast.

Grunting, Scott slapped the van into reverse and got its metallic ass away. The beast flew backward, the zombie wall falling away, and Scott realized in fright he didn't know *where* he was driving in reverse as he had no mirrors.

"Oh, Jesus!" He slowed to do a ninety-degree turn. The ass of the beast smashed into something unseen and grated a metal squeal when Scott put the van back into drive. Something scraped the underside of the rear as he pulled ahead and swerved to the left. A side road loomed, and he took it, hoping beyond hope that he was right and the road led to the highway.

He slowed to forty and forced his breathing to calm. He drove down a long throat of a road, noting how the houses were the townhouse kind, built together in narrow plots with very little space between them.

Then his heart sank, and his jaw dropped.

The side street he had driven onto emerged into a fishbowl swath of pavement, hedged in by large houses built close together, with fenced-off backyards and deserted cars in some of the driveways.

A cul-de-sac.

"Sweet fucking monkey!" Scott jerked the wheel to the right, feeling the van ride the curve of the turn and circle back to the road leading out. He drove back the way he had come, revving the engine in his growing panic.

"Oh, fuck me . . ." he trailed off.

Just ahead, the concert crowd of undead shifted and oozed into the street like a massive carnivorous amoeba, sensing the entrapment of its prey. Scott slowed and stopped, glanced left and right. There was no way to drive the beast through the narrow walkways between the houses. In some cases, huge dead elms blocked any exit for the beast, unless he dragged Gus out and made a run for it. One look at Gus' dead man's stare killed that notion. The beast couldn't penetrate the thing bearing down on them. They would plough into the first few ranks and stall against the press of dead bodies, perhaps even spin out on the corpses underneath while the remainder bashed and thrashed against the metal hull, until they broke through the windows or even rolled it over. It all ended badly for him and Gus.

The mass slid toward the beast.

Shaking his head, Scott did a ninety degree turn up over a small front lawn and turned back to the cul de sac. The van stopped in the middle of the pear-shaped dead end, and Scott focused on one two-story house. He saw the garage, the doors, the flimsy-looking windows. He looked around at all of the houses, seeing most were two-story, indefensible death traps. He had no other choice. No other choice at all.

"Fuck." Scott head-butted the steering wheel with his lightning bolt helmet.

Then he reversed the van and backed it up in front of the front doorway of the house opposite the mouth of the cul-de-sac. He got up, went to the back, and locked the rear door. Gathering up four boxes of shells from where Gus had stowed them under the seats, he unzipped his coat and plopped them all inside, tucking the front of his jacket down the front of his jeans.

When he got out of the van, the advancing dead were spilling toward the mouth of the cul-de-sac. Scott raced around the front, shotgun in hand, and dragged Gus, still clutching at the tablecloth, out of his seat. With anxious glances over his shoulder, he dragged Gus to the front door and tried turning the knob. Locked, *of fucking course*, Scott seethed. He drove the butt of the shotgun through a pane of glass set into the door, then reached in and unlocked it. Grunting, Scott threw open the door and shoved Gus inside. He looked over his shoulder again and saw the mass of walking corpses coming into the far end of the cul-de-sac, beginning to fill up the bowl.

Hunting, his mind whispered.

He slammed the door and locked it. Scott looked about for a chair. He ran down a short hallway and entered the kitchen, swearing to the Lord above that if he walked into another nest like the last one, he'd shoot Gus first and then himself. He grabbed a wooden chair, carried it back to the front door, and shoved-wedged it under the knob. It didn't feel secure enough.

High ground. Grabbing Gus by the shoulder and directing him forward, he pushed the man up a staircase to the second floor. They turned down a narrow hallway, and Scott found what he had hoped.

A trapdoor for an attic.

Frantically, Scott looked around. There was a linen closet nearby, and he opened it. Right inside was a long pole that ended with a hook. He grabbed and used it on the metal eye hanging from the ceiling. Scott pulled the door down to expose a folding stairway. He unfolded the stairs, the springs protesting loudly.

"Up!" Scott whispered and pushed Gus up the stairs. The wooden joints groaned at the weight, but held.

Scott thought he heard something down below.

Gus stopped halfway up the stairs, and Scott jabbed him in the ass with the pole, propelling him forward. On impulse, Scott glanced back into the linen closet and saw it stuffed with towels and blankets. Not thinking about why, he grabbed armfuls and threw them up into the attic.

Below, glass shattered.

Something crashed against the outside door. Wood squealed.

"Holy shit." Scott climbed the steps to the attic. Darkness surrounded him, pierced only by light from a metal vent in a nearby wall. The attic had flooring in the main area, but bare black loaves of insulation lay beyond. Gus lay on a thick plank with his hands still holding the tablecloth to his chest.

Placing the shotguns to one side along with the ammunition, Scott got flat on his stomach. He stretched his arm over the edge and hooked the stairs. Grunting, he slowly folded the lower section into the middle part.

More glass shattering below. He wasn't certain if the moaning was coming from Gus or the advancing fiends.

Grimacing, Scott hauled the stairway up into the attic, the springs squealing softly. Laying down the pole, Scott carefully moved over to Gus and covered him with blankets. He snatched the tablecloth away and gave him a clean towel for his face and beard.

"Shhhh," Scott warned and looked around in the dark. There were boxes and suit-cases stored in the attic, as well as books. He dropped to his hands and knees, and listened at the ceiling door.

Sounds of banging, followed by crunching of glass. Thudding. Wood squealing. Another crash of glass. Moaning. Moaning that, even as Scott listened, seemed to swell as voice after voice joined in, until a dreary river of sound filled the lower levels of the house. Sounds of crashing and wood being shoved aside punctuated the growing cacophony.

Well, fuuuuck, Scott's mind stated in awe and became silent.

Then, the noise began to rise.

Coming up the steps, *Scott thought*.

Behind him, Gus whimpered softly.

Scott crawled over to where Gus lay. The man's face was almost dead white in the dark, his black beard a mound of fresh ash. Gus squeezed his eyes shut as the fingers on one hand did a crab-like river dance on the flooring. Scott grabbed the twitching digits and covered them with the tablecloth.

"Listen to me," Scott rasped, putting his mouth close to Gus's ear. "Listen. They're coming up the stairs. They'll be here any second. You *have* to be quiet. Can you do that? You *have* to be still. Hold it together, okay? *Okay?*"

Eyes still closed, Gus nodded once.

Scott looked around the attic space and found an open box full of blankets. He quickly spread two dark ones over Gus before the moaning and hissing below became louder. The smell of the zombies' approach reached his nose and made him screw up his face. Scott crouched down and lay on his belly, placing an ear to the edge of the trapdoor. Through the wood, he heard the river of corpses. They thudded into the walls and wailed a graveyard's chorus. They passed under where Scott lay listening for any sign of being detected. Behind him, Gus remained quiet. For all he knew, Gus could be transforming into one of the dead. If that happened, Scott made the decision to finish him first and, if necessary, try and take his own life if escape proved to be impossible.

Scott didn't want to end it in an attic.

The wailing continued, filling the whole upstairs. It sounded like a goddamn convention, and he struggled to control the impulse to do something. Something crashed, the sound muted by the attic flooring, then more glass broke. The stomp and shuffle of the unliving surged through the upstairs, until it seemed walking corpses filled the entirety of the upper floor.

Clenched fists near his face, Scott listened to the bodies moving around under him. His own heart threatened to beat its way out of its cage, and still they shambled along below. He glanced back at Gus and saw only a dark lump in the scant light.

We wait now, Scott told himself. There wasn't much else to do. They were stuck in the attic until one of two things happened: Gus turned or the masses discovered them.

Closing his eyes, Scott forced himself to wait.

19

Four hours later, the light in the attic shrank away, leaving them in darkness. The dead-heads still moved around underneath them, incessantly crying out and bumping into things. Just when Scott believed there was nothing left for them to break, something else would give with a clatter. Wood squealed. Glass cracked. And the dead did not retreat. Their smell permeated the wood and gassed the attic, making him regret every breath.

At the five hour mark, Scott discovered he had to urinate. He moved back to the boxes, creeping along the flooring like a mouse fearing nearby predators, and slowly went through the exposed boxes stored in the attic. He needed to find some sort of receptacle, ideally a bottle with a stopper or lid of some sort. He found skates, winter clothes, boxes that contained old board games, more books, and what felt to be an old flat-screen television or computer monitor. He felt around the insides of another box and cringed when metal softly rattled against metal. He froze in place, waiting for a reaction from below, fully expecting the door to be yanked down to reveal a hallway full of rotting faces.

Nothing happened, and Scott realized the scuffle of moving bodies must have masked the noise. After a minute, he continued feeling around inside the box, ever so carefully, and realized it was full of pans. Scott backed away from the box as if it were a land mine. His bladder began to bother him, threatening consequences if he didn't find something soon. Gus remained still and as silent as stone, and Scott was careful not to bother him. He soon found two large suitcases made of hard plastic, and it took him long minutes to turn them both on their sides and unlatch them, his hands covering the latches to muffle the sound, while his bladder began to really complain, sending uncomfortable pangs through his midsection. Inside the suitcases were soft clothes, sweaters and shirts by the feel, even balled-up socks.

His bladder demanded release, and Scott considered a suitcase. They both had seals of sorts inside, and the clothes would absorb the urine. As long as the lid remained shut, there shouldn't be any smell, or at least very little. Unzipping the front of his jeans, he positioned himself across and inside the suitcase as if he were about to spoon-fuck it, and let go. His bladder heaved in relief and emptied into the suitcase and onto the clothes without a hiss. *Jesus Christ*, Scott thought, one of the most under-appreciated feelings in the world had to be a satisfying piss. He finished a minute later and rolled away from the suitcase, closing it as quietly as possible.

Feeling much better, Scott carefully crawled over to Gus, feeling the edge of the trapdoor and realizing if he had backed up, he would have been on it. The place had its share of pitfalls, and Scott committed where things were to memory. He reached out a hand and felt the mound of his companion.

"Gus," he whispered.

"Yeah?"

"How you feel?"

"Need a piss."

"No, but, y'know, otherwise."

"Feel fine. Nerves just got a little rattled, is all."

"No shame in that, man."

"I . . ." Gus's voice faltered in the dark. "I think I'm okay. I don't think I swallowed anything. I don't think. Or I puked it out. It's been a while."

Scott considered. It had been a long time. "You might be right."

"I think, but . . . be prepared to shoot my ass if you need to."

That brought a smile to Scott's face. "Already was."

"Thanks."

"You're welcome."

"Now, like I was saying, I need to piss."

"You're going to have to crawl a bit. Follow me and be quiet. You know what's below?"

"I know." Gus's voice trembled, but held.

"There's a suitcase over there. You can take a leak in that. There's clothes in it. I used one just now. It should absorb everything."

"Okay."

Scott led him out from beneath his blankets to what he decided would be Gus's suitcase. With painstaking care, he lifted the thing up and slid it across his legs.

"Take this and put it on your side. Take your time with it." Gus took it, and Scott heard him move it slowly around, a soft dragging sound that put Scott's teeth to the grind. He winced at the sound of a latch popping, and for another long minute, the two of them froze. Gus started moving again after a while, and Scott heard him sigh in relief.

Minutes later, he heard the soft scuffling of Gus retreating back under his blankets. It made Scott wonder how loud *he* had been. With the night coming on, the temperature in the attic dropped. Scott located what he believed was a sleeping bag. Confirming that it was, he laid it out and got inside.

"You know . . ." Gus began. "Those were once people down there, who now want . . . to *eat* us."

"You feelin' better?" Scott whispered.

"I think," Gus answered, then allowed the silence to be filled with the sounds of the moving dead. After a minute, he said, "Thanks again, man."

"You're welcome."

"We'll have to sleep in shifts," Gus said. "Just in case one of us starts snoring."

That was a good idea. Scott was glad Gus was back. "Sounds good. Go ahead. Don't think I could sleep anyway with them below."

Gus didn't answer. Moments later, Scott could hear his breathing, steady and strangely comforting, while the dead underneath them continued to stir, like things caught and bobbing in a moonless tide.

Every now and again, something bumped a wall just to help keep Scott awake.

When sunlight crept back into the attic the next day, Scott woke up to a loud thud that came from directly underneath the trapdoor. He opened his eyes and stared in the direction of the door, waiting for it to be pulled down and the dead to swarm upward. Another loud clunking happened, but the door remained closed.

"Maybe," Gus whispered, "they're stacking furniture."

Though he was glad Gus was still able to make comments and that he didn't have to kill him, his remark didn't make Scott feel any better. He remembered being a kid and having a distinct fear of the attic. That was the place where ghosts hung out. It was also, ironically, the same place where Santa stuffed his Christmas presents. He no longer had a fear of attics, but he found it funny that the terrors resided in the part of the house usually reserved for the people, while he and Gus were stuck where the ghosts belonged.

"Gotta take a piss," Scott said, and grabbed his suitcase. He opened it to the faint smell of uric acid and did his business as quickly as possible. Finishing up, he closed the suitcase and inhaled the air. "Can you smell that?"

"Yeah," Gus answered in a low voice. "But it's not, like, strong or anything."

"Not much to do about it up here."

"Nope. That's what I figured when I took a dump."

"You what?"

"Every morning I squeeze pipe. This one was no different."

Scott sniffed. "Oh, fuck. I can smell it."

"Just a little, though, right?"

Scott thought about it. "Yeah."

"All right, then. We got some time."

"Wonder what time it is?"

"Morning," Gus said. "That's all you need to know."

They became silent then, listening to the rustling below.

"Can't believe you took a shit in the suitcase," Scott muttered.

"Wiped my ass with a T-shirt, I think. Don't let it bother you. You'll have to take a squat sooner or later."

"Not me. I get constipated when I'm scared."

"Really?"

"Yeah."

"Well, then . . ." Gus words sounded as if they were framed in a smile. "The things you find out about a person."

Scott positioned himself facing Gus across the way. "Back is stiff from last night."

"Plenty of beds downstairs."

"Fuck off."

In the morning light coming in through the vent, Scott saw Gus's beard smirk. "There you go. Wondering if you had it in you or not. By the time this is all over, you'll be calling me names, too."

Scott grinned back. "You got any breakfast over there?"

"Hold on, now, and let me run down to the kitchen."

"Make it fast."

"Ah, wait. I put a loaf in the suitcase here. Fresh this morning."

Laying his head on the flooring, Scott sighed. Below, the moaning continued. "S'all I need to think about now. Dead people underneath me and your shit in a suitcase."

"I understand a person can eat their own chocolate at least once."

"Yeah? Why only once, I wonder?"

"Tastes like shit, I imagine."

"How long do you think we'll be up here?" Scott asked, wanting to get away from the subject.

"Until they go."

Scott had no reply to that. When they could go was the million dollar question. They could still be below next week. That didn't set well on his mind, starving in an attic. *I'm starving.* He thought about the expression and realized that he had come close to that several times since the collapse of civilization, but he, Teddy, and Lea had always found something before it got too bad.

"Relax," Gus said. "It'll work itself out one way or the other."

"You're pretty calm about this. Yesterday, you were a mess."

"Yeah, well, yesterday was . . . the first time I thought I died."

Scott kept silent. He didn't think Gus was completely out of danger yet.

"For a while there, when you were sleeping," Gus went on, "I paid attention to every twinge I felt. I swear my mind was inventing it as it went along, but I don't think I was ever so aware of my own body as I was last night. I'm in the clear, I'll have you know. But . . . fuck. I was worried to say the least."

"You freaked out."

"I freaked out," Gus agreed quietly. "And the thing was, I wondered if I would be aware of going over to the other side. If I would be really dead when I turned, or still be alive and somehow know—or not know—what I'd become. And if I did, whether or not I could stop myself from attacking you."

Jesus. Scott's mind cringed.

"But I'm okay," Gus continued. "We do have the problem below, though."

"Yeah."

"So, Chico, the one thing—the *only* thing—we can do is sit on our duffs and hope that the morning tide takes them out of here and away. And if not, maybe the afternoon tide will. Or the night."

"Maybe they'll take the van and just go," Scott whispered.

"Maybe. You got the keys?"

"I do."

"Well, scratch that off the pissability."

"Did you just say *pissability*?"

"Did."

Scott grunted with a smile and rolled quietly onto his back to stare up at the shadowy beams of the ceiling. He exhaled and saw his breath. Listening to the sounds of the dead, he tried to think of anything but the idea of food.

And if the dead starved.

They waited until the afternoon, still hearing the unliving thump into walls and furniture below. The smell no longer made them wrinkle their noses, but it was still foul. Scott took the time to carefully root around in the semi-light, and found several Tupperware dishes. Two he handed to Gus, while he kept one for himself for any emergency voiding. They both suspected that to open either suitcase would kill them. They whispered in low tones, making jokes at times, and it made Scott glad that the episode with Gus yesterday appeared to be only a one-time ordeal. They talked about what they would eat when they escaped from the attic. They then went on to talk about what they would drink. They napped when the urge took them and felt increasingly sure that as long as they stayed quiet, they were safe.

Time dragged on into evening, when the light started to retract from the attic, like a wary gunslinger with both guns drawn. Scott watched it go, all to the irregular beat of dead people searching the house for meat they instinctively knew existed, but couldn't locate. The unliving proved their fearlessness and resolve time and time again, but they were displaying another trait every bit as lethal.

Patience.

Or dumb fuck stupidity, Gus pointed out as if he didn't want to give the corpses any flattering characteristic at all.

They each filled a Tupperware dish and sealed it, noting that they weren't urinating regularly.

"This," Gus informed him, "is where it might get bad. We can probably last without food for a while, and I'm talking a couple of weeks, but the dehydration won't let us."

"How do you know?"

"Watched a lot of Discovery Channel."

"Oh."

"We could drink our own urine if it came down to it."

"What is it with you and this fascination with consuming your own waste?"

A thoughtful silence answered Scott, before he heard an almost embarrassed, "Just sayin' is all."

The sound of something falling silenced both men then, and kept them quiet until sleep took Scott away.

Scott dreamed. He dreamed about baking on the midnight shift. Every morning, after he had completed the day's supply of baked goods, he would ready the day-old cookies and muffins for the garbage. It wasn't something he enjoyed doing, and when he first took the job, he carried home as much as he could eat. That practice didn't last long, as he soon grew tired of bringing the food home. His co-workers, mostly university part-timers, were of the same mind. The food was great for the first couple of months, but then the novelty wore off, and no one wanted to touch it thereafter, or until a new worker arrived.

He bagged food to be thrown out and left it in a stout shed out back. Sometimes, the shed would be opened, and the bagged food would be taken and eaten by the homeless. Scott had no problem with that. It was food. They were hungry. No questions asked.

But the manager found out and placed a padlock on the shed.

Scott dreamed in that slipstream of dream cinema, where he was both the viewer and the actor, lugging out a bag of day-old muffins—still fine to eat, but not up to the fresh standards of the company. Scott opened the back door and stepped out, the shed's front door to his immediate left.

Then, they showed up.

Except in his dream, the homeless had died years ago, their flesh the color of decomposing meat, and their sightless eyes fixing on him. They voiced their need, backing Scott up. He turned to the door only to realize that it had closed on him, and there was no knob on the outside.

The dead closed in, barring any escape. Their clothes reeked from the grave. Fingers, missing and ground to the dirty bones, reached for him, reached for the garbage he held. One finger, its bony tine hooked and sharp, sloughed out in nightmare fashion from the dark and pawed at the plastic bag, cutting it open with barely any contact. The contents spilled forth and splashed the concrete step and Scott's work sneakers.

He screamed.

The bag wasn't full of day-old baked goods any longer.

It contained something with more sustenance.

The dead clawed and feasted upon the meaty chunks, chewing on every piece in nauseating detail. Both the scene and smell rooted Scott in place, but there wasn't anywhere to run, anyway.

And the dead were *famished*.

Stale, one of the corpses rasped at Scott. *Staaaale*, it complained with a throat full of scum dredged from the bottom of a sea bed and the things that lived and writhed in it still. Scott wanted to run, but the nightmare wouldn't let him. He knew he was going to scream, he knew he was going to scream loud, and that was the horror of it because he knew he was in a dream, and *to scream in the attic would mean they would hear below*.

As the first of many clawed hands reached for him and hooked into his skin, tearing and stretching lengths of meat that bled in runny gouts, dreamtime Scott opened his mouth and *shrieked* . . .

Scott woke up. He inhaled, catching a full whiff of the dead's lingering stench. His mouth possessed an earthy taste. The last image he had from his nightmare was bony fingers reaching into his mouth and trying to fasten onto his tongue. It was still night, and his stomach felt empty.

Stale. That voice echoed in his brain, like something sinking into the depths of a dark lake.

He didn't know what time it was, but he relieved Gus from his watch.

20

They believed the house began emptying sometime on the third day. The sounds and smell began to lessen.

By night, the interior of the house was silent.

They stayed in the attic anyway, just to be safe. Just to give the tide of the dead time enough to completely clear out and, if they were lucky, maybe even leave the cul-de-sac entirely. Cul-de-sac. There was a joke there, somewhere, but they were in no mood to figure out exactly what it might be.

On the morning of the fourth day, Gus woke up and felt no need to pee whatsoever. The day before, he had urinated once, and at that time, he experienced a burning sensation that wasn't at all pleasant. By the evening, he was pissless. And he wasn't even scared. He rolled over and listened to the house below, straining and hearing nothing. He listened for a long time, until Scott woke up.

"Hear . . . anything?" Scott whispered weakly.

"Nah."

"What . . . d'you think?"

They suffered from thirst, headaches, and fits of restlessness to weariness. Four fucking days they had been stranded in the near dark, hiding out in fright at first, which bled away into monotonous boredom. In the end, the boredom was their greatest threat, as any momentary lapse in maintaining quiet would have alerted the dead still in the house. It only took one mistake, and their fears of dying from a lack of water or food would be forgotten in the surge of corpses trying to access the attic.

Gus had had enough of attics.

"Get ready," he said.

"Are . . . we goin'?" The thirst they both felt raked their throats, and Gus believed that even his tongue was swelling, if such a thing were possible.

"Yeah," Gus answered in his own parched voice. He swallowed and felt the sinker of his Adam's apple clink thickly in his throat. "I'm gonna have one huge fuckin' Mai Tai when I get outta here."

Taking a breath, Gus slipped his fingers around his shotgun. He reloaded the weapon, hearing the soft clicks and snaps coming from Scott's side of the attic. They each took an equal share of shells, stuffing a box inside their tucked-in shirts and the remaining shells into their pockets.

"Not gonna . . . miss this place," Scott muttered, putting on his lightning bolt helmet.

"Nope," Gus agreed, doing the same with his helmet. "Ready, Chico?"

"Why do you call me Chico? You don't hear me calling you anything except your name."

"Oh, sorry." Gus got to a sitting position, feeling the aches in his limbs from sitting and lying down for so long. He felt the drag from the lack of food and water.

"You got the keys?" Gus asked.

Scott patted his jeans pocket.

"All right, then . . ."

Using his feet, Gus pushed down on the door and lowered the steps. When the stairs were extended, he slowly stretched out his legs and, holding onto the door frame, flipped the lower sections down. Springs yawned at the extension. Setting the stairs firmly against the floor, Gus gripped his shotgun, and adjusted the bat on his back.

"Let's go," he whispered.

They descended into the upstairs level and, for a moment, marvelled at the destruction to the house. The recent press of bodies against the walls had left them cracked and bowled in. Dark smears of bodily fluids ran in wavy lines the length of the hallway. The reek of the dead hung throughout the house like a popped blood blister. It would have made their eyes water if they had the moisture to spare. The only thing missing from the party, Gus thought, were strands of toilet paper hanging from the ceiling. The rooms he glanced into were empty, in shambles, soiled, and battered by the recent invasion of the dead.

Gus heard a thud behind him and whirled to spot Scott leaning against the wall.

"You okay?" Gus approached the man.

"Yeah, just . . ." Scott's eyes squeezed shut and opened a moment later. "Just dizzy is all."

"Can you move?"

"Yeah. Yeah, I'm behind you."

Nodding and hoping Scott was indeed behind him, Gus turned and covered the last of the hallway, peeking around corners to bedrooms and bathrooms to see if any corpses remained. He reached the stairs and placed his back against the wall, his own dizziness suddenly making things swirl. Taking a breath and hating the taste of the air, Gus angled his shotgun to cover the living room. Descending the steps quietly, they faced another wreck of overturned furniture, grotesque markings on the walls like thick streamers, and smashed glass from the destroyed picture window.

Gus edged into the room and peeked around the corner. Empty. He looked toward the driveway. There the beast waited, seemingly untouched. The cul-de-sac appeared deserted.

"All clear," Gus whispered. "Move it."

Gus opened the front door and sped to the van with Scott following. They got into the vehicle, checked the interior, stowed their weapons, and buckled themselves in. Scott placed the keys in the ignition and turned it. The engine coughed and started faithfully, and Gus exhaled his relief.

"Would've shit right here if it didn't turn over," Scott said.

"I would've shit out a tumbleweed," Gus added.

Scott accidently placed the van in reverse before stomping on the brake and getting the right gear.

"Take 'er easy," Gus whispered

"Watch the road," Scott said. "I got lost the last time. That's how we got here."

"I gotcha."

The van rumbled across the asphalt, the daylight hidden behind a thick carpet of clouds. The streets were deserted, and for that, the two men were thankful. Scott drove slowly, and they caught only glimpses of dead, until Gus directed Scott to the main road. Once, Scott had to pull over as a wave of dizziness assaulted him, but only once. Moving a steady speed of thirty, the two weary men reached their mountain home by early afternoon. They barely possessed the strength to move the gates and close them, and by the time they finally parked the van in the garage, both were exhausted.

"Home again, home again, jiggity jig," Gus said once they were safely inside.

Not bothering to unload the van, they moved into the house, dropping gear as they went, until they got to the kitchen. They sipped water pumped from the well, replenishing their fluids, and Gus got around to heating up a can of Chunky soup. He stopped cooking when it was just lukewarm, and slopped half of it into a bowl for Scott. Standing around the island in the kitchen, they devoured the food, and opened up another can.

"You're not drinking?" Scott asked him at one point.

"Too thirsty to drink." Gus grinned. "Don't you worry. When I'm ready, I got a bottle of Canadian Club with my name on it."

"You'd probably puke it up if you drank it, anyway," Scott smirked, eyeing the man over his second bowl of soup.

Gus nodded and got back to eating. "Once this is done, I'm going to take a bath."

"Thought we couldn't do that."

"Today's an exception. You got one, too, if you want it."

"Sounds good to me."

Gus spooned another mouthful and paused. His hand shook hard enough that he dropped the spoon.

"You okay?"

Gus studied his fingers for a moment, making a fist and shaking it loose. "Better than ever."

"Glad to hear it."

Having eaten and drunk enough water to rehydrate, Gus later went up to the master bedroom and his bath. He made it hot, but not so hot to be unbearable as he usually did. He filled the tub and grabbed a bottle of nearby shampoo and body wash. Steam rose and covered the black-and-white checked tiling. He stripped and slipped into the deep-set old-fashioned tub, submerging himself to his woolly chin. He thumped his head against the side of the tub and relaxed. He held up his hand, watched it shake for a moment, and let it drop back into the water. Shaking or not, he was thankful to be able to see it without an urge to bite it off.

He soaped his head, his beard, and eventually his body, feeling the taut cords of muscle that were previously covered by about a hundred and fifty pounds of fat. He felt the scars around his lower abdomen, from back when he had met crazy Alice in a hospital so long ago. He had sported a beer belly then. It was ironic that the layers of fat there had actually saved him from being disembowelled when, for years, his doctors had told him to lose the gut. He couldn't remember much about what had happened at the hospital—shock had wiped that particular slate of his mind clean—but he remember what had happened just days ago, and how he thought that he had swallowed a piece of the undead. The pure fright of knowing what might have happened, what *could* have happened, made Gus shudder for a moment.

Then, it all came out.

Not wanting Scott to hear him, Gus plunked his head against the metal of the tub and wept as quietly as possible.

The next day, they decided to take it easy and replenish their strength. Neither of the men wanted to return to Annapolis so soon after escaping it, so they stayed on the mountain, safe behind their wall. They ate breakfast and went out to the van to look over what they had taken from the city.

"Map," Gus said. "This goes inside. We can hang it somewhere. Look at this." He unrolled the map and held it up for Scott to see.

"That's a good one."

"Everything is on this. Places I didn't even think of looking." Gus let one end drop as he scratched at his beard. "This is a prize."

"Didn't you have two crowbars?"

"Lost the other at the house." Gus frowned. Thinking of the old dead guy in the rocker with the gold teeth made him shake his head. It chilled him still.

"Look at this, though." He held up the ninja hoods. He tossed one to Scott and pulled on his own, struggling to tuck in his chin whiskers. Once done, he turned to Scott with the hood and mask in place. "Huh? How's that? Great, eh?"

Scott was wearing his, too. "Jesus, this is great. It's warm."

"And I bet it's fireproof, too."

"Or fire retardant."

"What's the difference?"

"One can burn if it's exposed to open flame long enough. The other can't."

"Oh." Gus pulled off the mask and rubbed his bald head. "That's going on when we head back down. This, however . . ."

He pulled out the fireman jacket and pants and put them both on. "Heavier than the leather."

Scott tried on his. "Yeah. Warmer, though. Especially with a sweater on underneath. Thicker, too."

"Won't need the heat on in the van with these things on."

"Nothing going to bite through these things."

"Heavier armor," Gus remarked, checking himself out. "But it'll slow us down."

"A trade-off."

"Yeah."

"Hey, Gus, how much ammunition do you have here?"

He thought about it. "Left? About, maybe, somewhere between a thousand and two thousand rounds. Remind me to get a few boxes to put in the beast."

"All for twelve gauge?"

"Yeah. I got most of them in the storeroom of a gun shop a long time ago. Someone took a lot of the other stuff, but the place was well stocked. The places in the malls were cleaned out. And I found some in basements, sheds, yada, yada."

They went through the rest of the goods, stashing one of the first-aid kits and a fire extinguisher in the beast, as well as the remaining crowbar. The rest of the gear they placed in the lockers.

After unloading the van, eating, then cleaning their shotguns, they bundled up in sweaters and doubled up in track pants before retiring to the deck. They lounged outside, drinking only water, which lasted until mid-afternoon when Gus broke out two bottles of Canadian Club whiskey. They toasted their fortune of being alive, drank, and respectfully regarded the quiet cityscape stretched out in the distance. They talked and relaxed in the lawn chairs.

"What time is it?" Scott asked at one point.

"Hmm?"

"What time is it?"

"Why? You have to be somewhere? I don't know. I don't wear a watch."

"Just like to know what time it is."

"Look." Gus pointed to the city with his bottle. "Time was left behind in the old world. Nothing around here is concerned with the time of day anymore. You think this mountain cares about time? Any animal? That is if they even exist 'cause I ain't seen any. There is nothing down there that is nine to five anymore. Nothing. There's just you and me and . . ." Gus belched. "You and me and . . . and this."

"This?"

"This moment."

"Thought you said there was no time anymore."

"There isn't."

"Well, if there's no time, how can you directly reference one moment in it?"

"Huh?"

"You," Scott pointed at him, "just went on about how time doesn't matter, but then you said that this moment—which is a part of present time—does matter."

Gus made a face. "I said that?"

"You did. Just now. I heard it."

"I'm full of shit," Gus slurred.

Scott broke out laughing.

"I think it's December tomorrow," Gus added.

"You think the mountains care if it's December? The animals? God knows I haven't seen any," Scott said with a sly gleam in his eye.

"Fuck off." Gus smiled and took another drink. "Tomorrow we go back down there. We gotta stay on course. Winter is here, man, and we aren't ready yet. I'd like to find more food. If there's any left."

Scott nodded. "Think there's any down there?"

"I do, but how much is the question. There're two of us now. We'll be okay," Gus said, studying his bottle. "We'll be okay."

When dark came, they went back into the house and drew the curtains over the windows. They ate beans and wieners from cans and continued drinking straight whiskey. They got out the Scrabble board, but abandoned it when Gus pointed out he was "too shit-faced to spell anything."

They loaded up a copy of John Carpenter's *The Thing,* then rounded out the night watching old Benny Hill comedy shows.

Somewhere before midnight, both passed out.

And were spared dreams.

21

Gus woke up and thought he was still in the attic. He flailed on the sofa where he'd fallen asleep, looked over, and thought for the briefest of time that the snoring figure in the recliner was the gold-toothed deadhead. He rubbed his eyes, then his hairless scalp, and took a deep breath. He needed to piss and get a drink of water, in that order. He looked toward the TV and saw that it had been turned off. Scott must've done that at some point. He had turned off the lights as well and draped Gus in a blanket before settling back in the recliner and covering up himself. He watched the blond man sleep, mouth open, displaying a slight overbite. Light snores emanated from him.

Gus went to his chamber bucket and relived himself, covering it when done. Then, he headed to the kitchen. He filled two pitchers with water, staring out at the clear pre-dawn sky. He drank half of one pitcher before going back downstairs and placing the second pitcher on the coffee table for Scott, hoping he'd see the thing before coming upstairs.

Coughing lightly, Gus went back up and stepped outside. The biting December air cut around the corner of the house, grazing his face and making him shiver. He listened to the morning. The evening star, or at least he thought it was the evening star, shone right next to the bare face of the full moon. Gus stood for a moment and simply studied it.

Then, he heard the engines.

The noise hooked him by the jaw, a roar of motorcycles speeding away, their mufflers gone. The raucous sound ripped through the morning quiet and made him look in the direction of the dark city, the moon causing some of the rooftops to look like dull slabs of silver. The sound faded in the distance, and Gus willed it to happen again so that he could get a better sense of where it was. It had been at least a year since he'd heard another engine. One as loud as the one he had just heard went against all he practiced when he went into Annapolis. Almost as if it wanted to be heard . . .

Nothing. The wind smothered any other sound and left him cold. After lingering for a few more moments, he retreated back inside to the warmth of the house.

Going through the pantry, Gus decided on instant oatmeal with dried apples and cinnamon for breakfast. He boiled the water and sat at the kitchen island, listening to the growing huff of the kettle and thinking about the motorcycles. He was certain they were motorcycles with the mufflers gone, raising hell on some car-littered street no less, but just before the crack of dawn? The question hung in his head. What could they have been doing?

Or had they just arrived in Annapolis?

That thought had merit.

He ate his breakfast while mulling over who was in the city. The idea that there were others around had never left him, but rather got pushed to the back of his mind in his day-to-day foraging. Scott was the only person he had met who wanted to be found, it seemed to him. Others kept to themselves for whatever reasons. Or . . . His next thought made him pause with his spoon in his mouth. Maybe he was the one avoiding contact. He'd always thought it was better to be alone, but Scott saving his ass had gotten him to think otherwise. Civilization had to rebound at some point, and people, not the dead, would eventually band together to do it.

"Morning," Scott muttered as he came around the corner, looking like a huge, fluffy bear just emerging from his cave. "Thanks for the water."

Gus nodded.

Scott pointed to the second bowl. "This for me?"

Gus nodded again. "Just add water from the kettle."

Scott did so and settled down for his first bite of the day. "This tastes so good," he muttered between bites.

Gus let him finish before informing him of the noise. "Heard it this morning."

"Who could it be?" Scott asked.

"Don't know," Gus admitted. "But once you finish, let's go take a look."

With the sun partially obscured by thick clouds, they drove the beast down into the city. They passed intersections and even the turn-off leading to old Port Williams, but didn't see any sign of motorcycles or any other moving vehicles. Zombies, moving slower with December's chill, spotted the roads like dark sores and looked up at the sound of the approaching van. These dead posed no threat and were soon left behind. They continued into the downtown section of what was once known as Kentville, the office buildings blocking the sun even further and making the streets feel like unearthed tunnels of a tomb best kept sealed.

There, Gus spotted the brother to the beast.

"Stop and back up," he said and pointed a thick glove. Both men had clothed themselves in the firemen outfits recovered from the station. The ninja masks were tight, but warm, and they made their motorcycle helmets fit even more snugly, although Gus found himself shouting more often to be heard.

"What? Oh." Scott slowed the beast and stopped before an alleyway between a vandalized outboard motor shop and a gutted supermarket. Far back from view and partially hidden by a rust-coated dumpster gleamed a red SUV, a tinted windshield eyed them while the grill bared metallic teeth.

"Oh my," Scott said.

"Been down this way, but never spotted that before."

"It's far enough back from the street that you'd have to be looking straight down there to see it."

"I'll check it out," Gus said.

"You sure?"

"What's that supposed to mean?"

Scott didn't add anything else. Gus supposed he didn't have to. "I'm fine. Wouldn't have come here today if I didn't think I was."

"I'll back in."

"Not all the way, just enough to see what's coming down the street."

"Fine."

Gus got up and slung his scabbarded bat across his back. He took down his shotgun and clomped to the rear of the van, feeling the weight of the fireman boots. *Steel-toed nastiness*, he thought. Scott backed the beast in blindly, opening his door to gauge where he was at times.

"Don't be long," Scott shouted when he finished parking.

Slapping down his visor, Gus threw open the rear door and jumped out. He closed it behind him and walked down the length of the alley, noting the fire escapes on each building and the metalwork's rust. He approached the SUV, looking like a firefighter that had forgotten his proper helmet. He felt his breath on his face, hotter than before because of the ninja mask, and for an instant, a stab of fear stopped him in his tracks. Jesus. He was *out* of the van. Gus felt a cold sweat break out over his face. His breath quickened. He blinked, and the visor-tinted form of the old fuck with the gold teeth hunched over him, the zombie's jaw *clicking* open.

Grunting, Gus pressed against the side of the alley and gripped his shotgun. He opened and closed his eyes. The old dude disappeared. The alley was just an alley. He took a deep steadying breath and calmed himself, fighting the impulse to rip the tight helmet from his head.

I'm fine. I'm fucking better than fine. Another breath and he continued forward, hoping to God that episodes like the one he'd just experienced were only a passing thing—some residual by-product of freaking out, and not regular.

He just didn't need it.

Easing around the dumpster, Gus moved to the passenger side of the vehicle and, holding his shotgun one-handed, yanked open the door.

And grimaced.

He could smell the body, but thankfully the corpse behind the wheel wasn't the re-animated kind. A man—Gus could tell by the light rugby shirt and jeans—sat behind the wheel as if listening to a tune on the stereo. The bare flesh was decomposed black, but because of the SUV's seals, no insects had found the chunk of meat.

"Shit," Gus whispered, studying the face and the shrivelled eyeballs. An empty blue plastic prescription bottle rested on the floor. Gus leaned in, smelled a faint whiff of long-dried fecal matter, and picked up the bottle. *Seconal: 100 mgs* was typed on the label in bold-faced lettering. It meant nothing to Gus, other than the ripe bastard behind the wheel had taken enough of it to end himself. He studied the man's dead face, the slumped position of the body, and shook his head. *Smarter than you look,* Gus thought. *Braver, too.*

Gus closed the passenger side and moved around the SUV. He opened the driver's door, and pulled the body out from behind the wheel. Dried up as it was, the body was easy to drop unceremoniously into the dumpster, making Gus glad that he had taken the precaution of wearing all the new gear, right down to the new gloves with whole fingers.

The key fob dangled from the dash, and two keys jingled against it. The third key was in the ignition. The SUV was a hybrid, a Dodge Durango. He studied the plush black leather interior and decided the dead guy must've been rich. The dash gleamed with information controls. Checking out the interior in the rear, Gus saw that there were a few containers in the back. He would check those out later, but at the moment, it was enough to know that the thing was free of corpses.

He got behind the wheel, put his shotgun in the passenger seat, closed the door, and turned the key. The engine turned over smoothly.

Well, well, Christmas comes early. Gus smiled behind his mask. It was the first bit of good news, other than him not changing into a zombie, he'd had in a while. The dash lights glowed, and he saw that it had half a tank of gas. *Cool.* Finding the right buttons, he dimmed the lights and put the vehicle into drive. Depressing the accelerator, he moved forward slowly, pebbles snapping underneath the tire treads. Gus drove it to the rear of the beast and jumped out.

"Look what we got," Gus said as Scott stuck his helmeted head out the driver's side of the beast.

"Running, too," Scott said in approval.

"Yep."

"Drive it back now or . . . ?"

"Let's hit a few houses first."

"Port Williams?" Scott asked. Gus thought the man might be smiling.

"Fuck that," Gus muttered as he turned back to the Durango. "I'll drive in front. You keep up."

They stopped and searched five houses without much luck. Gus scavenged a few cans of mixed vegetables, meat balls, packets of noodles, and mixes for lemonade. It wasn't enough to fill the bottom of one bin in the van, but it was food, and it allowed them to live a little longer.

The two vehicles inched up a street that looked to loop back out toward the bay and stopped in front of a sixth house. Three zombies appeared from across the street, lumbering with unsteady steps and opening their mouths as if shouting. Scott pointed to them as he backed the van into the driveway. Already out of the SUV, Gus moved to deal with them, feeling his heart starting to race.

Three deadheads, spaced apart, just stepped onto the asphalt. Gus sized the three of them up and propped his shotgun against the rear bumper of the SUV. He smoothly extracted the aluminum bat and practice swung it like a sword. He reached up and adjusted his helmet just a bit and watched the zombies come to him. They were a family of three, an older man dressed in the remains of beige casual pants and a sweater, his wife whose long blond hair had sections torn from her black scalp, and their teenage son who was the size of a football player, in jeans and a T-shirt that was probably once tight on him, but hung loosely off his large frame, and the dull gleam of a splintered collar bone jutted from his dead flesh. Their faces were intact and hissing.

Instead of being afraid, Gus felt a surge of annoyance. When the father figure got close, he cracked the bat off its head and crumpled one side of the dead man's skull. The impact spun the corpse around to fall to the pavement.

"That's one, you fucks," Gus hissed and slipped into a swordsman's stance with his bat, raising the weapon high above his head. The oversized teenager came on, large arms stretched out as if wanting a hug. Gus caved in the sinus cavity with one bash of the bat. A second bash squashed in the thing's decayed forehead and dropped it to its knees. Gus then spun and rocked the head from the side with one loud crack, putting the dead thing down.

Taking a breath, Gus confronted the mom. She hissed, exposing a mouth full of stained smoker's teeth.

"So sick of you. So goddamn sick of being scared of you."

He butted the tip of the bat into the creature's chest. The mother staggered back, hissed again, and crept forward.

"I'm through being afraid of you," Gus said quietly. He pushed the zombie back at bat's length. "Now, I'm just pissed. With you . . ." He tapped her again, ". . . with this whole situation."

He snapped the bat up and swung it as it trying to smack a fastball. The creature's knee exploded. The thing lurched over and fell to the ground, rapping its face on the pavement. Not even acknowledging the hit, the zombie crawled toward him, its hiss unchanged, but he noticed that several front teeth had been broken.

"No more goddamn sense than flies on a pile of shit."

He smashed one of its arms. The zombie dragged it along, moving the upper portion while the section below the break, just at the elbow, twisted slowly backward as it crawled forward.

Gus broke the shoulder. He stepped over the creature, avoiding the slow moving left arm, and shattered the shoulder and hip of that side. The zombie still inchwormed its way toward him, pushing its head into the rough grain of the asphalt with each thrust. The mother hissed again, biting at air, as it checked where Gus stood before slinking in his direction. Gus stepped over the crippled dead thing and then stepped over it again. He gnawed on his lower lip in distaste. In a horde, they were terrifying, but like this, he felt only contempt.

Worse, he felt pity.

He trapped the mother in place, placing one heavy boot against its skull. It mewled and squirmed under his foot like a huge pissed-off nightcrawler, while he lined up the top of the skull with his bat. It would be just like that summer game with the mallets, except he didn't have any little wire arches to knock the head through. He tapped the skull once, then twice, before breaking it open with one swing and crushing it with two follow-ups.

The mother lay still. Gus stepped back and inspected his bat, then wiped the tissue matter on the red shirt of the mother. He sighed, feeling conflicted. He looked around and met the eyes of Scott staring hard at him, his hands on the wheel of the beast. He recognized the expression of concern even though Scott's mouth and the edges of his face were covered by the helmet. Without a word, for there really wasn't anything to say, Gus eased his bat back into his scabbard and retrieved his shotgun. He proceeded up the driveway of the house, passing by the open window of the van.

"You okay?" Scott asked.

"No . . . but I will be."

Then he was breaking in the door of the house. Gus dove into the doorway, not even bothering to check the corners before he went in.

22

After getting back to the mountain and stashing away the few things they had found in town, they went into the kitchen, speaking very little, and ate. After supper, they went down into the den with their bottles of Canadian Club and drank. Sitting in the recliner, Scott swallowed the first shot and grimaced, then studied Gus on the sofa.

"You want to talk about it?"

They had only turned on one light, near the stairs, and the shadows made Gus's beard and face all the darker. "About the zombies?"

"Yeah."

"Figured you'd get around to it sometime."

Scott eased himself back into the recliner and rubbed his ankle.

"How's that doing?" Gus asked.

Scott shrugged and ran a hand over his thickening beard. "Getting there. Not as sore now."

"You'll be able to play soccer soon."

"Hockey, you mean."

"That, too."

"So how about it, then?" Scott fixed him with a pensive look. "You okay?"

Gus leaned back into the softness of the sofa and didn't say anything for a while. The wind rose outside, and the timbers creaked.

"I think I hit my limit," Gus said quietly. "For the last two years, I've been scared of those things, living up here, away from the city and everything. But when I thought I was about to turn into one and didn't . . . that did something to me. I ain't never been scared of much in my life, and I think I'm tired of being scared of these things. They're nothing. The only thing they got goin' for them is they don't stop comin' at you. Ever. That one deadhead I bashed up today? The woman one?"

"Yeah?"

"I fuckin' immobilized her ass, Scott. Crushed her. And all she did was just squirm and try to gnaw her way through my boots. There was no pain there. No fear, but I used to think there has to be a bit of thinkin' going on up here for that." Gus tapped his bald head for emphasis and took a heavy shot of whiskey.

"There ain't nothin' goin' on up there. Not a goddamn thing. They really are as mindless as . . . as fuckin' rocks. As shitcakes. And I, I ain't afraid of that. I broke down, or at least I thought I broke down. I didn't. Not completely anyway. I think all the fear's gone from me now. Like . . . therapy."

"Therapy?"

"Yeah, like you know how some folks are scared of spiders? And their shrinks force them to confront the spiders? Let small ones walk on their arm, then work their way up to big ones, right? Until you have like wharf spiders or tarantulas there. Big, mean, scary fuckers that would shock a person dickless."

"What if it's a woman?" Scott smirked.

"Pay attention here. You asked if I'm all right, and you're bein' a smart ass."

"Sorry, man. Go on."

"Yeah, well, anyway, my point is, being exposed to the spiders gets a person over their fear of them after a while. When I thought I had swallowed a piece of them, I thought . . . man, *everything* was goin' through my mind. But in the end, I thought that was it. I was done. Dead. I freaked out—and you can only freak out for so long—and I remember being okay with it. Just waitin' for the change. Then, the change didn't happen, and I realized I was worked up over nothin'. Scared over nothin'. Swallowin' that piece of corpse, or at least *thinkin'* I did, was my big fuckin' spider on my arm. I'm not scared of them anymore, Scott. If anything . . ." Gus thought about it for a while, his dark eyes looking grim in the scant light.

"If anything, I hate them. For puttin' me through hell for the last few years. For forcin' me to pen myself up here. I hate the things now."

"That could be dangerous," Scott offered.

Gus nodded. "I agree. Just as dangerous as being terrified of them. And I'll have to be just as careful of that. But I'm *through* being scared of those dead fuckers. I'm through. Christ above. I'm having visions of goin' on a fuckin' safari for the packs of them."

"Not sure that's wise."

Gus regarded him. "I know it's not. I'm not stupid, man. I'm not. So don't worry, I'm not gonna start doing stupid shit like risking my life or anything. Even though I was up here, here *is* the best place to be. With the heat and water and electricity. Here is the best place to be. No doubt. But I'm not scared of them anymore. Not those brain-dead fuckers. Not ever again."

Scott listened and remained silent. After a long considering moment, he nodded and took a long drink of his whiskey.

Gus sat and stewed on his emotions a little longer. He felt he spoke the truth, and it felt good to do that. He wouldn't do anything crazy, either; he promised himself that. But he also promised to kill them all. Pick them off where and when he could. He figured he had one hobby in this new world, and that was getting drunk. Gus took another drink of whiskey and considered adding a new one.

Two mornings later, under an increasingly overcast sky, they suited up, gassed up the beast, and headed for the city. Scott drove while Gus rode in the passenger side with his bat in gloved hands. It neared the end of the first week in December. Snow would be coming any day, and any day might be the last for access to Annapolis. They had to get what they could before winter dug in. Gus figured they had enough food, water, and booze, but he wanted to be sure—especially on the booze.

They passed the landmarks on the road they had come to expect and appreciate in some lost old days nostalgia: billboard with semi driven through it, motorcycle on its side with a gutted seat. Wrecked cars became a blur of colors splashed against a canvas of asphalt and steel.

Up ahead, two figures wandered into the road. They turned at the sound of the van. The way they staggered, it was easy to identify them as long dead.

"Wait," Gus said quietly.

"What?"

"Stop alongside those two."

Scott looked at him, his brow crunched up in a question. "Huh? Why?"

"I got an idea," Gus said.

Scott did as he was told, though his expression said he didn't understand why.

"Hold on for a minute." Gus got out of the van, taking his bat with him. He walked right up to the first undead, who had already detected him, and clubbed the head so hard that a pulpy jawbone flew from its mouth. Gus crushed in its skull with an overhead strike, driving the dead thing to its knees before watching it fall over.

Rolling his shoulders, Gus stepped up to the second zombie and bashed in one side of its head. Then the other side. When it dropped to the pavement, he clubbed it a third time.

A fourth and final time just to make a point. He no longer feared the once-thought-of-as predators. And he'd had enough of them. He went on to crush the joints of their knees, elbows, and shoulders.

He cleaned off his bat on one's shirt. Studying both of them for any sign of movement, Gus stood in the highway for a few moments more before returning to the van. He got in and slammed the door.

"What the fuck was that?" Scott asked, looking at him.

"What?"

"That!"

"Experiment."

"An experiment in what?"

"Remember I said I thought these things were thinning out? And how when I killed them, they up and disappeared from sight?"

Scott hesitated before answering, "Yeah."

"We take this road every day. There's another marker. Let's see if they're still there when we come back this way."

"We could just wait."

"I don't think we got the time to waste to do that. Winter's coming."

"Winter. Yeah," Scott agreed.

"Those things are dead and as fucked up as I can make them with a bat. If they're dead, *truly* dead, they'll be here when we get back. If they're gone, we'll go to phase two."

"What's phase two?"

"Kill more and wait to see what happens."

Scott gazed out onto the road. "Drive on, then?"

That sounded good to Gus. "Yeah."

They drove past familiar sections of the city, old garbage hugging the sides of the road like a rotten fur lining. Gus directed Scott back to the street that had previously been cut off by the massive herd of dead.

"Keep going," Gus instructed, looking at each house as the van went by it.

"How do you know, anyway?"

"I leave the doors open on the houses when I can."

The van crept up the street until Gus lifted a gloved hand into the air. Scott stopped the vehicle and turned it, backing it into a driveway that had tall grass on both sides, buckled over with frost.

"Back in a flash," Gus said and picked up his shotgun and bat. He jumped out from the rear and closed the door behind him, leaving Scott to watch the street and drum nervous fingers off the steering wheel.

Gus went up the stone steps to the front door. The house was a two-level affair with red plastic siding and a black roof. An older house, charming, but Gus wondered what was inside the place. He tried the door and found it unlocked. Taking a deep breath, he turned the brass knob and swung open the door.

Gus stood there for a moment, staring into the shadowy interior. Musty air reached him, but it didn't bother him. He tapped the barrel of the shotgun on the frame and waited, wondering if any deadhead would answer. Elongated thoughts of what had happened in the Port William's home stretched and snapped through his mind in disjointed black and white. Some bits were graphically recalled, while other pieces were missing. Shock, he supposed.

With a shake, he realized he'd been standing in the doorway for several minutes. Feeling a grimace on his face, Gus went in.

He cleared the main floor and the upstairs. There wasn't a basement, so that made life easier. In the living room, he found a dusty collection of *National Geographic* magazines, the cover of the top one showing a mosquito poised with a gossamer proboscis on a bed of flesh. Gus made note to take the magazines later as he enjoyed looking at the pictures. A collection of at least two or three hundred Blu-ray discs were arranged in an almost ceiling-high shelving unit, but Gus left those. Most of the titles he had back at the house on his terabyte, except for several Japanese animated cartoons that looked borderline triple X. A gas fireplace dominated the room, along with the usual living room furniture. He found two plastic ten-liter bottles of water, along with several cans of food, including instant noodles and the oatmeal he'd grown fond of having for breakfast.

Making note of those items, he came to a locked door with an old-fashioned keyhole. Gus knocked on it, listened, and stepped back. He kicked the door with several heavy connections of his new boots, and when the door finally burst inward, he took a moment to compose himself, feeling the sweat running underneath his gear. Bringing up his shotgun, he eased around the corner, into a home office area. A desk with one of the newer nano-desktop computers faced him, along with a printer and two small speakers. Bookshelves lined one wall, filled with names like George Eliot and Elizabeth Gaskell, including some books on self-improvement, world history, and an ample collection of military fiction. On a small table was a dust-covered model of a group of intrepid fantasy adventurers heading down into a dungeon area where a sleeping green dragon lay. Gus bent over it, admiring the detail of the miniatures pieces, from the weapons and armor possessed by the fighters, to the wizard wielding a magical staff.

Smiling, Gus straightened and looked at the wall behind the door. A glass cabinet filled it and inside, on display, was an arsenal.

His mouth dropped open. Well, he knew why the door had been locked. He didn't wonder why the weapons were there and not with the owner; he only hoped they worked.

Guns and ammunition, arranged on hooks against a red felt background, lay ready for the taking. He had no idea what manner of firearms they were. A closed cabinet below the glass gave Gus hope that more ammunition was stored inside. The cabinet was locked, so Gus smashed out the glass.

A pair of sleek black pistols hung at the top, facing each other, each sporting sound suppressors. Ruger was stamped into their grips, while SR-9 lay across its short barrel length. Two foot-long Bowie knives with their blades crossed hung beneath the pistols, just above a small pedestal with a miniature ceramic skull, black-eyed and grinning. A tin-colored derringer lay on the bottom of the cabinet, as if tossed in as an afterthought.

But the item that took Gus' breath away, the thing that made him place his shotgun on the desk, was the weapon placed straight up alongside the others. Gus took it out of the cabinet and looked it over, his mouth hanging open in awe. He had no idea of the reputation of the gun, but the sheer spectacle of it spoke military grade.

The word Benelli was stamped in the gun metal, just above the trigger, right next to "Made in Italy." It looked like a shotgun, but with a pistol grip and a skeletal shoulder stock. Gus marvelled at the sleekness of the boomstick. *Combat shotgun*, that much he knew, with what looked to be a removable stock. He looked down the sights and got another surprise. It carried a mounted scope, which made Gus shake his head. It could not have come at a better time. God above, he *wanted* to go hunting for gimps with this beast.

"Sorry, Betsy," Gus muttered, glancing at the shotgun on the table. "Think I just divorced you." He looked down through the scope again. "Fuck me gently."

Not wanting to release the shotgun, he reluctantly placed it on the desk and went back to the cabinet. The lower cabinet doors were locked, so he kicked his way through with his steel-toed boots. Clearing away the flimsy wooden fragments, Gus mouthed the word *yes*. Ammunition. Seven twenty-shell boxes of regular shot and seven five-shell boxes of what was marked on the box as sabot slugs.

Sabots. The name sounded familiar, but he couldn't place it. He felt as if he'd just found a thunderbolt. He opened a box of the copper solid sabots and took one out. An impressed whistle left him as he studied the green plastic shell casing and the inner copper top.

"Wow." He knew they were special rounds, but didn't know exactly *how* special. He looked over the boxes for anything to give a description to what he'd found, an owner's manual perhaps, but there was nothing else. He did find ten loaded maga-zines for the Rugers, in addition to a heavy tackle box filled with what looked be another two hundred or so loose nine millimeter rounds—little brass shells with red tips.

"Christmas came early," Gus muttered. He pulled out the ammo, checked the mag-azine loads, and found gun cleaning kits for both the pistols and the Benelli. Behind the boxes of shells were two brown leather bandoliers, which Gus looped over his head and under his arms, making an X on his chest. He rooted around for more good-ies and felt genuine disappointment when he found nothing else useful.

Knowing he shouldn't complain, he took what he could carry out to the van.

"Find anything?" Scott called when he opened the rear doors of the van.

"Yeah," Gus replied. "A fuckin'armory."

"What?"

"You heard me. A fuckin' armory."

"Like what?"

"Like this."

Gus held out the combat shotgun, which pulled Scott out of the driver's seat so he could see the weapon closer.

"Ho-ly *shit*," Scott exclaimed softly, taking the weapon.

"Eh?" Gus nodded emphatic agreement. "Mine, though. I call dibs on it."

"Aw, man."

"I got you something, though, if you want 'em."

"What?"

"Hand me the duffel bag, and I'll bring it all out in one trip."

"Man!" Scott admired the shotgun. "Where the hell did the guy get this thing anyway? Something smells illegal here."

"Private collection probably. I once knew a guy from Truro who said his father had an old AK-47 in a seventeen-gun collection. And what do you mean *illegal*? If we're gonna be finding guns, the *illegal* ones are the ones I want."

Scott had nothing to say to that. He was too interested in staring down the scope of the Benelli. He aimed up the street and made gunshot noises.

"I'll be back," Gus said, and returned to the house.

23

They cleared seven houses, pulling in a bin full of canned peaches and pineapple, as well as fruit cocktails. Gus found some boxes of beer, but he left those for the several additional bottles of gin and vodka. Fourteen rolls of toilet paper were found and taken. Loading up what they found at the seventh house, Gus got aboard and glanced up at the overcast sky. He felt exceptionally good about what they had scavenged, and then realized where they were.

"Hey, guess where we are."

"Where?"

"Near the liquor corporation."

"Oh."

"Yeah, *oh*. Why don't we head on over there?"

Scott looked out at the overcast sky. "I wonder what time it is."

"There you go about the time again. Where do you have to be? Hmm? Where?" Gus looked over at Scott, watching him shrug. "You don't have anyone waitin' for you except me, and I'm right here."

"You're the big baby who wants to be back on the hill before dark."

"Hey, now," Gus said, feeling mildly defensive. "That's just plain good thinking. You want to get caught down here if anything goes wrong again?"

"That's what I'm sayin'. It's cloudy out, and I don't know if it's one o' clock or four."

"It'd be darker if it was four."

"So you want to go over there?"

"Yeah."

"You're an alcoholic, you know that?" Scott said pointedly.

"You're not?"

Scott shook his head. "Where to, Budweiser?"

"Hey, if you're going to give me a nickname, make it Jack. Or even better, *Uncle* Jack."

"What kind of name is that?"

Gus shrugged. "Popular in the movies."

"What movies?"

"Movies, man, movies."

"Yeah, *bad* movies."

Gus shook his head. "I think I like you better when you're drinkin'. Head on down this street and take a left. One quick stop. Load up on some Mr. Daniels."

"Whatever, man, I just drive here."

"Use the name."

"I'm *not* usin' that shitty nickname. So drop it."

The helmet hid Gus' smile.

Ten minutes later, with the sky becoming increasingly sullen looking, the beast rolled into the parking lot of the liquor corporation. The building was built low, single story, and reminded Gus of an aboveground, red brick bunker. With so much cash generated for the crown-owned store, one would think they could splurge a little on the building's design. Cars dotted the wide lot, some with their doors opened and others with smashed windshields. The van did a ninety-degree turn in reverse, and backed right up to the two main doors.

"Don't take long," Scott said.

"I won't." Gus brought up the Ruger SR-9 pistol with its suppressor.

"You're not takin' the shotgun?" Scott asked.

"Got this right here," Gus said, thumbing the safety on the gun. "Thing's got like a ton of bullets in the clip."

"Mag."

"Huh?"

"It's not called a clip; it's called a magazine. A mag."

"How do you know?"

Scott shrugged. "I hear things."

"What's the difference?" Gus wanted to know.

"The difference is *those* things are mags that use a spring to feed bullets into the gun, while with a clip you can see the bullets. Like they're stuck to this piece of metal, all exposed like. And don't call that a silencer, either."

"You mean this? What is it, then?"

"Called a sound suppressor," Scott said and turned back to keep watch.

Gus regarded the length of black metal at the tip of his gun, and then Scott. "Knowledgeable fucker, ain'tcha?"

Scott shrugged. "Get a move on. Time's wastin'."

But Gus stood in the rear of the van, sizing up the sidearm and thinking about the new terminology he'd learned. He finally got a move on and slipped out the back, feeling a chill in the air, even through his gear. He looked inside the shop, seeing how dark it was. Taking a step into the entryway, Gus stopped and stomped his feet before slapping the doorframe with his free hand. He waited.

No reaction.

Feeling a little disappointed, Gus crossed the threshold and went inside. The gloom was periodically speared by sparse light from windows. Gus thought about going back to get a flashlight, but decided against it. If there were any gimps inside, they would've heard him slapping the wall. He kept the pistol pointed at the floor, dearly wanting something to appear so he could shoot it. Pushing his way through a turnstile, he walked by a series of cash checkouts and proceeded past shelves that still had a few bottles on them. He grabbed a shopping cart and wheeled it down the aisle, carefully checking the remaining bottles on the shelves. He knew he'd taken most of the Jack Daniels and Captain Morgan off the shelf, so that meant a trip to the storage room, and for that, he'd need a flashlight.

Gus filled up the cart with boxes of Bacardi amber and white rum before returning to the van.

"Holy shit," Scott said as Gus loaded the booze into the beast. "That's a lot of liquor."

"They got wine in there, too. You want any?"

"Nah, I don't know anything about wine."

"I feel the same way. But I do like the sweet stuff." Gus reached to the side of one bin and pulled out a rechargeable flashlight. "Everything clear?"

"Thus far."

"Be right back, then," Gus announced and returned to the dark cave of the liquor corporation.

"Hey, get me some cider if they have it," Scott called after him.

Gus stopped at the mouth of the store and raised his hand, but then he tensed.

A scream from beyond the lot. A woman's scream.

Scott stuck his head out his window and looked back at Gus. They froze, waiting for more.

"Whaddya want to do?" Scott asked.

"Follow me." Gus bolted around the van. He jogged across the lot with pistol in hand and visor up, moving in and around the derelict vehicles. Upon reaching the edge of the pavement, he listened once more. Behind him, the van crept up to his position.

Looking left and right, Gus couldn't see or hear anything. In front of him, there was a ditch filled with rotting debris. Beyond that was the broad side of a Chinese restaurant, along with an alleyway and fencing fringed with crumpled yellow grass. The fencing was part of a nearby subdivision.

"Well, shit." Gus headed down the embankment. He sprinted through the back alley behind the Chinese restaurant, hearing his boots click on the pavement as he ran.

"Let me go!" came from ahead, prompting him to run faster. He held the pistol out with his finger on the guard. He ran past one long side alley filled with dumpsters, then another, until he heard a clanging noise. That made him worried. If he could hear the noise through his helmet, so could *they*.

Slowing at a corner of a white building which had a half-hanging sign reading, "—son's Electronics," Gus took a breath and peeked around it.

There, between two dumpsters and only visible from the chest up, was a tall man, dressed in a winter coat and wearing a red toque. He held a woman by the throat, her dirty blond hair splayed out over her shoulders, topped off with a white toque. Raising the Ruger, Gus eased around the corner. With the sound suppressor, he had no qualms about shooting.

"Let me—" The woman's words mushed into a breathless growl, and Gus saw the man bring a knife to her throat.

"Whattaya think you could do? Hmm? Whattaya think you could do? I gotcha now, and I think you need to be punished. Whattaya say to that? Hmm? You just be good to me, okay?" the knife wielder said, gazing at the woman as she grunted and squirmed in his grasp. "You just be good this *one time*. Don't make another peep, and I'll—"

"Hey."

The knifeman whipped around and stared at Gus, blinking in astonishment. Pale-faced with thick lips and a shitload of dirty stubble, he switched back and forth from Gus to the woman, whose eyes flicked white trying to see the owner of the new voice.

Gus aimed his gun at the knifeman. "Let her go."

"D'fuck you come from?" the knifeman demanded, flashing a mouth full of yellow teeth.

"I said . . ." Gus held the pistol in a shooter's stance he'd seen in the movies. "Let her go."

"I'll cut her." The guy brought his knife, which looked to be nothing more than a kitchen blade, up to the right side of the woman's face. "You shoot me, and I'll slice her open."

"You cut her," Gus said slowly. "And I'll fuck you up twice."

"Uhhh, uhhh," Knifeman half-wailed, half-grunted. *"I'll cut her!"*

Gus didn't bother answering. He kept the gun steady. Steady was the key. He took two steps toward the couple, aiming for Knifeman's head.

"You stay back!" the man shouted. It became obvious to Gus that Knifeman hadn't expected any trouble beyond deadheads, which was idiotic. No, Gus decided, he was dealing with a fucking moron caught in the act of probably getting around to a rape. That thought made him scowl.

"Stay back, fucker! *Stay back*! I mean it!" Knifeman bawled, his eyes wide with fright.

In response, Gus took another step, closing the gap to about three meters. He felt oddly distant, staring down the barrel of the Ruger. He'd wondered if he had the guts to shoot a *person*. He'd had plenty of practice on dead folks, and as terrifying as they were, there was a guiltless freedom in shooting them. They were *dead*, for Christ's sake, and putting them down and thus returning them to the grave could even be considered a *good* thing. Even if they were living and infected, Gus believed there was a place for mercy killing the doomed. Putting down a living person, however, even one as possibly deserving as the piece of moronic shit standing before him, was something altogether different. He wasn't certain he could do it.

Then, it occurred to Gus that *fuckchops* didn't know his thoughts. With dramatic flair, he squeezed one eye closed, as if aiming.

That, apparently, was enough for Knifeman.

"You fucker!" He released the woman in a near hysterical huff. "You fucker, you fucker, you *fucker*!"

Knifeman jerked himself out from between the dumpsters and bounced off the opposite wall. Intent on giving Gus as difficult a target as possible, he zigzagged in one direction, then the other, abruptly changing paths again and again, ricocheting off the close confines while scrambling out the front of the alley. Gus felt both impressed and relieved. He didn't have to kill a living person, and he got to see a man-shaped super springy ball in action.

"You fucker!" Knifeman bawled one more time as he disappeared around a corner.

Gus ran to the end of the alley, sparing only a glance at the woman, who was holding her throat. Looking around the corner, he saw Knifeman in full retreat, still screaming, *"You fucker!"* at the top of his lungs. Gus shook his head. The way he'd been brought up, he learned that the meek were supposed to inherit the earth, not the fucked-in-the-head. Knifeman bounded across the street and vanished up another alleyway.

Gus turned to face the woman. She stood between the dumpsters, regarding him with a red face while massaging her cheeks. Her teeth weren't as white as what they might have been, but Gus was close enough to see that she still had most of them. Fancy that. He hadn't seen a woman in damn near two years, he figured. A dirty white coat kept her warm, and she wore a pair of black jeans and brown hiking boots. Then, something else struck him that wasn't so funny. Back at the house, he had an extensive movie collection, which he had had plenty of time to watch. One of the flicks he enjoyed was one of the remakes for Tarzan, starring a simply stunning woman by the name of Bo Derek.

The woman looked like her, except slimmer. A little more grit . . .

"You gonna fuckin' take your shot now?" she grated, taking in deep breaths.

"Huh?" was all a startled Gus could get out.

"You heard me, fuckwad fireman." She pulled a gun out of her pocket and pointed it at him. The barrel of the weapon seemed big enough to launch a torpedo.

"Hey, now." Gus lifted his own gun skyward in a gesture of peace. "I just saved your ass."

"Yeah, saved it for yourself, I bet." She crept to the edge of the dumpster while keeping the gun on him. Positioned as she was, the corner of the trash unit gave her exceptional cover. "I should shoot you right now." She sniffed and rubbed one cheek.

"Wait. *Listen.* I don't wanna hurt you."

"Yeah, right."

That took Gus back. "Look—"

"Shut up!" She caught herself, and quickly regained composure. "Listen."

Gus obeyed. His mouth opened slightly behind his helmet. Moaning, coming from the street.

"Hey." Scott, poised with his shotgun, entered the alley behind her. Gus breathed a sigh of relief then, but the woman just glanced over her shoulder and didn't drop the gun.

"You shoot me, and I'll drop him. I swear to Christ."

"You drop him. I drop you," Scott informed her with a coldness that struck Gus as downright *hard*.

She looked from one man to the other. The moaning got louder and, for whatever weird reason, Gus thought he heard a distant "*You fucker!*" rolling over the concrete.

Trembling, she dropped her handheld rocket launcher.

"All right." Gus moved past her toward Scott. "This way."

"What?" Bo asked.

"They're coming."

Bo looked to the alley mouth. "Oh, sunny Jesus."

"Come on!" Gus shouted, following a retreating Scott.

She finally ran, and the three of them beat their way back to the beast, waiting atop the parking lot rise. Overhead, the clouds seemed to darken even more.

"You go around to the back," Gus shouted at her. He climbed into the passenger side as Scott clicked his seatbelt into place.

"We takin' her with us?"

"Can't leave her here."

"Why not?"

Gus stared at him incredulously. "I didn't leave you." Not waiting for a comeback, Gus made his way to the back of the van. He unlocked and opened the door, and there she stood, red-barrel bazooka dangling in her hand.

"Where're you goin'?" she asked.

Gus blinked at her. "You're fuckin' jokin' now, right? You want to be left behind or what? You hear what's out there?"

She looked back at the main road, confusion clouding her features.

"Get your ass in here," Gus commanded.

Appearing not to like it at all, she climbed into the van, shooing away his offer of assistance. Gus let her be and went back to the front.

"Holy shit," she said.

Gus looked back at her while he fastened his seatbelt. Scott started the van and put it into reverse.

"You guys been shoppin', eh?" She stared at the goods in the back. "Where'd you get all this?"

"Liquor corporation," Gus said. "Now hold on to something."

"To what? You got nothin' back—"

The sudden lurch of the van cut her off and sent her squatting on the floor. She gripped the bins for support.

"Home then?" Scott asked.

"Yep." Gus turned to the woman. "Anyplace we can drop you off?"

"No," she said after a few moments.

"You okay to come back with us?"

"Where?"

"Out of town."

"You better not rape me."

Gus looked at the ceiling, thought of a reply, but shook his head. Scott steered the van onto the main road, keeping clear of the dozen or so dead staggering into the daylight.

"Go that way." Gus pointed to the left, realizing he still had a hand on his pistol. Then, a bolt of horrible realization struck him. The woman was in the back.

With the weapons.

He looked back at her then, between the seats, and watched her study the goods they had taken from the houses. She glanced up at the shotguns, including the Benelli, but then looked back in the bins.

"You've got cans of fruit cocktail back here," she said.

"Yeah, got them today."

Her lips parted as she continued staring. "You've got lots."

Gus didn't say anything.

"Can I have some?" she asked.

That one simple question affected Gus more than he cared to let on. "Uh, it'll be messy to open that in the van. Can you wait until we're back?"

She thought about it. "How long will that be?"

"What's your name?" Gus asked so he could dispense with the Bo Derek imagery going through his head.

"Huh?"

"Your name?"

"Roxanne," she said, sitting cross-legged on the floor.

"I'm Gus. This is Scott."

"Hello," Scott said, keeping his eyes on the road.

"Okay. So anyway, it'll take about thirty minutes or so, depending on traffic."

That space between her eyebrows crinkled up. "Traffic? What traffic?"

"The dead kind."

"Oh."

"Who was that guy back there?" Gus asked.

"I thought he was a friend, right up to then, anyway. We—" she fumed for a moment. "We were coming in from New Brunswick. Making our way to Halifax. He's just a guy I paired up with. Strength in numbers, right?"

"He have a motorcycle?"

"Yeah. A loud one. Stupid prick. I kept tellin' him about it, but he doesn't know how to fix it."

Gus exchanged looks with Scott. "We heard him the other day."

"Yeah, well. He can go on and get killed now for all I care. I've taken care of myself before."

Gus supposed she just could. She struck him as being full of fight. "Roxanne?"

"Yeah?"

"What kind of gun is that?"

"Flare gun."

"Flare gun." Gus had thought it was a wicked blast laser or some other kind of mass effect weapon. Shaking his head in sad amusement, he looked back at the road.

"Scared you, did it?" Roxanne asked, a smile in her question.

"Damn right it did," Gus muttered.

He settled back into his seat and looked at the street rushing by, the skeletal trees reaching for Heaven.

24

The beast rumbled out of the city with smoke spilling from its exhaust. They linked up with the main highway and began the long, but comforting drive home. Roxanne remained quiet, and the two men left her alone.

When they came to the place where Gus had put down the two corpses, Scott slowed and leaned over the steering wheel. "See that?"

Gus saw. "Yep." The bodies lay where they had left them.

"What is it?" Roxanne asked.

"Nothin'," Gus answered. "Just an experiment."

Scott drove by, leaving the unmoving dead behind.

It was almost dark by the time they got back. They slowed to the gate on the road, the camouflage looking dead and thin. Gus got out and pulled open the latticed gate. He waved them through. The van stopped just inside, and Gus put the gate back in place, opened the door, and jumped aboard.

"You guys live up here?" Roxanne asked.

"Yeah," Gus answered. "We do. Doin' pretty good, too, except for the days we have to head into the city."

Roxanne nodded and removed her white toque. She shook out her hair and Gus looked away before making the mistake of staring. That was all she needed right now, he figured, after what she'd been through.

"You have to head down there often?" she asked.

Gus nodded, watching the dirt road ahead as the van travelled over the winding slope. Scott kept the headlights off as they approached the wall. "Snow will be down soon, though. Won't be able to get down there at all. That's why we were in your part of the woods today. Pickin' up supplies."

Beyond the tall stone wall, the dark peaks of the house rose up. The van came to a stop.

"Home again, home again, jiggity jig," Gus said, and got out. He went to the gate, a shadow among shadows, and opened it for the van. Scott drove through, heading toward the open garage. Gus closed and reinforced the gate, wondering how he had gotten all the shitty jobs. Once done bracing the gate, he half-jogged back to the garage.

Inside, he cranked down the door. Scott had backed the van in and opened the rear doors. He was eyeing Roxanne as he stripped off his firefighter gear. Gus joined them and started disrobing. Roxanne turned around so she wasn't looking at them.

"Don't worry. We wear clothes underneath," Gus told her.

"I'm not worried," she said. "So, how long have you guys been up here?"

"About two years for me," Gus answered.

"Couple of months here." Scott tossed his Nomex coat, pants, and fire boots off to one side of an open locker.

"We might stink a little, but it's a small price to pay for being safe," Gus said. "You want, you can get that can of fruit cocktail now."

That got her attention, but she remained cool as she climbed back into the van and got out three cans of fruit.

"Can I have the peaches, too?"

"Sure," Gus said, hoping his little smile was hidden by his beard. He turned to Scott. "I'll take her into the kitchen."

Scott nodded indifferently.

Gus walked into the house, and Roxanne followed like a deer wary of stepping into the sights of a hunter's rifle.

"My God," she said, glancing left and right at the kitchen area and the living room. "This is paradise."

Gus faced her from behind the island in the kitchen, spreading his hands on the black marble counter surface. He watched her size up the furniture and then the kitchen. A smile spread across her face, and her eyes lit up. She shrugged off her coat, and Gus couldn't help but take in her slim figure and the swell of her breasts covered by a black sweater.

"See anything you like?" Roxanne asked with a scowl.

Blinking and suddenly embarrassed, Gus diverted his gaze to the countertop and then the cupboards. "Ah, sorry. Uh . . . you can bring those cans over here. The fruit . . . I mean." He winced and shook his head, feeling the blood rise to his cheeks.

Roxanne came to the island and sat at one of the stools. Keeping an eye on Gus, she laid out the three cans.

"You got a can opener for these things?"

Nodding, Gus got her a plastic bowl and a spoon. "If you can wait, I'll put on some soup for you."

"Soup?"

"Soup," Scott said as he emerged from the hallway. He walked around Roxanne and sat down at the end of the island, placing both elbows on the counter and his chin in his hands.

"You forgetting something?" he asked Gus.

"Huh? What?"

Scott squinted at him, but Gus still didn't catch on. "Back home drinks?"

"Oh." Gus went to the kitchen table and got the two bottles of Canadian Club they'd been working on. He gave Scott his and returned to the other side of the island.

"We have this thing we do when we get back. In one piece."

"You drink?" Roxanne asked.

"I drink," Scott said. "He gets smashed."

Gus frowned at Scott and shrugged at Roxanne.

"So where's mine then? Or don't I get one?"

"You got fruit cocktail," Scott pointed out.

"Course you can," Gus quickly spoke. He looked around. "Uh, you want a glass?"

"You got those, too?"

"Yeah," Gus managed, getting a plastic one from a cupboard. "We've got pretty much everything here."

"Is that why it's warm in here?"

"Solar power," Gus said and poured her a shot from his bottle.

"My God. It's too cloudy for that, isn't it?"

"Sun's still up there. Okay, then. Cheers." Gus held up his bottle. Scott held up his, but Roxanne didn't share in the toast.

"And you're welcome," Scott said as he took a shot.

"What for? For bringin' me here?" Roxanne said with a hint of petulance in her voice.

"Yeah. That, and for savin' your ass," Scott reminded her.

Gus watched the exchange between the two and felt a little tongue-tied. He took a sip from his bottle and placed it on the island's surface. The burn of the whiskey still in his mouth and throat, he realized darkly that he felt something else as well, something he hadn't felt for a very long time, but recognized it as clear as daylight. Insecurity. Around *her*.

Well, shit.

"You were about to shoot my ass, if I remember it correctly," Roxanne said to Scott.

"Oh, I would've shot it. Guaranteed." Scott nodded, keeping his eyes downcast. "But you were smart about it. Right, Gus?"

"Um . . ." Gus cleared his throat. "That's right. You did the smart thing there."

"Thanks. Both of you," she added, with another glance at Scott.

Each time she looked at Scott, something in Gus *willed* her to look his way instead.

"If you like," Gus plunged on, "you can stay here."

Scott's eyes flicked up at Gus before he turned back to regard Roxanne.

"I just got here," Roxanne said. "Let me think about it."

Scott snorted a chuckle. He rubbed his blond beard and shooed his hand in a gesture telling them to ignore his little outburst.

Gus had to smile himself. "Sure. Go right ahead. When you want to leave, just say the word. We'll drop you off wherever you want to go."

"I thought you were going to make some soup."

"Hungry myself," Scott threw in.

Gus got a large pot and opened up three cans of it filled with preserved vegetables and chunks of chicken. He emptied all three into the pot and fired up a burner.

"Dig in with the fruit," Gus said. "This'll take a few minutes."

She opened one of the fruit cocktails. "Oh, God. This is so good."

Gus watched her from the stove. He glanced over at Scott, who shook his head at him while hiding a little smile with his hand. Gus inquired with a look, but Scott responded by turning away.

Roxanne finished her food and wiped her mouth with her hand. "Oh, God, that was delicious. I haven't eaten anything like that for years. Even before everything went to hell. You don't know how hard it is to find anything out west. Most food was taken by the army or police or gangs."

"We've got plenty of food here," Gus informed her.

"Yeah?"

"Yeah, we're pretty self-sufficient." Gus went on to explain about the well and electricity, as well as the food and drink in the basement. He finished cooking the soup and portioned it out in bowls that Scott got from the cupboard. They ate then, and the silence filled with the sounds of supper. Roxanne bolted hers down and eyed the pot on the stove.

"More?" Gus asked.

"Yes, if you can spare it."

Gus poured the last bit into her bowl.

"You have any bread or crackers?"

166

"Ah, no, sorry. We're well off, but we don't have everything."

"So you were just talkin' out of your ass a few minutes ago." Roxanne crossed her arms.

"Ah," Gus began, looking at Scott.

Scott didn't appear too pleased with Roxanne. "I think you should be a little more thankful for what we—more exactly, Gus—did for you today."

"How thankful I gotta be?" Roxanne fired at him.

"What the hell is this? Gus, I do believe you've let a bitch into the house."

"Fuck you," Roxanne shot back.

"No, fuck *you*," Scott said, squaring her with an incredulous expression.

"Hey, relax," Gus asked them both and, to his surprise, got it. "Look, Roxanne. We're goin' to do a little drinkin' here, me and Scott. I think you should just maybe relax. I got some extra clothes that'll fit you, and you can take a hot bath, okay?"

Roxanne's jaw dropped. "A hot bath?"

"Yeah."

"Well, shit, you want that blowjob now or later?"

Gus blinked, not knowing quite how to react.

"That was a joke. And I don't remember offering it to *you*." She directed the last at Scott.

The blond man shook his head in wonder.

"Well, boys, I'm going to finish my lovely soup here, and when I do, maybe one of you can direct me to that bath? And a razor, too, if you can spare it. I haven't had either for a while."

"A razor?" Gus asked in confusion.

Roxanne cocked an eyebrow. "You want to know what I'm goin' to shave?"

25

After supper, Gus took it upon himself to show Roxanne the bathroom and what would be her bedroom, next to Scott's. He tuned on the water, letting it run, and took her some clean sweatpants, a T-shirt, a sweater, and a disposable razor.

"Shampoo and soap are in there." He pointed to a cabinet as the flowing hot water steamed up the room.

"My God." She sighed.

"We'll be downstairs." Gus turned to leave.

"Hey," Roxanne said. "Thank you. For everything. There's nothing like this out there anymore. Nothing that we could find, and we were looking. I mean, solar panels? Not everyone can afford them and, really, who has the room?"

Gus nodded. He left her and walked downstairs to the den. Like always, they left only one light on, keeping the room in perpetual shadow.

Scott was in the recliner, his bottle of whiskey in his lap. "She in the tub?"

"Just about." Gus sat on the sofa.

"Why aren't you with her?" Scott gave him an evil smile.

"Huh?"

Scott shook his head. "Oh, man. If I can see it, you can sure as shit know *she* can."

"See what?" Gus asked in a defensive tone.

"You, around her. She's only been here what? An hour? And you're already *smitten*." He emphasized the last word with a horrified expression.

"You got an issue with that?"

"Gus, you listenin' to yourself?"

"Hey, I asked you a question."

Scott regarded him. "All right. Listen. You listenin'? I'll say this once, and that's it. You're welcome to her. I ain't interested."

Gus stared at him. "Why? You're not gay, are you?"

"What?" Scott rolled his eyes. "No, I'm not gay, you twat." He shook his head and took another shot of whiskey. "I'm not interested in her because I was married once. Remember?" He scratched at the space between his eyes. "Before all of this. Wife and daughter. They got infected and died."

"Sorry, man."

"Look, I didn't say this before. Hell, I didn't even tell Teddy or Lea. I . . . I had to kill them both."

That struck Gus like a hammer, leaving him dazed and speechless.

"I put them down. I killed my own daughter. She was . . . she was only two. She bit her mom's finger off. And while I made up my mind what to do with her, my wife changed on me. I don't even remember how I did it. All I remember is leavin' the apartment with a bloody rolling pin."

"Jesus Christ," Gus whispered.

Scott shrugged. "I'm lucky that way. Not rememberin', I mean. But sometimes I think I remember—nightmares. They don't come as often now, though." He sighed and ran a thumb over the surface of his bottle. "So, yeah, I'm not interested."

"I'm sorry, man."

"It's okay. I wouldn't have told you if it wasn't for the bitch upstairs. And listenin' to you going all bubbly over her."

Gus winced. "I went all bubbly?"

"Man . . ." Scott shook his head again. "I wanted to signal timeout there at one point when you went on and on about the house. That's what I mean by listenin' to yourself. I do want to say thanks, though. For includin' me in ownership of the house. And other stuff. You've truly saved me."

"As far as I'm concerned, you live here."

"Yeah. That's what I mean. Thanks, Gus."

Scott held up his bottle, and Gus leaned over and clinked his against it. They drank and let the whiskey burn it all away.

"She's a peach, though, ain't she?" Gus said.

"She's got a dirty mouth."

"I like it all the same."

"You would." They both chuckled. Scott cleared his throat. "Just don't be so god-damn eager, okay? If something happens, and you have to be ready, though nothin' might, but *if* something happens, just stay cool, all right? Be cool."

Gus nodded and, for a brief moment, thought of Tammy. "Thanks for the advice."

"All I can offer right now. So what are we doing tonight? Same ol'?"

"You know it. Maybe a movie, too."

"What one?"

"Been eyein' that old one there by John Carpenter."

"*Escape from New York?*" Scott's brow went up a notch.

"*The Thing.*"

"Oh, good choice. I can watch that again."

"I'll load it up."

"I noticed *Scarface* in there, too." Scott said. "Ol' Al Pacino, eh?"

"Sounds good, amigo," Gus answered with a rough Spanish accent. "But first, *The Theeeng.*"

Springing up from the sofa, Gus powered up the big screen television and, with the remote control, selected a movie in the 1050 terabyte digital library. He found the folder and brought up the cover display for the old 1982 movie.

"Great cover," Scott said.

"Great movie."

The opening credits came on, heartbeat music started, and the two men were suddenly in the Antarctic, watching the plight of an American research station as it came into contact with an alien once frozen in the deep ice.

One hour and change into the movie, Roxanne came down dressed in the clothes Gus had given her. "I haven't seen a movie in years," she said, and skipped in front of Gus. He moved his legs from where he was stretched out on the sofa, watching her as she passed. She sat at the other end of the couch, eyes glued to the screen.

"What is this?" she asked.

"*The Thing,*" Gus informed her.

"Oooh, sounds scary."

"This is a classic."

"I think I saw the remake as a kid."

"That what happen to you?" Scott threw in.

"Hey . . . don't start over there, unless you want a couple of letters thrown your way."

"Letters?"

"Yeah, F and U. You fugly ucker."

Scott went back to watching the movie.

"Yeah, that's what I thought," Roxanne said, but she was smiling.

Breakfast the next morning was oatmeal sweetened with white sugar. As he felt it was his kitchen, Gus took it upon himself to fix the morning meal. He lined up three bowls and filled them. He boiled more water and prepared coffee. Afterward, he settled down at the island and began to eat.

Scott emerged wearing his bum clothes and sat down. "Morning."

"Morning."

Gus had the light on over the stove, bathing the area in a soft glow. They both had half of their breakfasts gone when Roxanne appeared like a ghost, dishevelled and sour-faced. "What's this?"

"Oatmeal," Gus said. "Morning."

"Morning," she said, still partially asleep, it seemed. "Morning," she directed at Scott.

"Morning," he muttered back, not looking up.

"Oatmeal?" she asked.

"Yeah," Gus said. "That okay?"

"I used to hate oatmeal. Funny how a little bit of starving solves that." She sat down and yawned before digging in.

Gus caught a whiff of her morning breath and made a mental note to get her a toothbrush and mouthwash from the storeroom.

"Oh, my God, coffee even. This is so hard to come by," Roxanne said, as she sweetened it. She slurped, and her shoulders slumped. "Mmmm."

After breakfast, they piled the dishes into the sink and gathered around the kitchen island.

"I don't know what to say. Thank you for that," Roxanne said.

"Roxanne," Gus began. "We've gotta unload the van, all right? You want to help, that's fine. Later on, we're gonna head out again. Just a short run. See if we can't pick up some more supplies for the winter."

"Didn't drink enough last night?" Roxanne asked.

"That wasn't drinkin'," Gus said straight-faced. "That was us relaxin'."

"Oh. Well, where are you goin'?"

"We'll see later if we have time. Days are gettin' shorter now. I'll show you around a bit, too. You're welcome to move around the house, but stay outta my room please."

"Mine, too," Scott added.

"So that means you won't be comin' into mine?" Roxanne asked Gus.

"Of course."

"Hmm. Fine."

"All right, then," Gus said, drumming his hands on the countertop. "Let's get dressed and get to work."

Minutes later, they met up back in the garage, dressed and ready to move things from the van to the house. Gus and Scott moved the alcohol carefully, treating it like a wounded child. They divided up the firearms and ammunition, with Gus claiming the Benelli shotgun as his own.

"Do I get a gun?" Roxanne asked.

"You don't," Gus said. "You just got here."

"Well, I *need* a gun," she stressed.

"You got a flare gun, don't you?" Scott asked.

"Yeah, but—"

"That's enough for you. For now, anyway."

"Next one we find can be yours if you're workin' with us," Gus added.

"I'm workin' with you, okay? Give me something to do," Roxanne pleaded.

Gus said, "Okay, grab some of the food and follow me below. Scott, leave one of those gun cleaning kits in the van."

Taking some of the canned food, Gus led her to the basement storeroom.

"Oh, my God," Roxanne said as she took in the sight. "You've got a shop down here."

"Well, two little ones anyway."

"My God, I see shampoo, soap, toilet paper."

"Yeah." Gus took what she had in her arms and placed it on one of many shelves. "Here," he said as he plucked out a toothbrush, still in its original wrapping, and gave it to her with a tube of toothpaste. He handed her a pack of dental floss as well.

"You tryin' to say something?" Roxanne said as she took the items.

"Yeah, without comin' out and sayin' it," Gus said, smiling. "But I will if you really want me to."

"I can take it."

"I think you can. But I think I'll let this one go. Those are yours. Enjoy."

"Floss," Roxanne said as she studied the packaging. "Shit."

"You couldn't find any floss out there?"

"Everything's been picked over, man. You don't know. That's why we came east to the smaller cities. Better chance of finding anything. I mean, there are people out there now that will literally *kill* for floss."

"Well, what you see here is mostly good. Sometimes I'll find something in a house that's exploded from gases or bacteria or some shit. I don't know how it happens, truthfully. Or bugs got in through the packaging. I once heard that for all the food out there, a small percentage has like bug eggs in it. Which sometimes hatch. Best test is, if it's still sealed, it's a good chance it's still good, but if you open it, look and smell before digging in."

"Good to know."

"Yeah. I got my hands on some freeze-dried stuff before. Well, once in a blue moon. That stuff's *always* fresh. I consider it like Christmas turkey."

Roxanne stood sizing up the many goods in the room. "I can't believe you have all of this."

"Yeah, well, with three people here, we'll go through it pretty fast. That's why we should head out today and see if we can get more. House picking, I call it. Winter's comin' on."

"You're scared of winter?"

"I'm scared of being isolated up here and not being able to drive anywhere so, yeah, I'm scared of winter. Don't want to run the chance of gettin' stuck in the valley when the snow's on the ground."

"But I thought the snow and cold slows them down."

Gus regarded her. "Doesn't stop them, though."

They ate an early lunch of crackers, canned chicken, and cheese, while doing a slow cleaning of their shotguns and Ruger pistols. The pistols took longer than any of them expected, as none of them had ever cleaned one before. It took an hour before they figured out how to get them apart, clean them, and put them back together. The smell of gun oil clung to the air. They talked as they worked, and learned that Roxanne was from Ontario and had struck east with the man called Edgar. The knifeman. He had been fine up until a few days ago, and Roxanne believed he had simply lost it.

Around early afternoon, they suited up. They didn't have any firefighter gear for Roxanne, so she simply wore her white winter coat and toque. After loading up the van and their weapons, they headed out, opening and closing the gates as they came to them.

Gus looked back at Roxanne for a moment.

"What?" she asked, the lip of her toque pulled down almost to her brow.

"What can you do?" Gus asked.

"Huh?"

Gus waited.

"I can drive," Roxanne said. "And I can shoot a gun."

"A flare gun," Gus said.

"Well, yeah. I only have three shots left, though."

"Anything else?"

Roxanne grimaced. "Not really."

"What did you do back in the real world?"

"I was a manager for a fried chicken takeout."

"Really? Good job?"

"Not really," Roxanne said. "I put on something like forty pounds, I think. And all on my ass."

Gus chuckled. "We'll find something for you to do. We all can do something."

They became quiet then, mindful that they were beyond the safety of the house and wall. The van cut its way through the landmarks on the highway until they came to the place where they had left two of the dead on the highway.

"You see what I see?" Scott asked as he slowed to a stop.

"Yeah," Gus said, looking ahead and then around.

"What?" Roxanne asked.

"That experiment I mentioned yesterday?"

"Yeah."

"It ain't there anymore."

"Huh?" Roxanne got to her feet to peer out the windshield. "Tell me again."

"Shit." Gus ignored her and opened his door to exit the van. He glanced around at the road, taking in the wrecked cars, as well as the motorcycle behind them and the billboard with the semi driven through it. He felt a pang of wary excitement in his gut. It was the place, sure as hell it was, but no zombies. He looked back into the van at Scott and Roxanne and shrugged. He studied the area and located some faint stains where the dead had fallen, but couldn't find anything to suggest that they had gone off. He reached for his bat and realized it was back in the truck.

"Give me my bat," Gus said, opening the passenger door.

Roxanne handed it to him. "Here you go."

"Anything up?" Scott asked.

"Don't know. Keep a lookout."

"Will do," Scott replied.

Gus closed the door and walked to the side of the road. He got down on his knees and peered under a few of the wrecks. Nothing. He stood and walked over to the guardrail. He had looked forward to smashing a deadhead, but the side of the road and the area leading up to some sparse trees were empty. The sun crept out from behind a cloud and lit the area. He looked up and down the highway, but didn't spot anything. He finally turned and headed back to the van.

"Anything?" Scott asked.

"Not a goddamn thing," Gus grumped. "Damn funny."

"What do you think?"

Gus looked at him. "I think we have a problem. Something just occurred to me, and I don't like the sound of it."

"All right. What? You don't like the sound of what?" Roxanne asked.

"I first noticed that bodies were disappearing down in the city. That was the first place. Now it's here they're disappearing. And I smashed the joints of those last bastards . . ."

"So?" Roxanne prodded.

"So something's dragging them away. Or something is eating them."

They became quiet, listening to the idle chug of the engine.

"What could feed on the dead?" Roxanne asked.

"Dogs," Gus said. "Maybe raccoons? Bears? I dunno, but I'd say dogs. They'd be strong enough to carry off a body. Wild ones would eat anything, I imagine."

"Dogs," Scott said.

"That might be a problem." Gus said.

"Why?" Roxanne asked.

"Well, I know how the disease affects people, but I don't know how it'll affect animals. And if it's all the same to you, I don't want to meet up with an infected bear or dog."

"A lot of the animals died in the first year, I figure," Scott said quietly. "But there's bound to be a few that adapted. That survived."

"Until they got infected," Gus added. "Well, shit."

Silence ruled once again as they contemplated what might lurk out there beyond zombies.

"Well," Gus finally said. "No use worrying about it now. Dead is dead until I see it walking."

26

Their first stop was the liquor corporation. They filled up one bin of the van with cases of Bacardi rum, various bottles of whiskey, alcoholic cider, and moscato wine. The loading went quickly with Roxanne helping Gus with lugging the cases from the gloom of the storeroom to the van. Next, they decided to look for a new street to house pick.

"Why not the malls around here?" Roxanne asked.

"Been picked over already. Nothin' in there. When the fall happened, that was the place that was the most looted, and dangerous. The dead zoned in on it like it was a magnet. Most of the big shoppin' centers are like that. I stay away from them. Nah, at this point in the game, the big stores are done. Too dangerous. I stick with the houses now. Most don't have anything because the people that lived there took what they could, but some are treasure troves. Like the shotgun and pistols we found the other day."

"Could be more out there just like that," Scott added.

"Oh, I guarantee it," Gus agreed. "We just gotta keep lookin'."

"To what end?" Roxanne asked. "I mean, sooner or later, probably sooner, this is going to be all looked over right? Everything that could be found will be. What're you gonna do then?"

Good question.

Gus looked back at her. "Move?"

"Where? It's the same out west, if not worse. It's the Dark Ages all over again out west. I mean, I came from it."

Gus looked at Scott. "Like your Tenner."

Scott didn't reply, but his face became pensive.

"Who's Tenner?" Roxanne asked.

176

"A killer," Gus said. "Anyway. Good point on what happens next. I'm thinking on it."

"Think faster," Roxanne said.

"Well, right now . . ." Gus looked up at the cloudy sky. "I think we can get in a few more houses. You guys up for it?"

"We have time," Scott said.

"Oh, guaranteed you're keepin' track of the time," Gus said, shaking his head. "No worries there. Nerd."

The sun descended behind the hills as they returned to the mountain and backed the van into the garage. They had done well for the six houses they managed to search—more toilet paper, stationery supplies, history books on the world wars, and sealed condiments. Roxanne had also made the suggestion of taking blankets found in linen closets for the upcoming winter, which filled the rear of the van and gave her something to sit on for the ride back to the house. Scott and Roxanne unloaded everything that same evening while Gus prepared canned beef ravioli for supper. They had their welcome home shots of whiskey and settled in for a night of Scrabble.

That night, Scott lay in his bed, staring at the ceiling. He heard Roxanne go to the washroom and return to her room minutes later. She was a little rough around the edges, but she wasn't a bad person. She also played a mean game of Scrabble. Of course, he and Gus had been pleasantly buzzed at the time.

Then, Tenner crept back into his mind. Tenner was still out there.

Tenner was unfinished business.

It disturbed Scott how easily Tenner had gunned him down and executed Teddy and Lea. It disturbed him that the man still lived and was probably killing whoever crossed his path for whatever reason. The pleasure? The thrill? Or just because people were there?

Scott exhaled.

Then, he heard a soft knock on the door.

Roxanne opened the door and stepped into his room. He could tell it was her from the shadowy outline. Her hair fell over her shoulders as she eased herself inside, keeping a hand on the knob. Even more interesting, she wore only a T-shirt that halted just at her upper thighs.

"Scott?" she asked quietly.

"Yeah?"

"You up?"

"Mmhmm. What do you want?"

"Gus is asleep, so I thought . . ." Her shape leaned up against the wall, and Scott was aware of her T-shirt slipping upward. "I thought you might like . . . to talk."

Well, *shit*.

Scott took a moment to collect his thoughts. He realized he was on extremely delicate ground. "Uh, no, I'm fine, Roxanne. I was about to drift off when you came in."

"Really?" she said softly. She lifted one leg, running her toes against the instep of the other, before placing it behind her as if stretching. She thrust her chest out, and he saw that she wasn't wearing a bra.

For a moment he didn't say anything, then, "Yeah, really. Good night."

She didn't leave right away. Scott closed his eyes and then opened one just a crack. She remained in place, and for a moment, he felt a bolt of awkwardness surge through him. *Oh, sweet Jesus*, he thought. *What if she strips down in here?*

He didn't need that. He closed his eyes again. Then, he heard the door click closed. He cracked open an eye and relief flooded through him. Roxanne was gone.

Exhaling, he shook his head. He didn't need that. He hoped it wouldn't make things awkward. He was, in his mind, still married.

And then there was Gus.

He wouldn't mention the episode to Gus. He couldn't.

He wasn't certain, however, what Roxanne would do.

Over his bowl of instant rolled oats sweetened with sugar, Gus watched Scott emerge from the hallway, yawning and scratching at his belly.

"Morning, sunshine." Gus smiled with a spoon in his mouth. "How you doin'?"

"Good," Scott said. "How you doin'?"

Gus winked at him. "Pretty good."

"This mine?" Scott pointed at the bowl on his end of the island.

"Yeah."

"Clear weather out there today."

"Hmm," Scott grunted.

"Hey." Gus lowered his voice. "Guess what happened?"

"What?"

At that moment, Roxanne came around the corner, dressed in white socks, sweatpants, and a sweater. She nodded coolly at Scott, before running her hand across Gus's hand and planting a kiss on his cheek. Without a word, she went to her chair and picked up a spoon.

"Wow," Scott said sardonically, and resumed eating.

"Yeah." Gus squinted at Roxanne. "Well, someone got lonely last night."

Roxanne gave him a half-scolding look, then started eating.

Scott inspected his coffee mug, then got up to pour more. "Well, that's great."

"I thought you'd say that." Gus beamed.

"I hate to ruin your morning, though," Scott said, sitting back down at his breakfast.

"Why? What's up?" Gus asked.

Across from him, Roxanne looked up with concern on her face.

"I've been thinking. It's time for me to get movin' on," Scott said.

"What?" Gus dropped his spoon.

"Yeah."

"Why?"

"Something's been botherin' me," Scott said, softly stabbing his rolled oats with a spoon. "Tenner's still out there."

"What?"

"Yeah. I'm not one to forget things. I mean . . ." He met Gus's gaze. "The prick shot me and gutted down two people I knew."

"What?" Roxanne said, shocked.

"Yeah," Scott took a spoonful of rolled oats and tasted it. "Well, the way I see it, I'm the only one that knows of him. Sorta. Knows what he sounds like anyway."

"You're kiddin'." Gus stopped eating and stared at him. "You're serious. You're goin' after this guy?"

"Yeah," Scott answered, taking another bite.

"Will you stop eatin' for a second? I mean, he could be anywhere out there. Anywhere, Scott. And fuckin' winter's comin' on, for fuck's sake."

"I know."

"And you're still goin'?"

Scott didn't answer right away. "Yeah."

Gus sat and stared at him as he continued eating.

"You'll be okay," Scott said, glancing furtively in Roxanne's direction.

"That's not what I'm sayin', man."

"What, then?" Scott asked.

"You saved my ass out there," Gus said quietly.

"You saved mine first. We're even. Well, there is one more thing."

"What?"

Scott pursed his lips as if in pain. "Can I take the SUV?"

The request stunned Gus. He couldn't believe this was happening. Last night, when Roxanne came knocking at his door out of the blue, he'd thought he might have been dreaming. For the first time in two years, he felt as if he didn't need a shot of whiskey in the morning. Then, Scott had dropped his bomb.

"You're really doing this?"

Scott looked him in the eyes and nodded. "Never said I'd be stayin' here forever."

Silence bloomed around the island.

"No," Gus said finally. "I guess you didn't. Sure, you can take the SUV. We can get another from the city."

"Thanks."

"You'll need food, too. Supplies. I'll . . . I'll outfit you."

Scott nodded.

"So, when are you headin' out?"

"This morning, I guess. Daylight and all."

"Yeah. Smart."

Gus got up from the table, his appetite suddenly gone. "I'll start things then." Feeling dazed, he moved away from the island.

27

"All loaded up," Gus informed Scott, with his arm on the open rear door of the Durango. The back was filled with bottled water, cases of canned food, a first-aid kit, his share of the Ruger ammunition, shells for his shotgun, one of the bandoliers, a bowie knife, clothes, a few books, and anything else he might need while on the road. Two filled gas containers were tucked in tightly with the supplies. A dozen rolls of toilet paper were even pushed in there. Everything and anything that Scott had found while he was with Gus was freely given. Gus had thought that Scott might reconsider, but the blond man never said a word on the subject. He merely loaded things aboard the SUV in grim fashion like a hunter about to go on safari, only asking Gus if it was "Okay for this?" or "Fine to have that?"

Gus didn't refuse him.

Roxanne watched from the doorway leading into the house, her face drawn and pensive- looking, her arms folded across her chest.

Scott faced Gus and nodded. "Thanks for everything."

"You're really going to head out there?" Gus asked.

Scott nodded. "He's out there. And he's worse than the deadheads. He's hunting whoever's left."

Gus nodded. "You . . . you got a place to come back to, you know that, right? Anytime."

"I hear you," Scott said and smiled. He looked at Roxanne. "Take care of this one. And yourself."

She nodded, still brooding.

Scott held out his hand.

Frowning, Gus took it and pumped it twice.

"Time to get goin'," Scott said.

181

"Yeah."

"Get the garage door for me?"

"Yeah."

Sighing, Gus opened the door, cranking the lever with both hands. He heard the SUV's door slam behind him and turned to see Scott wearing his lightning bolt helmet, visor up, sitting behind the wheel. He gave a thumbs-up.

Shaking his head, Gus walked down to the wall and removed the timbers bracing the gate. As he worked, he heard the SUV growl toward him, closing, and finally idling. He opened the gate and stood back, looking once from the wilderness beyond at the man behind the wheel. Standing in the open garage bay was the white figure of Roxanne, watching with her arms still folded.

Fighting down the sadness he felt, he walked over to Scott's open window.

"You can get the gate below. It's a long walk back for me."

Scott nodded.

"Well, this is it then. Happy huntin' out there. And watch your ass."

"You, too."

Gus smiled. "We'll be fine."

"Yeah. Have a good winter."

"You think you'll be back this way?" Gus asked.

Scott looked him in the eye. "Don't know."

"Yeah."

Giving one last nod, Scott put the Durango into drive and eased through the gate. Gus watched the vehicle pull away, the brake lights flaring red and smoky in the tail exhaust. The SUV rose and fell in the ruts of the mountain road before sinking out of sight. Gus leaned against the gate wall, listening to the hybrid's motor work until the sound lessened.

Gone. Just like that.

Feeling his throat tighten, Gus stayed until he composed himself. Minutes later, he turned and made his way to the garage. Roxanne hugged him, and Gus stood and breathed in her scent.

After a moment, he hugged her back.

"What do you want to do today?" she asked.

"Nothin'."

They ate lunch a little later, washed up, and retired to the den, where they cuddled up on the sofa and watched old Disney animated movies. With a bottle of Captain

Morgan, they stayed below ground where it was warm and comfortable. After the first movie, Roxanne stole Gus's attention by removing her sweater, then her T-shirt and her black pants. Next, she helped him out of his clothes. He removed her bra and panties, and somewhere along the line, they started kissing. Then came the fondling. Finally, the fucking.

They exhausted themselves in their lovemaking, surprising even Gus. Roxanne had been even more demanding and physical, much more than the first night together, and once they were done, Gus collapsed on the sofa, and she covered him with her naked body.

They watched another movie, drank and ate a late supper. Very little was said between them, except the little words of new-found lovers. More rum. They had another bout of sex after moving up into the master bedroom, where Gus showed her the rubber trophy from a previous episode of house picking. The sight of the dildo made Roxanne peal laughter, and in the soft bell-like quality of the sound, Gus forgot that a friend had departed the mountain that day.

Sometime later—Scott would have known the time exactly—they feel asleep while the night deepened, the temperature dropped, and winter's breath made the house creak.

In the morning, Gus slipped away from Roxanne's form and got out of bed. He stood above her for a moment, taking in her bare breasts, the light brown nipples sunken in sleep, and her curves beneath the comforter. She whined softly, seeming to feel the chill on her exposed skin, and Gus covered her up to her chin, basking in the design of her face and how her hair splashed against her pillow. With effort, he turned away from his lover. He dressed in fresh sweatpants and a sweater, warm socks, and left the room.

Descending the stairs, Gus looked toward the black-curtained windows and noted the sunlight glowing around the edges. He went over to one and peeked outside, and his mouth dropped open at the sight. Moments later, dressed warmly in a black parka, he opened the sliding door and headed outside.

A thin layer of snow covered the ground, the deck, and the deck furniture facing Annapolis. The morning sun set the snow sparkling, almost blinding. Gus squinted and wondered if he had any sunglasses stashed somewhere. He stared out at the city and wondered if Scott might be there still. Doubting it as soon as he thought it, Gus inhaled the cold air and tasted its freshness. The gimps would be cold, if not frozen. He had noticed last winter how their activity seemed to lessen during the cold months, only to resurge in the spring with the warmer temperatures.

Exhaling, he watched his breath dissipate in the morning brightness. With a shrug, he headed back to the house, wondering if apples and cinnamon rolled oats would be an acceptable breakfast for Roxanne. He went into the kitchen, poured water from the tap, and told himself to keep an eye on the solar panels. He hadn't had to clean them of snow in previous winters, as they generally melted the snow when the sun came out, but there was always a first time. And with the light snow, he wondered how treacherous it would be to get into town. He would have to go into Annapolis later. They didn't have much time left before the heavy snows came.

He'd eaten half of his oatmeal before Roxanne appeared, looking sleepy.

"Mornin'," he said.

"Mmm." She sat down at her place. "You have coffee?"

"Yep." He got her cup.

"Thanks."

"Snow fell last night," he said.

"Really?"

"Yep."

"So what does that mean?"

"We've got to get down to the city. Do some last minute house picking. Won't be long before we get snowed in up here."

"Snowed in?"

"Yeah."

"You mean trapped?" She looked worried.

"Mmm, more like sealed off," Gus said. "We'll be fine, though. Haven't had any deadheads up here in the winter time. Too cold for them, I guess. Too much trouble sloggin' through the snow."

"How will we make it?"

"Oh, we're fine. We got the panels. And the batteries store enough power to get us through snowstorms. The only thing I'm worried about is if we get a real blizzard and the panels get covered up. Even then, we just clean them off."

"Hmm."

"You're worried about something?"

She fidgeted on the stool. "Maybe you should show me where these batteries are."

Gus grinned. "Maybe. Definitely for sexual favors."

"I'm serious here. If anything happens to you, I'm fucked."

That made him frown. "No, it's pretty self-sufficient. I'm not even sure how the thing works. That's a con, especially if something does happen to the system, but nothing has yet. So don't worry. And nothin's gonna happen to me."

"Mm," Roxanne said in sullen fashion, looking lovely as she did so.

"I'm goin' to get ready for the day. The sooner we get started the better. You up for drivin' the beast?"

She nodded while eating a spoonful of rolled oats.

"Excelente," Gus said in his bad Spanish accent.

After a quick run to the outhouse, he was out in the garage, suiting up in his fire-fighter's pants and jacket. The boots were the last items to go on. He inspected his old shotgun and the new Benelli and figured he didn't have to clean either. Eying the rest of the equipment in the locker and packing it away, he wondered for a moment about the roof of the house, and felt a momentary pull to the outside. Gus placed the two shotguns on the floor of the van and went through the house and out onto the deck.

Outside, the sun remained cold yet bright. Roxanne had dressed in her white coat and toque, and stood at the railing, facing the city.

"Hey," Gus said. "You see anything wrong with the roof?"

Roxanne turned around, and for a moment, Gus didn't think she was going to answer. She finally looked up at the roof and squinted. "No, but I don't know what I'm looking for."

Gus turned about and walked in reverse while looking up. Something was wrong. He felt it. Studying the length of the timberframe, he shook his head. "Well, looks fine to me too."

"Something wrong?" she asked.

He turned and noticed that she wasn't wearing gloves. "We'll have to see if we can get you some gloves today."

"You're still set on headin' down there?"

"Didn't get dressed up for nothin'," he informed her brightly.

"You should show me the batteries first."

He shook his head, smiling at her little scowl. "I think later. After that sexual favor."

Roxanne's face went from drawn to having a little smile at the edges of her mouth, like a sun peeking out from behind a storm cloud.

"Oh, Gus." She slowly unzipped the front of her coat.

"Mm," Gus said, approving.

Roxanne opened her coat to reveal a tight-fitting sweatshirt.

It was one of his, Gus realized. "Gonna haveta get you some women's clothes, too."

"I can't wear yours?" She arched her back, making the sweatshirt tighter across her chest.

"Well, I can see your points. Point, I mean."

With a giggle, she laced her fingers around the back of his head and pulled him close for a kiss. She tasted of toothpaste, and Gus momentarily lost track of everything else.

She broke away after a while, her blue eyes twinkling. "Here's that favor then."

"Oh."

She gently lowered his head to her breasts. Gus complied. He kissed one through the cotton, then moved to kiss the other. He felt her hands tighten around his neck, and before he could back up, he saw her knee coming toward his face.

28

Gus flew backward and landed hard on the deck. His world went black. Somewhere in the soupy black of his off-line consciousness, he heard elongated words directed at him, but the meaning was lost. He heard a far-off explosion, or at least what *felt* like an explosion, and wondered what was running down his throat. *Something* was running down his throat. He was aware of swallowing gobs of it, feeling the reflexive click of swallowing. A hard lump, or lumps, got caught in there, and he coughed. Another swallow and another rock went down. Pain. Pain was inside his skull and gouging his darkness like thunderbolts. He grimaced and felt the embers of a distant fire closing in like a tide of white noise.

He opened an eye and thought for a moment he was falling into the sky. Realization crept in that he was on the deck. The white noise rushed back. He blinked. His nose and mouth exploded with torrential agony, lighting up his returning consciousness like a soundless alarm klaxon. Feeling as if concrete blocks chained his arm, he reached up and felt his face.

And gasped.

He struggled to sit up. He got to his elbows and gazed down at his bare hand covered in blood. His face sizzled as if a hot grill had smashed into it. Blinking again, he became aware of Roxanne standing on the deck beside him, fiddling with something in her hands. As he watched, she lifted the item to the heavens.

Flare gun.

The gun went off with a loud cough, and a second sun cut the sky with a smoky line.

Jesus Christ. What was she doing?

"Roxanne . . ." Gus got to one knee.

She jerked as if caught doing something criminal, and her face quickly morphed from startled surprise to one of violence. She ran at him and kicked at his face. Gus got a hand up in time to have her foot smash into it, flipping him onto his back. She stomped on his stomach, and the wind left his guts. A kick to the side of his face flipped him over onto his side. He felt the follow up boot to the ribs.

"Sexual favor, huh?" she snarled. "Here's your goddamn sexual favor. How d'ya like being boot-fucked? *Huh*?"

She kicked him in the ribs again. He sensed her drawing back for another shot, and he protected his crotch, knowing it was all over if she got him there. Her foot crunched on his hip bone. She punched him in the face, and he felt his senses tilt once more. More punches to the face. Claws. She was *clawing* him.

"Rox—"

He heard her scream and felt thumbnails graze his eyebrows. A split second later, they found his eyes. His lids closed in reflex, and he twisted away from her fury, hiding his face as another bolt of agony crackled through his skull. His shoulders were grasped, and he felt himself bent backward, straightened out on the snow.

What he thought was her elbow slammed into his face, bouncing his head off the deck.

Another elbow and he felt bone crack.

A third impact . . .

But he was floating, and the force of the connection felt muted, as if something had splashed down beside where he drifted in a dark tide of unconsciousness.

Then total blackness.

Breathing heavily, Roxanne looked down at the pulped mess that had been Gus's face. The bastard brought out the worse in her. Why couldn't he have just shown her the batteries? It would've been easier. Once Jonathan got there, he'd take Gus into a back room and work him over—no, he'd *torture* him—cutting off parts until Gus screamed what he wanted to know. That wasn't Roxanne's way. She liked a softer touch, but she could be hard if she had to be. It was all a fluke meeting up with Gus and Scott, anyway, a wonderful fluke for her, even though Edgar actually *had been* trying to rape her. The fucker. He'd be with Jonathan and the gang, and they were all down there somewhere, starving and freezing.

Roxanne remembered her dues. The gang had protected her in her travels from Ontario. Jonathan had taken a liking to her, which was fortunate as he was the leader. He'd saved her ass and treated her good. As good as Gus had.

It was just that she'd met Jonathan first.

And she remembered her dues.

She dropped Gus' bloodied head to the deck with a thud. He was tough, she'd give him that, but she knew how to fight. She knew how to defend herself. Gazing down at the way Gus's\ nose was squashed to the right and how his front teeth were missing, she figured she'd subdued him enough. If he'd shown her the batteries and explained them a little more, she could've just shot him outright. She *had* planned to divide and conquer, but Scott up and left. Half of her thought he might return. What was the stupid prick *thinking?* To leave a goddamn *oasis* like this to go off and hunt for some lunatic? *Insane.* They had power, for Christ's sake! Running *hot* water! She'd even told them what it was like out west.

She had let him go, happy not to have to fuck him.

The thought made her seethe. Denying *her.* Who the fuck did he think he was anyway? *Insane.*

But not as insane as Jonathan.

Or more correctly, insane with gratitude that his bitch had found such a perfect nest for the winter. It would be a tight fit, but that wouldn't be an issue. Some of them could bunk up together. Jonathan shared his bed with her, and even Tiff when the mood struck him.

She backed away from Gus's body, noting the blood bubbles swelling and bursting with each shallow breath. Bringing up her flare gun, she cracked the barrel and ejected the spent flare, tapping against her thigh. Then, she loaded the last flare and shut the gun with a snap. She had never thought she'd actually have to use the gun for its intended purpose. She looked toward the cityscape coated in snow. *Last shot.* She hoped the others would spot it. She wasn't sure about firing it off during the day, but she didn't want to wait until evening. She couldn't bear the thought of the group being down there, hungry and freezing, another moment.

"Don't."

Roxanne turned around and saw sun flash off the metal of the derringer in Gus' hand.

"Where," she gasped, "where the fuck you get that?"

Gus' eyes tweaked and twitched. Pain stitched his ribs with each intake of air. His face felt broken, and he knew he was in bad shape. He simply couldn't believe Roxanne had kicked the shit out of him. Perhaps even kicked him to within a hair of losing his life. He didn't know why she had done it, nor did he care.

"Drop it," he gasped, feeling the pain of his wind sawing at the spaces left by his missing teeth. He only had his incisors left upstairs, and he winced when the cold air attacked the exposed nerves of the broken enamel, as the roots were still in his gums. Two of them anyway. He supposed he looked like an old school hockey player.

Roxanne didn't drop it. Instead, she screamed.

Gus shot her at close range, the bullet blowing through her stomach. A soft girlish grunt passed her lips, and she flew back, crashing off the railing and crumpling to the snow-covered deck.

Growling, Gus sat up, keeping the derringer pointed at her. He had kept the little gun in his boot since the day he had found it, even envisioned himself shooting off a foot when he pulled his boots on if he ever forgot it was there. The little weapon had saved his life. He knew it. He also knew that he only had two shots for the thing, which made him wonder why the hell there was so much ammunition for the other guns, but nothing for his little lifesaver.

Moaning, he got to his knees. His limbs worked, and for that he was thankful. Keeping an eye on Roxanne where she lay on her belly, he saw the hand holding the flare gun move. He heard a little bubble burst of pain come from her mouth. She pouted her ass up into the air as if offering it and pushed herself to her hands and knees.

"Don't move," Gus ordered.

Roxanne moved. She raised the flare gun to her chin. Another gasp of breath and a long thread of blood dropped from her lips. Blood tap-tap-tapped the deck, dripping from where she'd been shot.

With a rasp, she shoved the flare gun upward, as if cocking it against her ear.

Gus emptied the other shell into her, puncturing her right lung and dropping her to the deck. The flaregun fired. Light shot out over the edge of the deck, snaking an angry path toward the city and soon spiralling out of sight.

He dropped the derringer and crawled toward her, enduring terrible pain from his beating. He fastened his hand onto his Roxanne, and turned her over, grimacing.

Her eyes were open, and they fastened on him. Blood smeared her not-quite-dead features. "Why?" he sobbed into her face, his blood dripping onto her chin.

Blue eyes, perhaps as sharp as sapphires, twinkled at him.

"They're . . . coming," she choked out.

And died.

29

The words frightened him into action.

"Who?" he demanded, grabbing her shoulders and shaking her. "*Who?*"

He paused to get a grip on his emotions, and the last soft expulsion of air left her lungs, grazing his features.

Gus lowered her to the deck and left her staring at the sun. He shuffled backward, snarling in pain, and skidded against the railing.

They're coming.

He looked toward the city, searching the snow-glazed rooftops for an answer. The sun beamed down, lying to him that all was right with the world.

And then, he heard the distant roar of a motorcycle without a muffler, soft yet alarmingly gruff. Gus's breath caught in his blood-coated throat.

They're coming.

Then, nothing.

Snorting, Gus started crawling on his hands and knees toward the house, a growing urgency in his shuffling movements. Blood dripped from his mashed face, and he realized that when he breathed through his nose, a whistling noise perked his ears. He paused to touch it and felt how it was squished to the side. Mewling in agony, he stopped and squeezed his eyes shut. He placed his fingers against his crushed nose, feeling the bone pebbles shift. A laser of pain blossomed over his face, and he yelped, but he didn't let go.

Instead, he took a breath through his mouth, feeling the bright rub of air making contact with his broken teeth, and snapped his nose back into position. He swooned. His eyes watered. His sinus cavity filled with fluid, and he spat blood and snot out onto the snow, grimacing. He got unsteadily to his feet. His face probably wouldn't be as pretty anymore, but after Roxanne, he couldn't give a flying squirrel fuck about the opposite sex.

They're coming.

Grunting in anger, he staggered to the sliding door and opened it. Jesus Christ. Had it only been minutes ago that he was preparing to head into the city? The thought made him cringe. Images of Roxanne on top of him, her shadowy face contorted in ecstasy, her hips rocking and her bare breasts quivering, played out soundlessly in his mind, shifting to her smiling face as she laced her fingers behind his head. Then, he remembered the abrupt tightening of her fingers on his throat, and the pulling of his face down to meet her knee coming up with jackhammer force.

How did things go to shit?

And Jesus Christ, he had killed someone. He killed someone *dead*. Even worse, he had killed Roxanne. But he had to kill her, he had no other choice. But his soul was guaranteed to be heading to Hell. The thought of her stopped him in his tracks, and he looked back at where she lay in the snow. Again, his thoughts spun. He had been on the verge of *loving* that woman. He probably *did* love her.

Dead and gone.

By his hand.

He staggered into the living room, tracking snow behind him. He bared his teeth, knowing he must look like a monster. He pushed the images of Roxanne from his mind and tried to rise above the pain reports coming in from seemingly everywhere in his body. She'd fucked him over good. Real good. But he was still breathing, wasn't he? Yes, he was. He was still breathing and still in the game. Goddammit. He was *still* in the game.

And the game was coming for him.

The *end* game.

How long did he have?

Gus crashed off the wall twice before getting to the garage. The beast. He almost cried as he saw his reflection in the black surface of its hide. He whimpered and backed up, noticing his locker and his leather jacket, torn, but still serviceable. Gus ran his hands over the firefighter gear and made a face. No.

He had come into this world with motorcycle leather.

He had survived in this world with his unholy boomstick and samurai bat.

And if God gave a shit above, he'd die in it with his weapons on him.

The bottle of Captain Morgan dark rum stood on the top shelf of the locker, the foppish prick grinning at him as if he had a telephone pole jammed up his ass. Gus grabbed him, opened the bottle, and took three gulps before the burn of the rum smothered some of the pain. He stripped off his boots and his firefighter gear, throwing it everywhere. Leather pants went over his jeans, along with a hockey vest of protective padding for his chest. Hissing at the burn in his guts and the pain of his teeth, he pulled on his worn leather jacket. A thick neck brace clamped around his throat. Shin guards, hard plastic knee and elbow pads went on next, and Gus huffed when he slapped them into place. He pulled on black leather gloves, fingerless, and slung on his scabbard and bat. He paused for another three gulps of Captain Morgan cure-all medicine. Snarling, Gus loaded the shotgun. When he finished, he hefted the Benelli.

He looked back at the locker and saw the boxes marked "sabot shells."

The fuck they were anyway?

He didn't care. He stuffed seven of the green shells into the breach of the Benelli. He placed the gun in the back of the van and wrapped the bandolier about his waist. Then he thought better of it and threw it over his shoulder, crossing the strap of his bat scabbard. He loaded the remaining sabots into the pockets of the bandolier. When he ran out, he loaded his pockets with regular red shells. More rum was channelled down his throat. He noted that the pain of his mouth, nose, and ribs wasn't so bad anymore, and that alone made him chug another shot.

With a groan, Gus reached in and pulled out the silenced Ruger. He checked the load in the magazine. He gathered the five remaining mags, as Scott had taken the others. *Scott.* Gus shook his head. He could have used the blond bastard, but he felt good knowing that his friend had gotten the fuck out of Dodge.

After today, Gus didn't think there would be much of Dodge left.

He didn't have anywhere to put the pistol, so he stuffed it inside his hockey vest. It didn't feel comfortable there, but he was glad to have it.

Spitting a gob-sizzle of blood onto the floor, Gus sized up the locker for any other weapons. He hauled out the Bowie knife and stuffed its foot-long steel down his left boot. He took his pistol and shoved it down the other boot. That felt better. *He* felt better. He growled and had another two swallows of rum.

Spitting again, he turned back to the Benelli. Picking it up by the collapsible skeleton stock, he placed the butt against his shoulder. He cocked his head to gaze through its mounted scope. *Yes*, he thought. He felt *fine*.

He grimaced, baring teeth that were no longer there. Al Pacino's voice spoke in his head, spewing out quotes from the movie *Scarface*.

You fuck with me, you fuckin' with the best.

Say hello to my little friend.

Captain Morgan grinned at him.

And this time, Gus grinned back.

30

He heard the roar of the motorcycle in the distance like an approaching storm front. The loud, deboning sound cut through the quiet of the kitchen and made Gus open his eyes. He sniffed and grimaced when he did, still feeling pain, even though he was pleasantly drunk. He looked at the empty bottle of Jack Daniels on the kitchen island and, next to it, the drained bottle of Captain Morgan. The foppish captain still smiled.

"You both better . . ." Gus breathed, feeling the hiss on his broken teeth. It would be something he'd have to get used to. "Get out of here . . . Not going to be pretty."

The Captain didn't move.

Neither did Uncle Jack.

"Stay, then." He scowled, then added, "Y'fuckers."

He touched the bandages wrapped around his nose. It wasn't the best dressing he had ever done. Then he thought, what the fuck? It was the first field dressing he'd ever done. Roxanne had dropped a goddamn refrigerator on his face. He had inspected the damage in a mirror, and a sense of awe had washed over him. Black swollen eyes, swollen split lips, a two-inch cut in his forehead opened to the bone, the missing teeth—which had gotten a semi-drunken chuckle as it made him look like a stoned vampire—and bruised cheeks. His cheeks worried him the most, flaring pain when he wrapped his face with bandages. The cuts weren't so bad, as he'd filled them with Vaseline to control the bleeding.

Yep, he thought, Roxanne had certainly done a number on him. But she had missed his arms and legs.

Gus sighed, almost expecting to see Scott sitting in his spot at the island, chewing and mulling. He even expected to see Roxanne. God above, he even missed her, and a biting, scorching burn where his heart had once been flared up like a dying flame being blown on.

The sound of the motorcycle got closer.

Gus reached down and picked up his motorcycle helmet. He pulled it onto his head, crying out at the rude contact against his nose. He stood and walked over to the kitchen window. Keeping his visor up, he looked out of the slot over the kitchen sinks—filled with breakfast dishes—and studied the wall and gate. The roar of the motorcycle got louder, and Gus wanted to shoot the fucker just on the principal of being an annoying cocksucker. There was no need for that, he thought, swaying slightly. No need of it.

Shit like that would get a man shot.

Or eaten.

The last thought made Gus giggle, and *that* brought a dull ache to seemingly everywhere. It was just a damn good idea all-around to get juiced up before this fight. He hoped it was over before he sobered up because that was going to be a *bitch*.

He listened. The growing racket from the nearing engines diminished within seconds. Gus picked up the Benelli and cycled a round into the chamber, noting that he didn't have to pump it like a regular shotgun. *Different system*. He then wondered how they would deal with the gate, if they would try and ram their way through or pull it off the hinges. Sniffing and swallowing snot, he opened the kitchen window, and stuck the barrel of the shotgun out over the top plank. He had to lean over the sink a little, but at that point, leaning a little was nothing.

Gus realized he'd never test-fired the weapon. He had his other shotgun on the table and the Ruger in his boot, just for back up.

"Don't you misfire on me, baby," he whispered. The pistol grip of the shotgun already earned it brownie points in Gus's book. It was a great hold. He flipped off the safety switch, or what he thought was the safety switch, and took aim with the scope. The gate swelled in his vision.

"C'mon, you cocksuckers," Gus whispered, his words making his broken teeth ache. "Daddy's home. And he's fuckin' *pissed*."

Waiting for a moment and not hearing anything, he opened his other eye—which was a wonder in itself—and saw heads popping up along the top of the wall.

"Scouts, boys," he directed at the Captain and Uncle Jack. "What should I do?"

The bottles spoke.

"Fuckin' A," Gus replied. "And here I thought all you were good for was drinkin'."

"Roxy?" someone yelled from beyond the wall. "Roxy, you in there?"

Roxy? Stupid way to say her name.

"Roxy?" the voice shouted again. It became quiet then, the sun still bright in the sky. "If there's anyone in there listening, you let her go, and I'll kill you fast. I promise."

Promises, Gus thought.

"All I want is the woman."

Gus supposed that was all he wanted, too. Once upon a time.

"We're comin' to get you, babe," the voice hollered.

"Then come and get it," Gus whispered.

They came.

From the kitchen, he hadn't heard it, but Gus figured they must have parked something right next to the gate. Three men dressed in shabby clothes hoisted themselves all at the same time, swinging their legs up and over and dropping below. They all had long-barrel shotguns. They quickly started pulling away the timbers.

If Gus had been in a more stable frame of mind, he might have come up with a better plan than the one he had. His plan essentially had him firing at bodies as they came into full view. He targeted the first one through the mounted scope.

"Picked the wrong house, cocksucker," Gus muttered, his voice sounding as if his sinus cavity was brimming.

He squeezed the trigger three times, and hell erupted from the Benelli, hitting the first man and crunching him against the wall in a bloody print. Gus lowered the gun and stared at it as if it were a thing possessed. *Semi-automatic.* Green shell casings spat from the ejector littered the floor.

The two other men whirled and brought up their guns. Shots tore into the house.

Gus took aim at a second man and shot him through the chest, flipping him up and over a beam. The recoil was difficult to control in his drunken state, but Gus had never felt calmer. He looked through the scope at the third man, who collapsed to the frozen ground and shouted something. Gus lined up his head and blew it apart in spectacular fragmented fashion.

He shifted from the window, took more green shells from his bandolier, and shoved seven of them into the breech. When he looked up, more men were climbing over the wall.

Gus aimed and squeezed the trigger, the booze no longer a hindrance, but still grounding his nerves. He fired at the men and hit three, shredding them as they topped the wall. Two bodies fell on his side, hitting the beams as they dropped to the ground. The third fell back and dropped out of sight.

More bodies swarmed over. Men fired, and shots crashed into the wood. Gus fired again, snapping off a flurry of shots and hitting nothing.

Then, he whirled away from the window and reloaded.

"You fucker!" a voice shrieked from beyond. "You fucker! I'll fry you up and fuckin' eat you like the dead! Just like the goddamn dead!"

"There's only one shooter!"

"One shooter!"

"Fuck him up!"

Gus finished loading and stepped back to the window. *Relax*, he told himself. *Take your time.*

More figures flopped over the wall. They hit the ground running, moving right and left. Some carried guns, but most carried bats or knives. Some wore hockey helmets with cages; others had motorcycle helmets. Three men lay on the ground and fired as fast as they could load their guns, providing cover fire. Wood chips flew around the window.

The bottles on the island spoke.

"I hear ya," Gus snarled. He sighted the first shooter and fired, taking off the top of the man's head in an explosion of red cauliflower. Gus shifted to his next target, clearly seeing the fright on the man's features through his scope.

"Missin' some teeth," Gus observed. He blew away the face.

"Lookin' a little like strawberry jam out there," Gus said to the bottles.

Captain Morgan answered.

"Huh? Oh," Gus slurred, seeing what the Captain referred to. Two parties had split, rushing his flanks. They'd be trying to get into the house. "I hear ya," Gus said, stooping over and feeling the increased pressure in his sinus cavity. He moved from the window, reloading the Benelli. He regarded the sliding doors leading out onto the deck, as well as the windows around the house. Heavy wood comprised the front door and the rear one was boarded. He locked both of them. Then, he heard the breaking of wood and glass coming from Scott's bedroom.

"Oh, no, you—" Gus ran toward the bedroom and flipped around the doorframe. Two figures were coming through the ruined window, one holding an axe. The other held a shotgun and snapped off a shot, splintering the upper frame with a crunch. Gus roared and fired, emptying the Benelli in a maelstrom of sabot shot that flung the two invaders backward as if they'd been hit by a freight train.

He pulled green shells from his bandolier and reloaded. He looked about furtively.

More windows breaking.

"You fuckers."

Shadows passed in front of Scott's window, right across from where Gus stood in the hall. He rushed into the room, and when a hockey-helmeted head popped up, he unleashed three shells, blasting the man backward.

Wood cracking. Being forced. Gus moved back into the hallway and looked at the main door. It held. He eased ten feet forward, toward the open area. He checked the sliding doors, still covered in dark curtains. The dining room window remained boarded up on the outside.

He saw the extra shotgun and Captain Morgan and Uncle Jack on the island. The Captain had his hip cocked and a smirky grin in place.

"Likin' the . . . ?"

Shotgun blasts came from the opposite hall, from the direction of the garage and the second door. Gus retreated and waited. No further shots. There wasn't any way for them to get in from below or above, unless one of them was a fucking squirrel. Or a gopher.

The sliding door blew inward with a crash, sending fragments of wooden planks and glass across the hardwood floor. Two heads peeked in from around the jagged edges. Gus placed the butt of the Benelli against his shoulder and flexed his grip.

"C'mon, you fuckers!" he shouted. *"Come meet my little friend."*

One flipped around the corner, raising a long-barrel shotgun. Gus emptied the Benelli into exposed arms that got chewed up and spun the rest of the gunman into view. The last two shots slammed the would-be attacker to the ground. Gus retreated back into the hallway and reloaded, noting he had a helluva lot less sabot shells. He kicked the spent green casings on the floor away from him and realized he should not have done that.

"All right," he heard a voice call out. "On my count, rush him!"

That perked up Gus's ears.

"One."

The counting struck Gus as being a pretty stupid move. Bad tactics even. But then again, they were just ordinary people. Unless they had something else planned.

"Two."

Gus moved further back into the hall, hiding around a corner with his back to the main door to the house.

"Three."

Frightening war cries stabbed the air, and a thundering of boots and shotgun blasts ripped through the interior of the house. They unleashed hell as they came, laying down suppressing fire.

Then, it was over.

Gus wheeled around the corner and surprised about a dozen of them standing in the living room. He fired into the thickest mass, blowing two of them off their feet. He shifted and shot another road warrior though the shoulder, spinning the man around like a broken top. Screams cut the air. Shots zinged back at him. Uncle Jack exploded and simply wasn't there anymore. The wall and doorframe splintered and flew away in bursts of destruction. Gus blew the leg off one man, but missed with his last shot. He wheeled back into the front entryway, and two shots crashed into the wall at his back. He reloaded the remainder of his sabots, wondering where the hell they had all gone. Voices cried out.

Gus eased around the corner, looking into the kitchen. The shotgun was missing from the island. Uncle Jack was also gone, blasted into pieces.

Captain Morgan grinned at him, but the smile seemed forced, uncertain.

A man popped up from behind the island, raising Gus's shotgun. Gus shot him through the chest, punching a ragged hole in the guy and flinging him back. Another three carrying axes and bats came around the island. Gus blew apart the ankle of one man, making him howl. A sabot ripped the guts out of the second man, spraying the furniture behind him in gore. The third attacker had second thoughts and lunged outside headfirst through the wreck of the sliding door.

But more charged him.

Gus squeezed the trigger, and nothing happened.

The men closed in with axes and clubs and faces eager to take off his head.

Retreating into the hall, Gus flung the shotgun behind him, stooped, and pulled out the Ruger.

The faces went slack.

From a kneeling position, Gus fired into the mass of bodies. Four of the attackers yelled out and shuddered and shook with the impact of the Ruger's steady coughing. The others broke away. One man went around the island. Gus got up and ran into the kitchen. He shot the man twice through the chest just as the attacker tried to bring a shotgun—Gus's shotgun—to bear.

"I'll kill you!" a familiar voice screamed, and a huge man, football player size, charged him with a fire axe.

Despite having more than half a bottle of rum in his system, Gus turned and blasted the man in the chest. The impact stopped the screamer in his tracks. Pain screwed up his features behind a hockey helmet face cage. Gus shot him twice more before realizing the man still stood, so he switched targets and destroyed a knee.

That elicited a cry of pain, and the behemoth dropped to his good knee. Gus shot him through his shoulders and his navel. The shots bowled the big man over onto his back, into the living room. Gus looked back toward the kitchen.

There, still standing on the island, was Captain Morgan. His beaming features appearing much more confident.

"You fucker," a voice hissed.

Gus turned and recognized the contorted face of Knifeman. But Knifeman now had an axe. Gus aimed the Ruger at him.

"Fucker," the now-Axeman whispered at him through a mouth full of ugly teeth. "C'mon." He hefted the axe. "Drop the pistol and fi—"

Gus shot him in the face, whipping the man's head back and dropping him to the hardwood floor. After Axeman fell, the house seemed a lot quieter.

Except for the groaning football player.

Gus pulled out the spent magazine and filled the Ruger with one of the spare five. Gus sniffed again, noting it didn't hurt as much, and went on the hunt. He stepped out of the house through the shattered sliding door and spotted two men in winter coats pressed against the wall. One held a bat. The other held knives in both hands. They pleaded when Gus stepped into full view.

Gus shot them both, tapping each in the head with final kill shots as he looked around the corner. He walked around the house, looking for targets. He found out one of the men he had killed through the bedroom window had been a woman. A brunette wearing a toque. A shotgun lay just out of reach of her fingers. He found four other women and wondered how the hell they had gotten caught up in such a pack of raiders.

Feeling the energy leave him, he wandered around the house, seeing where they had peppered the exterior with shot. They had chopped off the doorknob to force entry through the second doorway. He circled back around, coming from the direction of the mountain and the wind generator. None of the solar panels were damaged, thankfully. All in all, the damage was mostly structural, with the odd broken window. Not as bad as it could have been. He figured the house had been important to the attackers. Of course it would be. The place was a gold mine, especially with winter coming.

Gus came full circle to the sliding doors and eased himself back inside the house. There, sitting up against the railing and facing him, was the football player. He snarled when he saw Gus, and Gus kept his gun on him. The man breathed weakly, and blood smears marked the hardwood floor where he had pulled himself across it. The bodies of the rest of the pack were sprinkled around, unmoving and quiet.

"Fucker," the big man said, and then coughed.

Gus stepped up to him and reached out. He removed the hockey helmet from the guy's head and placed the barrel of the Ruger against his shaven skull, just above his eyes.

The football player followed the weapon until it made contact with his forehead, then he closed his eyes for a moment, and made no move.

The aches slowly crept back into Gus, and he stood with the pistol ready, watching his target's pained expression. Gus thought about asking him who they were, and what Roxanne had been to them. He thought about asking if there were any more of them out there or in the city below.

In the end, he didn't ask anything.

In the end, he shot the football player between the eyes, the blow-through spattering the steps.

Gus stood and listened for a bit, noting the rising of the wind coming through the house, and felt cold. He inspected himself and found that nothing had hit him. Not one goddamn thing. *Superior firepower* flashed faintly in his head, and he rapped the barrel of the Ruger on the side of his helmet. Thinking about his hand, he stuck one out in front of him and inspected it.

Surprisingly steady.

Gus walked through the main level of the house, upstairs and down, but didn't find anyone else. The place was going to need paint and some screen doors. That thought made him smile. Tomorrow. He'd get at it tomorrow. He'd repair and seal the house once again before the temperature really took a dive. He shambled into the kitchen and opened a cabinet. Smiling grimly, he pulled out a new bottle of Uncle Jack and eased off his helmet. It still hurt. Sweat ran down his face and soaked his beard. He didn't care. He opened the bottle and looked at it at arm's length.

"I knew your brother," he muttered, hearing how his missing teeth affected his speech, and took two scalding swallows.

When he opened his eyes and turned around, the Captain smiled at him.

"Saucy bastard."

Noting that his ribs were killing him, he stepped over to the sofa and sat down heavily. He placed the Ruger in his lap and nursed the bottle of Jack Daniels. After another shot, Gus looked toward the sliding door and the sunshine blazing in. He knew that if he went there and looked out, Roxanne would be lying on the deck where he had left her, and a small part of him wished she was still alive.

Smacking his lips, Gus didn't know if there were any raiders remaining in the house. He thought that, if there were any left alive, he'd just sit and drink and wait to see if they came to him.

If they had the balls.

There, in his living room, the mountain man took shallow breaths and drank at leisure, listening to the weary moan of the wind.

31

Two days later, the red SUV slowed to a stop on the highway, the tailgates blazing in the drifts swirling around its base, hiding the wheels and making the vehicle appear as if it were hovering. The sun was up there somewhere, out-muscled by a brooding low pressure system that coated everything in freezing white. The weather had come early, much earlier than Scott had expected, and he supposed that the best place to be, if anywhere, would be in a town somewhere. He regarded the long white lick of pavement curving away around a shadowy fence of trees. He'd decided to head down to Halifax. Something had nagged him about the smaller town of Windsor, something that had hooked his subconscious and wouldn't let go. He checked it out, taking a couple of days to sufficiently explore it, but only found undead lumbering about as if trying to escape the cold. He suspected that Halifax might indeed be the place for a killer like Tenner, and thought he was wasting time with the smaller towns.

Looking out at the drifting snow drifting, Scott sighed, reflecting on the path he had chosen. An image of Gus popped into his mind. He wished the mountain man well, but didn't think he'd ever see him again. His was no longer a life of scavenging off the old world, and he didn't know how long Gus and Roxanne would be able to do it. He couldn't. Even before the world went into the shitter, he had been restless. That was one thing that could be said for the present day. It gave freedom to do whatever one liked, whenever.

But what a cost.

A gust of snow blew against his window, rasping it with a moan. Scott checked his blind spot. Nothing. He was still the only one out in this frigid shit. Gus had been right about that. The winter slowed them down. It didn't kill them, but the cold affected them enough that a person knew some deadhead wouldn't be running up from nowhere to pounce. He looked at the lit-up dashboard and figured it was time to get on.

Halifax called.

And he was going to see what it wanted.

32

One Month Earlier

Tenner slowed the black SUV at the city limit marker for Halifax before finally stopping at a green sign welcoming visitors to the coastal metropolis. Beyond the signboard, the dilapidated husk of the city appeared as a great dark shadow under the cloud-filled sky. Houses with their windows smashed out lined the highway leading into the city. Cars of all models littered the highway like poisoned metallic corpses.

Tenner got out of the hybrid and pulled his winter coat closer around him. He gazed toward the flat mirror of the sea and watched seagulls coast across the sky. They were the only animals he'd seen in a while, and he took a moment to appreciate them.

After a few moments, he turned his attention to the Welcome to Halifax sign. He didn't like the sign. It was behind the times. Tenner shook his head and proceeded to the back of his SUV. He popped the rear door and rummaged through his supplies. He stepped away from his ride, shaking the can of spray paint, and walked over to the sign. Tenner paused for a moment, chewing on the inside of his cheek, before spray painting the necessary adjustment. Once finished, he took a step back and inspected his work.

There, *he thought*. That's more like it.

Welcome to Hellifax.

He smirked at his own wit. The new wording meant everything to him. The old town was about to meet the new mayor.

Thoughts whirling and expectations high, he got aboard his vehicle and drove deep into the gloomy halls of the downtown area.

Intent on raising hell.

About the Author

Keith C. Blackmore is the author of the Mountain Man, 131 Days, and Breeds series, among other horror, heroic fantasy, and crime novels. He lives on the island of Newfoundland in Canada. Visit his website at www.keithcblackmore.com.

DISCOVER
STORIES UNBOUND

PodiumAudio.com

Printed in the USA
CPSIA information can be obtained
at www.ICGtesting.com
JSHW082204140824
68134JS00014B/412

9 781039 444140